and immediately encountered a thickset giant. The ogre's towering, gray-green, eleven-foot form was clothed in something like a burlap sack with holes cut out for his tree-trunk legs. His head was bald and lumpy, his ears big and pointy. A shimmering vortex was closing behind him, and he appeared confused.

"And just what are you?" Wes asked.

"Hungry," the creature said.

Wes nodded. "Yes, you have that inter-dimensional jet-lag look about you. No decent in-flight movies? No snacks along the way?"

"Food . . . ," the creature said, sounding ravenous—and deadly.

"I don't suppose it would interest you to know that there's a *sensational* bistro just down the street? The food's not alive, kicking, screaming, and begging for its life, but it is rather tasty."

"You . . . are . . . food."

Wes sighed. "Thought as much. Had to ask, though. Only polite thing to do." Wes extended his right arm out to the side and activated the release mechanism for the fold-away sword that he carried for these kinds of occasions. It *snikted* into place, and with the sword fully extended, Wes rushed the ogre with a take-no-prisoners look in his eyes.

Angel™

Buffy the Vampire Slayer™ and Angel™ Crossover Titles

Available from Simon Spotlight

ANGEL™

nemesis

Scott and Denise Ciencin

An original novel based on the television series
created by Joss Whedon & David Greenwalt

New York   London   Toronto   Sydney

Historian's Note: This book takes place during the last half of the fourth season of Angel.

SIMON SPOTLIGHT
An imprint of Simon & Schuster Children's Publishing Division
1230 Avenue of the Americas, New York, New York 10020
Copyright © 2004 by Twentieth Century Fox Film Corporation.
All Rights Reserved.

SIMON SPOTLIGHT is a registered trademark of Simon & Schuster.
The colophon is a trademark of Simon & Schuster.
Manufactured in the United States of America

First Edition 10 9 8 7 6 5 4 3 2 1

Library of Congress Control Number 2003113848

ISBN 0-689-86702-6

ANGEL™

nemesis

PROLOGUE

Night. The city of Los Angeles. Home to lost angels . . . and found demons. The round, pudgy little man in his perfectly tailored suit only caught a glimpse of the guy in the crowd who had jammed the flyer into his hand. He was wearing a black leather duster with midnight blue trim and *seemed* to have bloodred, blistered flesh.

The flyer read:

> *Looking for a little excitement? Bored with the same old scene you can find in any big city with a nasty rep? Then you've come to the right place. Just head to the dark side of town: Start wherever you like, pick a direction—any direction—and go. It's not difficult to get there—just ask anyone bearing the mark. The right mark is a shining bit of blue metal carved in the form of an ancient rune and slid*

under the skin directly above the left cheek-bone—find it, and you will be guided to the most fearsome and deadly dens of iniquity and decadence imaginable. In these places, all things are possible and all things are evil.

So come on out. We don't bite—except when we're tearing people's heads off. But as long as you have good credit and an appetite like ours, you'll be fine. Come and indulge yourself from dusk till dawn. Or don't . . . if you want to keep your soul.

The little man looked around, as if he was worried that someone might have seen him reading this. Or was he looking for one of the guides mentioned in the flyer? He frowned, feeling tempted to do exactly that. In his lifetime, he had faced many such temptations, and resisting them had always been difficult. Maybe that weakness, that potential for corruption, was why the strange man with the flyer had targeted him in the first place. Shuddering, the round little man crumpled up the flyer and tossed it in a nearby trash can.

A light rain began to fall, quickly growing more insistent, urging him to pick a direction, any direction, and go. The little man felt his pulse quickening. A vibration surged through him, a rhythm that seemed to rise up from the very pavement in order to worm its way into his nervous system.

A crazy thought, yet he still wasn't moving. He was on Beverly Boulevard, shopping for his wife's anniversary gift, as throngs of people rushed past him in either direction, giggling, speaking urgently, commandingly, into their cell phones. Some were even singing. He stood still, rooted to the sidewalk, feeling slightly disturbed. Why would anyone think he'd be interested in the "delights" promised—or threatened—in that flyer?

"Like calls to like," a young woman whispered. He turned and saw a swiftly moving barrage of pink hair, tattooed flesh, spandex, and spiked heels, swallowed up by the crowd.

"Evil has a voice." These words came from a seemingly disinterested man with a thick head of black hair, and a soul patch beneath his lower lip. He whipped past. "It's your choice if you listen."

The little man could still hear the steady rhythm of the street reaching toward him, its vibrations matched by the pelting rain from above. It was like heaven and hell, being pulled in two vastly different directions.

Why should these feelings call to him? He could be anyone. He had never done anything terrible. Why should the city target him? Why should the darkness, pulsing like a living thing in the heart of the city, choose him? And why was he frozen in place like this?

Was there no escaping? Had fate selected him for some dark and bloody future? Why would he even have such questions?

Then, just as suddenly as the nightmare had begun, it ended. The rain continued to streak downward, but the city's sensual beat no longer matched it, and no longer quested after him. He was safe.

Why had it happened in the first place?

Had he looked down only a moment earlier, he would have had his answer. He would have seen that, on the pavement, bathed in the golden light of the jewelry store window, there was not one but two very powerful shadows reaching out from his body.

One shadow was clearly his own. It mirrored his form perfectly. The other was something very different. Its shape was longer, thinner, with raking talons for hands and an ovoid for a head cut open to reveal long, sharpened, chattering teeth. This was the *thing* that had been searching for a partner in evil, a suitable host that would help it carry out its plans. The street hawkers and the demonic types wandering the street had nothing to do with the shadowthing except that they had drawn its attention. They sensed the little man's potential for wickedness and had tried to lure him to their club, but the man had remained strong.

The club . . . perhaps *there* the shadow would find what it needed. Little bursts reminiscent of sunspots flickered excitedly in the second shadow at the prospect of a gathering place of fully corrupt souls. The music would lead the shadow there . . . where the city's darkest rhythms traveled, the living shadow followed.

• • •

From the outside, Club K looked like a dump. For the rich and powerful gathered here, that was simply part of its allure. They were anxious for a look inside, greedy to know, literally, how the other half died. The thundering pulse of the techno-synth industrial pop—jacked either from Hong Kong on a direct feed, or one of the lowest circles of hell— made the walls shake like a heart about to explode.

The people waiting outside *loved* it. Being so close to this place of abject violence and terror was exhilarating, almost unbearably so. Several had to leave, the excitement proving too much for them, or they raced away because their dark passions were so stirred that they had to seek more immediate and certain relief elsewhere.

They were bad, every one of them, just—and this revelation would have shocked any of them— not quite *bad enough* to get in here. Not tonight. Money didn't matter this evening. Either one was chosen by the men making the selections to come inside, to dance, to watch, to drink in the sounds and smells Club K had to offer, to bathe in the spatters of blood, to soak in the pungent ambrosia of the most distilled forms of sex and violence in this city—or one waited out here. Being chosen had simply to do with one's capacity for carnage and blood sport.

The two men working the gate could spot the

hard core—those with the correct potential—a mile off. The people out here may have been cruel, shameless, and wicked, but they just weren't ready for what was inside. Only those with murder in their hearts and blood on their hands would do.

It was a karmic thing.

For tonight was fight night. The excited shadows of those taunted by the possibility that they might be allowed inside darted and danced, as their partners chatted and laughed and anxiously watched the door, praying they would be let in. Their shadows, dark with evil, swayed or shrank to nothingness as headlights hit them and moved on.

Only one shadow moved of its own accord, however.

Only *one* made it inside.

Bernardo Fulcia was in the fight of his life. He stood upon a stage in the center of Club K, the heavy metallic bars of the "cage" dropped down on every side of him. Music roared and the crowd cheered as he and his fellow fighter did their best to beat each other to death.

One, naturally, would succeed.

Facing life-or-death challenges was nothing new to him. He had been a soldier, an assassin, and a thief professionally, a murderer for pleasure and personal gain. It was all he knew, and all he would ever know.

Club K at least offered a fresh challenge—practicing

his art in front of an audience—and fresh rewards. Every Wednesday night for the past month he had come here to do battle and to claim benefits offered on the earthly and otherworldly planes, pleasures and excitements that would kill any mortal not blessed with the protection spells of the club's owner. He knew his run wouldn't last, of course. The same champion winning, week after week, would prove boring to the patrons. Eventually, he would be made to take a fall.

He didn't care. Death was meaningless, only the pleasures of life mattered. His five-foot, eleven-inch-tall body glistened with blood and sweat. The rough, tattooed, skinned and bleeding knuckles that had delivered dozens of punishing hits to the heavily muscled body of his opponent—an even taller, blond Russian, as muscle-bound and intimidating as Dolph Lundgren in his prime—had all been for show. Shaking his head sharply to flip his long black hair out of his eyes, Bernardo waited for just the right opening, then delivered a brutal strike to the other man's kidney, doubling him over. He brought his knee up swiftly, feeling the satisfying *crunch* of cartilage giving way in his opponent's face as he destroyed the man's nose. He held back just enough to keep from driving that cartilage into the Russian's brain and killing him instantly.

There had to be some drama, some satisfaction.

Raising his arms high, Bernardo pranced around like an overconfident fool, giving his opponent enough time to partially recover and come at him again.

Bernardo took all the punishment the Russian could dish out, the pain only making the upcoming pleasure after this bout that much sweeter. It was all part of the show for him. He was in prime physical and mental condition, ready to die, ready to kill.

Tiring of being on the receiving end, Bernardo head-butted his enemy and kicked him hard in the groin. The Russian doubled over again, still not blacking out. Bernardo had a sense that some mystical element had been added to the fight. A spell had been worked on the Russian, or the man carried a magical talisman allowing him to retain consciousness and stay on his feet despite his injuries.

The thought did not trouble Bernardo. He knew that it should have troubled him deeply, but he felt an otherworldly calm, as if some arcane force was at work within him, as well.

And so it was.

He drove an uppercut toward the Russian's jaw. An instant before his fist connected with his opponent's face, a black, magical sword seemingly made of thick shadow burst from the back of his hand and pierced the underside of the Russian's chin, streaking out through the peak of his skull without a single spatter of blood or gore. The shadowy sword killed the man instantly and then withdrew in a blink, as Bernardo delivered the final blow.

He watched the Russian fall, and waited for the music to stop and the shouts and applause of the crowd to give way to shock. Very few of these people understood that there was another world coexisting with their own, a world of magic and madness, and that Los Angeles was one of those ports of common entry—demon central, practically.

The spectators had come to see two *mortals* fight to the death. Bernardo was human, but something had been done to him—he had been set up. Now the club owner would deny him his reward, deny him the chance to ever fight again . . . and, most probably, spend several weeks slowly killing him.

You needn't fear, a voice whispered in his mind. *Allow me the pleasure of taking care of this little mess for you, and, I promise, you never need to be afraid of anything ever again.*

Bernardo had no idea if he could trust whoever, or whatever, had made the offer that only he had heard, but it sounded like the deal of a lifetime, and he had very few options.

Do it, the voice whispered.

Bernardo reached out, other shadows stretching from his hand. He grinned as a nightmare-black talon that was somehow a part of *him* sliced through the iron mesh of the cage as if it were made of woolen string. He felt himself changing, and reveled in the screams of his loyal fans.

Laughing, he wondered what he must have looked like, and suddenly, as the talon fell upon a man in the panicked crowd, he saw himself through that man's eyes: His body was pulsating with darksome energies, his head was elongated, his eyes blazing, his teeth sharpened to points.

He was a monster, but he didn't care. He felt so free and so . . . *ravenous*.

Had the voice been real? Had something within him been released? Or was some strange entity possessing him?

Could it be both?

All that mattered was that he had never felt so alive.

Leaping from the cage into the midst of the fearful crowd, he sated his hunger. He had only to gesture and his shadow would come alive, reaching out from his body, falling upon a dozen or more victims at a time. Their terror was satisfying, but it did not satiate his hunger. He drew more than the lifeblood from them before taking their lives: With their deaths came so much energy, so much knowledge. . . .

It was glorious!

The first shot caught him completely off guard.

There was a muffled bang—a firecracker pop, small and toylike, almost unreal sounding. He staggered back, feeling as if someone had shoved him by his left shoulder. He was not feeling any pain, though.

Three more shots sounded. Three more after it. His hands went wild, shadows flying everywhere. People screamed.

The power that flowed into him was so intoxicating that it deadened his mind, numbed his body.

More shots.

He was back against the cage now, his body flailing, dancing, and he was dimly aware that his blood was splattering everywhere.

A shot struck him in the face, followed by two more to the brain. He sank to the floor, no longer aware of anything.

His shadow, however, stood all on its own. Perhaps it was never his to begin with.

Certainly, it was still hungry.

The living shadow took the life of the shooter, relishing his wealth of experience. Then it reached out and held fast all three of the club's exits, while it greedily consumed all of the remaining victims. With each killing it learned more about this world it had somehow entered, effortlessly absorbing several of its languages, a host of customs and cultural singularities, and delighting in the wonderful, overriding cynicism and arrogance of the petty little fools populating this place. They feared death, yet thought themselves above the natural order of things . . . that is, when they conceded that there was anything greater than themselves and their own desires in the myriad number of realities that comprised the multiverse.

Fascinating—and useful.

From two of the club's employees, it learned the

otherworldly nature of this place's owner, and was slightly concerned at the idea that not all humans lived unaware of the truths behind what they commonly referred to as "reality" . . . and that this realm was populated by far more than humans.

That meant he would find competition here . . . and, naturally, opposition.

As the shadow creature contemplated this thought, words from the languages it had just stolen sped through its mind like cherries in a slot machine, finally alighting on—

Nemesis.

Yes, that's what it would call itself. Standing amidst a field of corpses, it felt refreshed from its journey, and wondered about the forces that brought it here. Somehow a tear had formed in the walls between the Forbidden Lands and the rest of reality. Had this been by accident or design? It had to know.

Nemesis was not the only one of his kind. There were so many more who were waiting in its home dimension, withering away to nothingness. They were trapped, alone with nothing to feed upon except one another. But Nemesis would change all that. It would be the one to free them to feast on this world.

Its reign of terror had only just begun.

CHAPTER ONE

The mild glow of indirect sunlight bathed the handsome, chiseled features of Charles Gunn's face as he stood in the lobby of the Hyperion, the hotel that Angel Investigations used as its base of operations. His piercing gaze narrowed as he set it upon the leather-clad ensouled vampire for whom the agency had been named. Cordelia Chase and Winifred Burkle were also present to "enjoy" the otherwise slow and boring afternoon.

"That's it, man," Gunn said firmly to Angel. "Get your hands off my joystick before someone gets hurt."

"Now that's something you don't hear every day," Cordelia observed, lazily stretching herself out on the wide, circular couch. "Unless you watch a lot of prison movies."

Gunn gestured at the Nintendo in Angel's hands. "You both *know* what I'm talkin' about."

It was the middle of the day, and there were no

cases for Angel Investigations. Not a demon was stirring, not even a lousy R'pnar shakedown artist. They had finished off the last of those finheaded extortionists two days ago, killing half the gang that was terrorizing a small neighborhood on the west side and sending the others packing.

"But I like this game," Angel said, disappointed as he handed over the game unit. The score was flashing on the new sixty-five-inch flat-screen television—a recent gift from a grateful appliance store owner whose life was literally being made a living hell by the demonic "protection" ring. Angel nodded at the screen. "I always win."

Snatching up the remote, Gunn clicked off the TV and protectively held the game unit close. Tall and muscular, he always looked formidable; it was just that he normally reserved his stone-cold killer's glare for the most fearsome emissaries of darkness and evil. Right now, he had that look directed at the vamp he had been all buddy-buddy with just an hour earlier.

Gunn shook his head. "Yeah, that's the point. I'm tellin' ya, man, step off and no more touchin' my gear. Got it?"

Angel shrugged. "Gotten."

"I don't know why you boys can't just play nice," Cordy said brightly. "When it was Gunn and Wes acting like a couple of twelve-year-olds, it never came down to, 'You don't play right, so I'm taking my toys back.'"

She hesitated, mindful of the looks she had elicited with the mention of Wesley Wyndam-Pryce, their former associate—and once, Gunn's close friend. His kidnapping of Angel's son, however noble he thought he was being at the time, had resulted in Connor being taken to a hell dimension and raised by a madman who taught him to hate Angel. Time worked differently there, and although baby Connor had only been gone a matter of months by their reckoning, he had returned a bitter and angry young man with superhuman strength and abilities—and a huge chip on his shoulder. To this day, Connor still had major issues with his dad.

"Right," Cordelia murmured, "don't mention the Wesley."

Both Angel and Gunn averted their gazes and studied the floor like lost children.

"Listen," Gunn said evenly to Angel, "I know all this everyday human stuff isn't exactly second nature to you."

"Can't imagine why!" Cordy buzzed in. Then, getting those looks again, she went back to her magazine, humming a little song and buzzing right back out of the conversation the same way she had come.

"I was winning too much?" Angel asked, struggling to understand the problem. "'Cause I could lose. It's easy. Just tell me how many times you need to win to keep it interesting—"

"Naw, man, it's not like that," Gunn said, his

annoyance seeping away. He set the console down on the floor, near the television, and sat beside it. "Look at it like this: A call comes in. Someone's in trouble. You go up against a bunch of guys you *know* you can take. Two minutes into the fight, they're toast and you haven't even worked up a sweat. What do you call that?"

"Satisfying?" Angel suggested. "The whole, y'know, 'save the innocent' thing."

"Didn't you ever play sports when you were a kid?"

The brow of the 243-year-old vampire furrowed. "Too busy working. Or avoiding working." He hesitated. "Things were different back then."

"Well, I'm trying to get you in touch with how things are now. If you'd played sports, maybe we could come to some understanding. It's no fun to play against that guy who can nail the hoop at fifty feet every time, or crash the end zone whenever he wants."

"Yeah, I'm feeling a little foggy on the whole getting in touch thing. And I'm not really sure how it's supposed to help with the mission. We're here to help the helpless. That's it. That's our mission."

"Yeah, but to carry out the mission better, you need to understand the people you're trying to help. You know what scares them, sure. You're even getting a handle on their hopes and dreams, but the things people do for fun goes right over your head a lot of the time."

Angel scratched the back of his head. "So you're saying this is about relaxation."

"In a way, yeah. But that's not all. It's about how people relate to one another, how they feel connected—"

Angel cut Gunn off. "If you're looking for pointers on trance-state inducement and meditative technique to deal with life when it's not all do-or-die, I've got some books I could loan you."

Gunn turned away in frustration and picked up the television's remote. "I'm just gonna channel-flip for a while."

"Suit yourself," Angel said, leaning back and going kinda glassy-eyed as he stared off at some speck on the far wall and let it become his entire world until he was called upon. Oftentimes, he would be upstairs, asleep at this hour of the day, but ever since Cordy had returned, her memories finally intact, he'd taken advantage of every opportunity that presented itself to be near her.

He didn't do anything about it; he knew they were at a fragile point in their relationship—if one could call it that—and that if he pushed her about her feelings for him, he might well be pushing her right out the door and back to Connor's small "apartment." Still, there was something wonderful and comforting just having her around, breathing in her scent, being able to study her reflection in the shiny spot on the wall he had chosen to stare into.

She was so beautiful. . . .

Across the room, sitting behind the reception desk, picking at the leftover Thai takeout she had *taken* out of the fridge less than an hour ago, Winifred Burkle had a sense of what was really going on with Angel. She had been alone quite a bit in her life, and she had also spent time loving someone from afar. That someone had been Angel, for the span of months directly following his rescue of her from the hell dimension known as Pylea. In the time since, she had let go of those feelings, and developed something very real and, she had thought, very lasting with Charles Gunn. Lately, her life with Charles had been strained, recent unfortunate events slowly pulling them further and further apart. Fred heard the squeak of the swinging door leading to the area in which she had set up her own little fortress of solitude.

"Hey, now, don't be like a Snacqunar demon," Lorne said teasingly.

Fred looked up at the Pylean crooner, earnestly attempting to get the joke. Her brow furrowed, her lips pressed tightly together, she squinted, then shook her head swiftly. She just couldn't place the reference.

"Um," Lorne said embarrassingly, scratching the green skin on the back of his neck, "they like to play with their food. Pick at it for days. Usually, it does a lot of screaming and begging." He sighed. "Never mind."

She knew exactly why Lorne was feeling nervous around her and wished there was some way she could reassure him that everything was okay. She had woken up screaming the past three nights in a row and, when asked about her terrible nightmares, had lied and said they were of the torturous five years she had spent in a demon dimension.

The same demon dimension that had spawned Lorne.

Pylea.

Even if it had been true—such nightmares *had* come back to her from time to time—that didn't mean she associated Lorne with the horrors she had experienced. He was an outcast from his people, as unable to "fit in" with his family's demonic warrior clan as Fred herself would be if someone invited her to a coffee klatch of suburban moms with bouncing burping babies in tow. She outwardly shuddered at the thought—and kicked herself inwardly at Lorne's little wince in response.

Lorne stood up, a delicious aroma wafting from his steaming plate of *paneer harialli*, a spicy Indian dish he had whipped up in the kitchen. His smile was as awkward and pained as his tense body language. Even his gaudy beyond words crimson leisure suit, yellow shirt, and purple and white pinstriped tie or his glittering golden jewelry couldn't detract from the hurt in his eyes. "I was going to see if you wanted some company, cupcake, but, ah . . . I don't want to intrude."

Fred's hand gently fell upon his wrist, and she drew him back to the chair next to her. "I always appreciate the company."

A moment ago, that hadn't been true. She had been alone and felt happy that way, but now she was feeling the isolation among their once tightly knit group, and Lorne's presence was exactly what she needed.

"So," she said brightly, "any mystical rumblings?"

"Only when I make the mistake of getting up in the middle of the night and giving in to my Shami Rajma Pizza crazings, which, I swear, have to be the work of something dark, demonic, and pure evil, considering I wake up with the runs every morning after. Sheesh."

"Spicy kidney bean pizza in a hot masala sauce, huh?"

"It reminds me of something my mom used to make for me when I was a little kid. It isn't until I'm at least halfway done that I remember how much Mom hated me and was always trying to poison my food."

"Still, sounds tasty."

"It is, pork chop. And speaking of tasty, have you been spending much time with our darling Cordelia lately? Truth be told, I'm a little worried about her."

Fred nodded. They had been through a lot lately, and Cordelia's warning that some big nasty of apocalyptic proportions was coming probably didn't help her state of mind—especially since little details like "where," "when," "why," and "how" were still up in the air.

At least she was here—though however long that might last, was anyone's guess.

Cordelia lay down the latest issue of *Allure*. The magazine was proving to be a bust; just the typical ramblings of a conspiratorial gathering of superthin supermodels intent on lowering the self-esteem of women everywhere by continuing to exist. She had been desperately attempting to reconnect with something, *anything*, that vaguely made her feel like her old self again. Her memories were back, but she couldn't shake the feeling that she no longer fit in with this place, with these people, even though she knew full well that they were her dearest friends.

Cordelia was still resting and recuperating from a journey down a long stretch of road that none of them truly believed was behind her. And there was the matter of her feelings for Angel, which were very mixed up right now, and her concern over how Connor was getting along without her, which was even crazier considering all the power he had and that his nickname back in that hell dimension where he was raised was "The Destroyer."

Yeah, right, there's someone who can't take care of himself, Cordy thought. But while Connor was physically strong, he was fragile emotionally, a truth she sometimes felt she was the only person on the planet who really understood.

Cordelia glanced up from her reading as Angel walked past and, for the love of Mike . . . had he actually just *sniffed* her?

This place was getting crazier by the day!

Fred excused herself for a quick trip to the ladies' room as Angel swung by, stopping on the other side of the desk from the former Host. "I don't get it, Lorne. Why's everyone so touchy?"

"Oh, gee, I don't know, let me guess . . . it couldn't have anything to do with where we last left our heroes, kinda beaten down and depressed after that fun-fun-fun round of 'We're all teenagers again, at least in our heads' and then coming back to 'Huh, y'know, this isn't at all how I pictured adult life was going to be. Oh, yeah, and the end of the world's coming. *Again.*"

"No need for sarcasm."

"Hey, it was my spell that went haywire, remember? And I spent most of that little adventure tied to a chair trying to talk you people out of cutting my heart out . . . or, at least, continuously clobbering me with blunt objects. Like your *wit.*"

"You're right, that is pretty depressing."

Lorne rummaged through a pile of large envelopes scattered around the reception area. He found one that had already been opened and he handed it to Angel. "Well, sweetness and light, maybe this'll cheer you up. Look at you! You're famous."

Angel slipped a comic book from the envelope. The color cover was printed on a thicker paper stock than the black-and-white interiors. The whole thing was crudely rendered, with some pasty-faced guy in a black leather duster holding a barely clad woman in his arms, his sharp, white fangs glinting in the moonlight as he stood upon an L.A. rooftop and threw his head back in torment. Angel didn't realize the guy in the drawing was supposed to be *him* until he realized that the jagged letters dripping crimson on the cover spelled his name.

Gunn sprang up and ran over. "Oh, man . . . why'd you show him that? I've been meaning to go down and straighten those punks out."

Lorne gave him a knowing smile. "Come on, cuddles. You're just upset because you're not in it."

"Not true."

Angel flipped through the pages of the comic book. He couldn't quite believe what he was seeing.

"This is me," Angel said, shocked. "This is about *me*."

Gunn nodded. "Sort of."

Angel picked a dialogue balloon at random. "'Oh. But no one understands. I live apart, plagued by my ravenous appetite, torn asunder within by my mountainous guilt. . . .' *Who wrote this?*"

With a sigh, Gunn revealed, "Remember that comic book shop I took you to?"

"With the chatty rooms?"

"Right. Those guys whipped this out in, like, a week."

Angel dropped the comic book onto the counter. "Great. For the first time in two centuries I want to sue someone, and the only lawyers I know are evil. This is unbelievable. I should just—"

"You should forget about it, sweetbuns," Lorne interrupted. "What are you going to do, sue for libel? Even if you could, would you want the world to know that people like you and me are walking around?"

"Good point."

"They do kind of deserve it," Gunn said, paging through the comic book again. "Just for the inking alone."

"People pay money for these?" Angel asked.

"Oh, yeah," Gunn told him. "It's a big market. Or . . . it can be. Something like this could turn up all over the world." He paused. "You really don't know much about comic books, do you?"

Angel shrugged. "I don't know. I liked *Archie*."

"Hold on, hold on," Gunn said, barely able to contain his excitement. "Critical question here: Betty, Veronica, or both?"

"I really liked Doris Day."

"So, Betty!"

Noticing that Cordy had taken notice, Angel

picked up the comic again. "At least I'm the hero. But . . . in here I'm always brooding. I'm not that one-dimensional!"

"Pfff!" Cordy said, the sudden exhalation of breath that came with the sound making her long bangs flutter. She came over and did her best Angel imitation. "I *brood*, therefore I *am*."

"I can be a fun guy."

"Yeah, right."

"Can *too*."

Gunn nodded at the comic. "Hey, you shouldn't complain about the way they make you look in here. Compared with us, you come out pretty damn rosy."

Angel read on. "'All my companions are dead and gone. I may not kill to survive, but I take and take from them. I drain their very souls. Without them, I feel my mask of humanity slipping. I feed, but in another way. I am but a lowly parasite, drawing all around me to their dooms. My need . . . my need is so strong!'"

"Yeah, that's what issue one is about," Gunn said. "All of us are toast and you put together a new crew 'cause you just can't help yourself. One of those lesser evil deals."

"Lesser evils."

"Yeah. You know what you'll turn into without people around, and you can't fit in with the world without folks to guide you, so you pick these people knowing you're going to see every one of them die sooner or later. Probably sooner. You try to keep your distance, but you can't. It's a real *Saving Private Ryan/Platoon* kind of theme."

"The me that's in the story," Angel said, wanting to make sure that was what Gunn meant.

"In the story, dawg," Gunn said with a smile. "Just in the story. That's why I didn't even want you seeing it."

"It's something, isn't it?" Lorne asked cheerfully. "The way we see ourselves versus the way other people see us, I mean."

Fred returned and called to Angel. "I just checked my e-mail. You know those computer-literate snitches we have working for us off the books?"

"We have books?" Gunn asked. "You're kiddin' me."

Fred didn't even look his way. "The three lower mischief demons you promised not to slowly torture to death for their crimes if they helped out now and then."

"Larry, Moe, and Curly?" Angel asked.

"Right, them," Fred said. "That crime scene you've been wanting to check out? It looks like things have finally died down over there. It's been three days; the bodies are gone. We should be able to get in."

"Excellent idea!" Lorne said, snatching the comic book from Angel. "I'll just file this under 'Let's not go there again.'"

"A crime scene, now that's uplifting. You guys go on ahead," Cordelia said, crossing over to their new television set. "I could still use some R&R and TLC and—hey, did this thing come with TiVo?"

When she didn't get any response, she looked back and saw that everyone but Lorne had gone. He held up that disgusting food he'd been eating.

"Hungry?" Lorne asked.

"Starved," she whispered, heading over to the couch with the remote. "But not for that."

What she was craving was even a trace of the joy she used to feel at seeing the team rush into action, and often joining in the craziness. She knew it was silly, but she couldn't get the words in that comic book out of her mind. Were they all pretty much doomed just by virtue of hanging around Angel?

Or was he the only one who just might be able to save all of them, when the time finally came?

She flipped through some channels, doing her best to put the question out of her mind though she knew she wouldn't be able to avoid the subject forever.

Angel met Gunn and Fred at the rear entrance to the building that had housed the illegal fight club. He had come up through the sewers, found a way inside, and opened the place up for them. Gunn and Fred hurried inside, looking over their shoulders for any prowling police cars that might pass by and notice them as they entered the crime scene. Once inside, they surveyed what little the police and all the others who had been through this place had left behind: a huge, dimly lit room with a bar, a stage, three exits, and the outlines of more bodies than Gunn had ever seen in one place.

"What happened here?" Gunn asked.

Fred removed her PalmPilot from her purse. She had transferred her electronic files about this crime to the handheld unit. "They're, um, they're calling it the 'Club K Massacre,'" she said, surveying the raw data once more, as if to convince herself that it was real. "Not like Special K. Not like the cereal. I mean . . . what does a cereal have to do with a mass murder, right?" Fred laughed nervously. "Except there's lots of the little bits in the bowl. Like lots of people killed. And it's flaky. Like what happened here is flaky, I mean." She sighed. "Right. I guess the point here is that killing one hundred and ten people in one place at one time doesn't happen every day. Especially when it looks like every one of them died of natural causes."

Angel was surprised. "That's what the police came up with?"

"Well . . . a couple were shot, a handful got trampled trying to get out, and three were listed as drug overdoses," Fred observed, doing her best to detach herself from the reality that these were people with lives and not just facts and figures in a report. It was working . . . kinda. "According to initial reports, though, SCD—or sudden cardiac death—was listed more than anything else.

Besides heart attacks, there were a dozen aneurysms and two victims who died of massive internal hemorrhaging and, may I just add, ick?"

"That's it?" Angel asked, wheels turning in his mind as he walked around, desperately attempting to pick up a scent of anything otherworldly. And there was something here, but it was nothing he had ever encountered before, nothing he could identify.

Fred nodded sharply. "Well, more or less. Kind of looks that way." She swallowed hard and shivered, wanting to be all hard-edged and analytical but feeling totally creeped out inside. "Yep! Yep, that's it."

"Has the Centers for Disease Control been here?" Gunn asked, sidling up next to her.

She nodded without looking his way. "They came up with squat. Diddly-squat. Less than nothing, nada, and zip all put together."

Angel leaped onto the stage, examining the bent-back bars on the steel cage that had kept the fighters in place. It was unlikely that anything human had done this—not without help. "One hundred and ten people were scared to death in this place. I can still smell the fear. But none of the people standing outside saw a thing. Nothing weird going in, nothing coming out."

Gunn was getting it now. "There're a whole lot of demons and other nasties out there that don't have to worry about doors and stuff. They can walk right through them."

"Or open a portal, do what they came here to do, and close it up again on the way out," Fred said distractedly. She had been walking around right on the verge of falling off an internal cliff into a swirling mass of disturbing memories. Every now and then she tread a little closer to the edge and, each time, it felt harder to draw herself back.

Gunn said nothing to that. Everyone had been making a point of not mentioning anything around Fred that might remind her of the recent events with Professor Seidel. Despite their care, however, all roads seemed to end at that same dark place.

"Gunshots mean there was something to shoot *at*," Angel said.

"And, y'know, people being *trampled* means there was, like, something to run away from," Fred added, surprised at her growing excitement. This was a terrible thing, yet it was also an intriguing analytical puzzle, something she could distance herself from and use to take her mind off her own concerns.

"Shooting victims?" Angel asked as he leaped down from the stage and crossed over to where Fred was standing.

Fred handed him the PalmPilot, the page he requested already pulled up. She knew he would want to see what they had on them.

Angel scrutinized the screen. "I recognize this Bernardo guy's name. He's an up-and-comer on the underground fight circuit. They keep trying to shut these places down, but more of them keep cropping up."

Angel had some personal experience with fight clubs. He had once been tricked into delivering himself into the hands of people who owned an underground club similar to this one—only with a distinctly demonic element. These fighters fought to the death, but they were human . . . which almost made it *worse*.

"So what was so special about this guy?" Angel pondered. "Why was he shot?"

Gunn suggested, "Could have been a stray bullet."

"He was hit twenty-two times."

"Probably not a stray."

Fred intervened. She was determined to stay unemotional. Clearing her throat, she said, "Initial investigation makes it look like the other poor schlep who died by gunfire was the shooter."

"So he just about *empties* two clips into this guy, then turns the gun on himself," Angel said flatly. "Why?"

Gunn seemed to think the answer was obvious. "Bullets weren't doing the trick. They stopped this guy, but they didn't stop something else. Possession, maybe?"

"Maybe . . . ," Angel agreed.

"But wait, there's more!" Fred said enthusiastically, taking the PalmPilot back from Angel.

"Everyone who died here had power and was into some nasty stuff. I'm not saying they deserved what happened to them, but this much bad karma in one place? I wouldn't be surprised if they were drawn here by something."

Angel's brow furrowed slightly. "Nasty stuff. Like what?"

"Murder, every one of them," Fred announced, still struggling to focus only on the facts. So long as she didn't get emotional about this, she had a chance of not dwelling too much on what happened to her and getting emotional about *that*. "Suspected, accused. A couple who were convicted then had their sentences overturned."

"Wolfram and Hart?" Angel asked with a scowl, figuring he already knew the answer.

"Maybe," Fred told him. "They were all into lots of other things, like corporate takeovers, black market dealings, kidnappings, white slavery, drugs—the list goes on and on. And it seems the people outside were into that sort of stuff too."

"But no murders," Angel asserted.

"Right," Fred said. "That was what everyone who got in, and everyone who worked here, had in common. One big happy family of evil, soulless worms." She hesitated. "Not literal worms. Not like people who turn into worms, or worms who turn into—"

"They were all human?" Angel asked, growing

more agitated. Fred's excitement seemed to be contagious. "We're certain of that?"

Fred nodded slowly. "You don't have to be a soulless monster to be, well . . . a soulless monster, if you catch my drift."

"True," Angel said, understanding her perfectly. Humans could be evil all on their own; no help from the supernatural forces at work in the city were necessary. "Maybe if we could find out who really owned this place, we might have somewhere to go with this investigation."

Gunn was getting into it. "You mean, like, someone sets up the fight club just to lure in a bunch of folks who're in negative numbers on the karmic scale, then harvest their souls or something?"

"A setup like this?" Angel said, continuing to survey the crime scene. "Anything's possible." He began to pace. "There are three ways out. Front entrance, back entrance, side door leading to the basement and ultimately the sewers. Three doors. No one got out."

"I can think of two possibilities. Whatever did this either didn't give them enough time to reach the doors or it held all three doors shut with some kind of low-level telekinesis, a stasis field, something."

Angel suddenly looked distracted.

"What is it?" Gunn asked, worried.

"Police are back." Angel sniffed the air and shook his head. "If we cross from here to get to the entrance to the underground, we'll be seen. I'll be seen. And I don't want to fight them to keep from getting dragged out into the sunlight. . . . I burn easily."

"They won't see anything—not if there's a distraction," Gunn suggested.

"I've got it," Fred said swiftly, the determination in her voice making it clear she wouldn't hear any arguments from her companions. She rushed ahead as Angel and Gunn slipped into the shadows.

Gunn let out a deep breath. "You go, girl."

"What he said," Angel added.

Fred didn't hear either of their comments. Instead, she started humming—loudly. The humming gave way to singing, and the singing was paired with dancing. Fred made just enough of a spectacle of herself to draw the attention of four police officers: two were silhouetted by the bright light coming through the now open front door, and two more crossed the entire length of the club to join the others, walking right past Angel and Gunn without seeing them.

Three of the officers wore uniforms; the other, a suit.

"Hello," the guy in the suit hollered, jumping in front of Fred and making her start.

She put her hand to her chest, which was rising and falling rapidly from her exertions. "You scared me."

Mr. Suit Guy pulled out his ID and flipped it

open for her. "Detective John Moffat. How are you today?"

Fred looked around, playing the space case. It wasn't hard; she'd had lots of practice, even by her own admission. Then she focused on the man before her.

Detective John Moffat was shorter than Fred. He must have *just* made the department's height requirement. He was balding, his fine red hair chopped into a near crew cut. He was a little thick in the middle, an intense fireplug of a guy who liked to do that "What're you lookin' at?" thing as his gaze darted from one of your eyes to the other and swiftly back again. He had rough, no-nonsense, almost cruel features. He reminded Fred of some actor who might have been cast as a thug in some BBC crime drama.

But when he smiled, the sky opened and he transformed, suddenly appearing jovial and trustworthy, like a favorite uncle.

His off-the-rack gray suit looked five, maybe ten, years old. It wasn't unfashionable, just cheap and well-worn. His tie was a faded red, his shoes scuffed. The only thing stylish about him was a neatly folded, natty little handkerchief poking out from his breast pocket. This guy was all about giving off mixed signals, but Fred was onto him. He was acting just like a cop—trying to keep her guessing in order to distract her into tripping up and feeding him a line. She got that.

So she made a conscious decision that she wouldn't allow herself to be thrown off. Yet . . . simply by making that decision, she understood that she was already on shaky ground.

"Oh! Hi!" she said excitedly.

"Can I help you?" Moffat asked.

"Gee, I hope so." She was attempting to turn her distress and its accompanying franticness into bubbly, perky, enthusiastic energy. She couldn't tell if it was working.

Digging into her purse, she pulled out and then handed over a folded-up sheet of paper she had printed off the Internet, which she had with her for just such a contingency. The detective squinted as he opened it and took in the information on the paper.

Fred laughed. "I'm trying to find this place and I think I'm lost."

"New in town?" he asked, his tone somewhere between wary and weary.

"Not exactly," she said, truthfully enough. "I'm just not used to this part of town."

He shrugged, scrutinizing the printout.

Fred realized that she'd been carrying this piece of paper around for weeks and she was not sure if the date of the apartment listing was on there or not. If it was, it might give her away.

"You're about ten miles east of where you want to be," the detective said. "And you're trespassing in a crime scene."

"Well, *yeah,* I can see something went on here. I just figured that's why the rent was so cheap."

She *so* hoped that he wouldn't ask for her name or ID.

He smiled, folding over the page. "No worries," he said, "*this* time. But, in the future, 'Do Not Cross' means—"

He tensed, his gaze shifting toward something over her shoulder. She heard someone coming. Had he seen Angel and Gunn?

"Yo, girl, there you are!"

Fred stiffened at the sound of her boyfriend's voice.

"Charles," she hissed, wishing at once that she could take back the utterance. What was he doing here? What was he thinking? The detective was about to let her go!

Gunn put his arm around Fred. "Listen, Officer, I can explain all this."

"Charles, I was explaining everything just fine," Fred said, shrugging off his arm.

Ignoring her, he went on, "See, this is my girl-friend. And she's a little, y'know, *crazy.* But, like, in a good way. Kooky. *Kooky's* a good word for it, wouldn't you say, honey?"

Fred was incensed. "If you're looking for a spiked heel in your instep—"

"It's just . . . the way she likes to get down, if you hear what I'm sayin'." Gunn kind of rolled his eyes. "The more public someplace is, the higher the risk of getting caught . . . y'all see my point, right? And a place like this, it's a little walk on the wild side, kinda creepy, but—"

Fred had heard enough. "I'm going to kill you!"

"Fine, fine, *enough*," Detective Moffat said. "Both of you, just go."

Fred and Gunn didn't need to be told twice. They hurried from the club and didn't talk again until they were in his truck, pulling away from the crime scene.

Gunn was triumphant. "All right, now *that* worked like a charm."

"Congratulations," Fred said icily.

Easing into traffic, Gunn chanced a look at Fred. "What? Something wrong? I don't get it."

"I don't expect you do."

He waited until they were stopped at a light, then looked over at her. "Listen, I'm sure you were gonna handle that just fine on your own. But Angel got away, and there had to be some reason for me to be there."

"You could have gone with him."

"I wanted to be with you."

Fred wanted to slap him. "You could have followed my lead."

"Yeah, I guess, but . . . did you see the look on that guy's face? Now *that* was funny."

"I didn't realize that was the point."

The light changed, and Gunn motored into a changing lane.

"Charles, you just don't trust me."

"Sure, I do. I'm sure what you were doing would have worked just fine. I just thought it could do with a little touch of my personal style, see what I'm sayin'."

"I do, yeah. And now we'll never know if I needed rescuing or not."

"Aw, baby, don't be like that," he said, reaching for her hand as he drove past a rundown grocery store.

She folded her arms over her chest, tucking away her hands.

He sighed . . . and focused instead on the road.

Three car-lengths back, a hooded figure wearing dark designer sunglasses watched the small shapes of Gunn and Fred as they strained not to talk to each other. There was a bug planted in Gunn's truck that provided the audio. The couple was clearly having problems, and it was only a matter of time before their emotional distance manifested itself in the physical.

"Fred, Fred, Fred," their observer mused. "We need to give you something else to think about."

The hooded figure smiled, ideas already beginning to form.

CHAPTER TWO

Night had wrapped itself around the hotel like a cool, comforting cloak. The potentially deadly grip of the sun had relaxed, and Angel could now move about freely in any place he so desired—as long as an invitation wasn't required.

Angel stood before his open weapons cabinet, mentally inventorying the spikes, pikes, blades, axes, bludgeons, and other assorted items of pure killing force standing at anxious attention. He assessed the merits and limitations of each weapon, carefully cross-checking the tools available to him against what intelligence he'd been able to gather about the nightclub owner and the creature that worked for him. The bright lights of the hotel lobby were gleaming off the perfectly sharpened edges and well-rounded curves of his collection.

There was a story behind each weapon that had come into Angel's possession. Most had once been used for evil and were now on a path of redemption similar to the one Angel was on, but a select few had been bequeathed by fellow champions.

Gunn stood beside Angel, sharing in his silent reverence. They were warriors, and whether they lived or died, this night might depend on the choices they made in this near-sacred moment.

"I'm worried about Fred," Angel admitted. "Maybe she should sit this one out."

"I don't know," Gunn countered confidently. "I was proud of her today. She seemed pretty on top of things back at Club K. She was the one who got us out of that mess with the cops. I nearly blew it for her."

Angel nodded slowly. "She was scared. I could smell it. The whole time, she was struggling just to keep it together. I know she wants us to think she's okay, but my instincts are telling me it's too soon to put her back on the front lines with something like what we're going up against tonight."

"'Nothing's more dangerous in combat than a soldier with something to prove,'" Gunn said, repeating a quote he had once heard.

"Exactly."

Solemnly, they went back to staring at the weapons, sidestepping, at least temporarily, the issue of who would break the news to Fred.

"Sheesh, and I thought the whole 'guys and cars' thing was bad," Cordelia said mockingly. She brushed past them, hauling out an ax and handing it to Gunn, then doing the same with a sword for Angel. "Hey look, kids. They're bright and shiny, and you can use 'em to hack stuff up. Wow, who woulda thought?"

Angel and Gunn sighed. Yet . . . the weapons Cordy had selected really did feel *right* for the job at hand. Maybe her ability to choose them so easily was some residual effect from having resided on a higher plane of existence for so long.

Cordelia crossed her arms over her chest. "Boys, after this, never *ever* complain again about how long it takes a woman to get ready to go out. *Capisce?*"

Angel and Gunn sheepishly murmured their assent. Footsteps sounded from one of the nearby offices, and they looked up as Fred approached, slipping on her jacket. She stopped dead when she saw the strange expression both men wore.

"What?" Fred asked. "Weather report said it was a little nippy out, that's all."

"Fred, we should talk," Angel said awkwardly.

Fred tensed. Suspicion flared in her eyes. "Really? Right now?"

Cordy crossed to the couch and sat down hard. "It's gonna be one of those, I can just feel it."

"One of those what?" Fred asked.

"One of those *rare* occasions when the guys act like doofuses."

"Not doofuses." Angel gestured at the couch. "Would you take a seat?"

"Oh, I have to sit down for this," Fred whispered. "Well, this should be exciting. I mean, heaven forbid we go out and stop a possible mass killer before he can do it again. You're right, let's chitchat." She sat on the couch beside Cordy, folding her hands in her lap. "Okay, I'm all ears."

"I thought it was all neck," Cordy muttered. Her eyes widened, and she looked at her companion. "Sorry! Did I say that out loud?"

Angel nodded. "Pretty much, yeah."

Cordy looked away. "I have *got* to get some action. I swear, it's making me so crabby."

"Still out loud!" Fred and Angel chorused.

The voluptuous brunette looked back in surprise. "Really?" She got up and excused herself. "I'll just go see if that new TV gets Cinemax," she said quietly.

"What's up with that?" Gunn asked as Cordy laboriously took the stairs.

"She's not herself," Angel said.

Fred shrugged. "Who is?"

"That's the thing," Angel said. "We think you should sit this one out."

Fred was floored. "Excuse me?"

Kneeling beside her, Gunn donned his most soulful and comforting expression. Fred guessed that it was supposed to be the spoonful of sugar to help with the bitter medicine.

It didn't do a damn thing for her.

"Baby, things have been hard on you," Gunn

said softly. "You've got a lot on your mind, and what we're doin' could be awfully dangerous."

"Excuse me, *Sarge*," Fred said sarcastically, ignoring Gunn and aiming the jab at Angel, whom she held with her fierce gaze. "Exactly *when* was I declared unfit for active duty?"

Angel's shoulders drew up. He looked pained and uncomfortable. He was good at that. Gunn got to his feet and started pacing.

"See, I usually handle the paperwork," Fred said, her annoyance mounting, "and someone forgot to hand me the memo!"

Gunn tried to calm her, but his demeanor came across as condescending even though he didn't mean it that way at all. "We talked about this, that you should take it easy for a while. Get back into it slowly. This, tonight . . . this is racing out of control."

"It's that bad, but the two of you can handle it on your own."

Gunn made the mistake of smiling. "Yeah!"

"Do not come within kicking range, Charles."

Angel threw up his hands. "We're going, you're staying. Deal with it."

"Really, honey, it's for the best," Gunn added. He tentatively closed in on her, and gave that hangdog look that used to get to her every time. Not anymore. He kissed her cheek. "Be back soon. Think about what you want to do with the night. I promise, it'll be sweet, whatever you want."

Fred wouldn't even look at him. "Charles, honey and sweetness are about the last things you've got to look forward to from me."

She watched them go, wondering if they had even thought to take the cell phone in case they changed their minds and needed backup after all. Fred knew that she should feel worried about them: Anytime they left this place and went to fight, there was always the chance that they wouldn't make it back alive.

But her anger forced out her worry. She almost didn't even bother to answer the phone when it rang, even when it got all insistent, ringing, ringing, ringing. . . .

She went behind the desk and snatched up the receiver.

"Angel Investigations," Fred said in her best fake bubbly voice. She was determined to calm down, not to let those guys get to her. Even if she thought, for a second, that there really was something to what they were saying, she was the one who should have been allowed to make the call.

Didn't she have any control over her own existence? And, if not, how did she let herself get put in a situation like that *again*?

The throaty feminine voice on the other end of the receiver asked, "Give me a good reason why you're not doing advanced particle research, young lady?"

Fred did a double take, actually holding the phone away, looking at it, then putting it back to her ear. She knew this voice. But . . . it was impossible!

Wasn't it?

"At least tell me you've got a boyfriend," the voice added.

"Alicia?" Fred said excitedly.

"Boys and physics, my two favorite subjects—though not necessarily in that order. Yep, it's me! And how is my long-lost Frederika of Hollywood?"

Fred clamped her hand to her mouth, barely stifling a high, shrill, girlish scream as she stamped her feet and bounced excitedly. She forced her hand away from her mouth. "Oh, my God!" she cried.

"No, I'm smarter than Her," joked the voice on the other end of the line.

"Alicia?" Fred said, totally shocked.

"The one and only."

"I . . . I . . . I'm sorry. I should have gotten in touch. I got back and—"

Alicia laughed. "My folks ran into your folks. I knew you were back. I just figured there was some reason you weren't calling. You needed time, or you didn't want your old life showing up and bothering you, something like that."

"No, really . . ."

"Then there I was in Amsterdam at a symposium on the theoretical application of particle theory to advanced weaponry and someone hands me this glorious story on supersymmetry by my old pal Fred, and that was it. You had me at deviant superstring theory."

Fred felt herself going all "oh, shucks" despite herself. "It's just a couple of crazy ideas."

Alicia cleared her throat. "Oh, really? Fermions mixing it up with bosons and challenging Planck's theory for an entirely new take on supergravity? Sweetie, you always knew just what to say to get me all hot and bothered."

Flushing, Fred said, "Um, you don't really mean that literally, do you?"

"Kidding, kidding! I kid. But this is thrilling work, and you are to be congratulated."

"Thanks."

"I mean it. If you could turn this into applied physics, you could win the Nobel. You know that, right?"

Fred was really feeling embarrassed now. "I suppose."

"Anyway, I just couldn't stay away any longer," Alicia told her. "I'd have flown home early to see you present it if I could have, but I just couldn't swing it. I'm in town now. I've got a job over at Norris Aeronautical Industries—all top-secret stuff."

"Really? Like what?"

"Remember that movie we watched? *The 4-D Man?*"

"Yeah?" Fred said eagerly.

"*Nothing* like that."

Fred laughed.

"Actually," Alicia said, her tone somewhat more serious, "Listen, Fred, I really want to see you. I know this is zero notice, but can we get together for dinner? There's something I want to talk to you about."

"Well . . . sure! There are *lots* of things for us to talk about." Fred drew a sharp breath. *Although it's not like I'm going to bring up those hellish five years I spent in Pylea courtesy of Professor Seidel. Or what I saw happen to him,* Fred thought.

She'd idolized Professor Seidel and trusted him completely. That trust turned out to be misplaced. Threatened by Fred's potential, he'd sent her to another dimension to die, just as he had other students before and after her. She'd been the only one to return, and when she'd learned the truth, she'd decided to take bloody revenge on him. Only . . . Gunn stopped her, taking the matter out of her hands by snapping Professor Seidel's neck and tossing his lifeless carcass through the dimensional rift to Pylea she had opened.

She sometimes wondered about the other students Professor Seidel had sent away. Had they all ended up in Pylea?

The others . . . could any of *them* still be alive?

One day, she was going to have to try to find out.

"Actually, I don't have any plans for the evening,

as it turns out," Fred told her, doing her best to keep any sharp barbs out of her voice. "In fact, there's a new restaurant across town I've heard about. They've got a nice outdoor area. It's called Pataki Mez. It's a little exotic, but you could always handle the hot stuff."

"Excellent."

"I'll call ahead and make reservations for nine. What's your cell, in case I can't get a table and we need to rethink?"

Alicia gave her the number, gushed a little more about how excited she was that they were finally getting together, then got off to take another call.

Fred set the receiver down and thought about her pal.

Alicia Austin was a knockout. There were no two ways about it. She had perfect hair—long, blond, and luxurious—kind yet electrifying green eyes, a radiant smile, cheekbones worthy of a supermodel, a perfect hourglass figure, a great sense of style . . . and she *loved* geeks. She could get along with anyone: jocks, wasteoids, preppies, punks, whomever—it didn't matter to her. Alicia was one of the least judgmental people Fred had ever met.

She was also every brainiac's fantasy come to life: a Mensa club member who would enter (and win) any wet T-shirt contest that was offering a cash prize. She'd do it to help defray the costs of her education and pay for her extracurriculars, which included such deliriously diverse things as an obsession with Japanese manga, an addiction to wild street fashions, unwavering devotion to the Oilers, and an affinity for creating small-scale models of particle accelerators. She was a trip, and it took this phone call to remind Fred just how great hanging out with Alicia used to be, and how much she'd missed her.

Right about now, this seemed like exactly what she needed.

Oh sure, there was something going on that Alicia needed to talk about, probably boyfriend trouble. When they had been close, Alicia rarely confided in anyone else about that stuff, though Fred was never quite sure why. In retrospect, maybe it was because, unlike so many of Alicia's other friends, Fred genuinely listened. She may not have had much advice to dish out, considering how lacking Fred had been in experience, but that probably wasn't what Alicia needed.

Just someone to listen . . . that was probably all Alicia needed now.

Lorne sauntered in. "Well, you seem a little more on the perky side. Who was that?"

"An old friend from college. One of the really good ones."

"That's great, pumpkin. Tell you what, in this town, real friends are hard to find." He glanced about the eerily quiet lobby. "Where is everyone?"

"Cordelia's upstairs, and the guys"—Fred shrugged—"They're off doing guy things."

Angel and Gunn were motoring down La Brea, the top down, the bracing wind cool and refreshing against their faces. Traffic was light, even for a weeknight, and the only people who gave them a second look were into the car, not the two of them. No cops, no lawyers, no vengeance-seeking abominations from the nineteenth level of some hell hardly anyone ever visited anymore. It was nice.

"I want to talk about our relationship," Gunn said from the passenger seat.

Angel shot him a confused look. "Yours and mine?"

"Naw, man . . . me and Fred."

"Dunno," Angel said warily. "Me and women. Hi, I love you, oops, evil again, yeah, okay, it was me who tried to kill everyone you care about, sorry, having kind of an off day, meant to get you, too. I mean, come on. What in our shared history makes you think I'm capable of relationship talk?"

"I just think that was pretty rough back there," Gunn said. "Leaving Fred behind, trying to make her understand."

"It had to be done."

Gunn looked over sharply. "Did it? The more I look back on it, the more I wonder. We've *all* been through some heavy-duty stuff lately. Who's to say *we* shouldn't be sitting things out too?"

51

"The job's got to get done. But, Fred . . . waking up screaming for I don't know how many nights in a row—that was a tip-off that maybe she needed a time-out."

Gunn nodded. "Man has a point."

The neon lights of expensive clothing shops blurred by as they drove. Angel turned down Melrose, miraculously found a spot only three blocks away from Pink's, and parked. They walked back, the scent of the place's famous chili dogs getting to both of them. Soon they were only a hundred feet from the restaurant that drew the richest of the rich, the poorest of the poor, the famous, the nearly dead and the newly wed. Everyone came to Pink's. The restaurant had been in business since 1939, and its atmosphere was that of an old-fashioned diner, with a blue-white luminescence filtering from its windows and the sounds of laughing, satisfied patrons within.

"Come on, now," Gunn said, his stomach growling with desire even though he had already eaten. "You can't be implyin' that this place is evil."

"Course not. You know what they say. Everyone loves Pink's."

They walked the restaurant's perimeter, then went down a dark alley. "Bad guys, too, huh?" Gunn asked.

"Put their hideout close by. So I'd go with a 'yes' on that."

Ahead lay nothing but darkness . . . and an empty square where the back entrances of several businesses could be seen.

Gunn shook his head. "This is gonna be another one of *those,* isn't it?"

"You mean a hideout hidden by a temporal and spatial phase shift?" Angel asked casually.

"Oh, now, come on!" Gunn complained. "Don't tell me you're goin' all big-brained on me."

"That's what Fred called the last three or four of these."

"So it's only there if we believe it's there and if we have the right magical password or key or both, is that it?" Gunn asked.

"Hate to say it, but it takes blood. Human blood." Angel reached into the dark recesses of his leather duster and withdrew the sword Gunn favored. The vampire handed it to his companion. "Just do me one favor?"

"Besides opening a vein?" Gunn asked, his upper lip curling in displeasure. Why wasn't he ever told about this stuff ahead of time?

"Yeah, besides that," Angel said, stepping away from him. "Do it quick, and when the door appears, don't wait for me, just go."

Gunn nodded. He had an idea of what was coming, and he knew it wasn't going to make their task this evening any easier.

Running the sword over his left palm, Gunn

drew the blade away and squeezed his hand into a fist, his blood leaking to the dirty ground. The instant the blood connected, a fiery *whoosh* sounded and a crimson and yellow door carved itself out of what had been thin air only seconds before.

Gunn heard a low, tormented growl behind him—and threw himself at the door.

CHAPTER THREE

"Welcome to The Netherworld," a leathery-skinned demon said to the mildly disoriented Charles Gunn. The eight-foot-tall demon wore a white shirt, black vest, black slacks, and black tie. His tree-trunk neck was spotted and crimson, but had a golden cast to it because of the lighting. And his twisting horns moved when he spoke. The creature's goatee and thick black eyebrows were perfectly trimmed. He carried a serving tray with two dishes in one hand, a small receipt book in the other. "Will you be dining alone tonight, or—" the demon's gaze went past Gunn to the other new-comer, who was still snarling—"perhaps you are the meal?"

Gunn spun around and was just in time to see the grotesquely protruding brow ridges and fangs of his partner retreat. Angel looked pale in this light—which was normal enough for him—but also a little shaken. Gunn wondered if being exposed to the blood of a friend was what made this more difficult for him than normal—especially since the last person he had fed upon was Buffy Summers. He was kind of bent over, old-movie-villain style, and holding himself as if something inside had pained him greatly.

"Separate checks," Angel said, drawing himself up to his full height.

"As you wish," the demon waiter said. "A table should be open in just a few moments. Would you like to wait at the bar?"

Gunn blinked, and the reddish mist that had nearly blinded him as he went through the portal quickly dissipated, revealing a posh restaurant reminiscent of Spago . . . except, maybe, Spago of the undead. The clientele here looked like it had been transported from Lorne's old club: lots of ugly, inhuman faces, horns, tails, tentacles, and the like. Elegantly dressed monsters ate with two or three sets of jaws, making crunching and squishing sounds as they feasted on things that were, at least, kind of dead, and certainly not of this earth.

"Actually, we're here to see Moesha P'athar," Angel said, sounding like his old confident self once more.

Gunn looked down—and saw that the slice in his hand had been cauterized shut by the fiery energies of the magical doorway he had passed through. He thought it a shame that so much magic existed in the world yet was only rarely put to any kind of humanitarian effort. Instead, those with the power kept it—and charged through the nose whenever they had the chance.

In Gunn's other hand was the sword . . . an object the demon hadn't chosen to comment upon up to this point.

Yet now the demon appeared displeased. "Our darksome lord and master, as he likes to be called—everyone's got their thing, I suppose—left strict instructions that he's not to be disturbed. However, I can offer you our plasma menu, including several fine vintages, some from the eighteenth century. Virgin's blood, even."

"Probably a guy's," Angel said to Gunn. "It's all in the details."

"Heard that."

"Would blood of a fresher vintage be more to your liking?" the demon asked. "Compliments of the house, of course."

"P'athar will want to see me," Angel said, withdrawing his ax and hefting it with gleeful and apparently malicious purpose.

Following Angel's lead, Gunn raised his weapon menacingly.

"Ah. Sir and *sir* are both self-starters, bringing their own cutlery for the evening's repast. Such effort is to be applauded," the demon waiter said calmly. "But it is entirely unnecessary. Our blades are plenty sharp, I can assure you."

Angel ignored the waiter's thinly veiled threat. "Word on the street is that he's got something big brewing tonight and he won't want anything messing that up for him. Leave me standing here and I *will* cause a ruckus that's bound to screw up his plans one way or the other."

"I'm sure that sir would make a fine go of it too," the demon said with a reassurance that came off more like condescension.

Angel smirked. Couldn't help himself. "Tell him Angelus is here. He'll *want* to talk to me."

The demon sighed. Angelus was a name that was not to be taken lightly in their circles. "Very well. I'll make inquiries."

Angel and Gunn waited in a corner while the demon trod up a velvet-covered set of stairs and disappeared into a shimmering pool of energy that only appeared when he reached the second-floor landing. There were tables and customers up there who seemed real enough, but something literally didn't smell right to Angel.

"Playing the Angelus card, huh?" Gunn noted. "Pretty hard core. Feelin' kinda testy, or is there anything else I should know?"

"I'm trying to time this right," Angel said, nudging Gunn's arm and nodding at the stairs. "Come on."

Angel and Gunn slipped past a couple of other inhuman servers who quickened their pace when they saw the pair heading for the stairs, but refrained from breaking into a run for fear of causing a panic. Repeat clientele was critical in the restaurant business.

"So when exactly are you going to fill me in on the plan?" Gunn asked, not bothering to mask the annoyance he felt.

"Thought you liked surprises."

"I hate surprises. You should know that."

"Actually, I'm kinda surprised myself." With that, Angel touched a certain spot on the banister that he had seen the demon waiter touch—and the rippling gateway at the top of the stairs appeared. They bounded through it and . . . again, they were somewhere else.

Moesha P'athar sat upon his throne and surveyed his kingdom. It was a place of strange beauty. Emerald hills and onyx plains. A sky the color of blood. Two dozen stone altars surrounded his throne, marble boxes laid upon each. Inhuman-looking guards stood before each altar, one in front, the other behind.

P'arthar's skin was dark blue, with red and green veins visible beneath the surface. The club owner's head was small and blocky, with tiny, heavily hooded eyes, a minute slit for a mouth, and pulsating openings along his neck to allow for the intake of air. The man's body had a roughly human shape, but his flesh quivered like jellyfish under tremendous pressure in the ocean's depths.

His guards were even less human-looking than he was. Each looked as if it had been sewn together from the bloody remains of corpses on a battlefield and squatted on four arms, each pointed in a different direction, and each had a thick, ball-like torso, the head drooping and poking out from between their cages of legs. Their heads held no features except gaping, jagged-tooth maws, and their limbs were sinewy but strong, tipped with insectlike pincers.

"Yuck," Gunn said, all thoughts of food that had been awakened by passing Pink's now officially put to rest.

"The service here is lousy," Angel said, whipping his ax back and forth, cutting neat little hisses through the air with each swipe. "Our waiter just disappeared."

Moesha P'athar smiled—a truly hideous sight. "You'll be happy to know he's been eaten alive for his impertinence."

"Don't suppose he delivered my message first?"

"That was one of his crimes, yes." The club owner sighed. "What can I do for you, *Angel?*"

"He didn't go for the Angelus bit," Gunn observed.

"Evil has a ripe and delicious scent that is strangely absent in this vampire," Moesha P'athar explained. "I don't think I caught your name."

"Charles Gunn."

The monster thought about it. "No. Sorry. Doesn't ring any bells."

Angel cut to the chase. "So . . . Club K? What's the 'K' stand for—'Killer'?"

"I'm just partial to the ring of it."

"Man, what is this place?" Gunn asked as he looked around. Something about his surroundings just didn't feel right.

"Just another room," Angel told him. "I can smell the AC. The pretty landscape and everything is just an illusion."

"What about the nasty-looking things near those altars?"

"Those, I'm afraid, are real." Angel sniffed again. "And so is what's in the boxes on top of the altars." He looked at the club owner. "Come on . . . babies?"

Gunn had heard faint sounds when they first arrived here that he had mistaken for the wind. Now he understood his error.

Angel shook his head. "Tell me they're not for eating. The babies, I mean."

"None of us has that particular appetite," the club owner said, deflecting the direct inquiry. And that suggested to Angel that perhaps whatever being they were planning on calling to this place had a different take on eating infants.

Whatever was coming *liked* it.

"You seem to be lost in thought," the club owner

observed. He glanced at the closest child. "Oh, I understand. Yes, you had one of these not long ago, didn't you? And you lost him."

"No, he was taken from me," Angel corrected firmly.

"Can't trust anyone these days," the club owner taunted, clearly aware of Angel's history with Wes. "Ancient wisdom, bold and true. Just like the one that says there are no second chances. Don't confuse this situation with the one you faced. You can't change the past. Your boy was taken from you, that's that. It has nothing to do with me, or what's in front of you now."

"Except I know what their parents are going through," Angel let him know. "And I can't allow that. Then there's the whole good-versus-evil thing." He hefted the ax once more. "Let's do this."

The jelly-bodied club owner grew distressed. "Wait! Before we start with the bloodshed, let me put a proposition to you, one businessman to another."

"Not in your line of work. Not interested."

"Hear me out. It's not just your life you're gambling with right now. It's his, too. And all the others you've gathered to you."

Angel's entire body tightened. He thought of that stupid comic book and the things the writer said about the people with whom Angel allied himself, how he would lose them all. First, it had been

Doyle. Now Wesley was gone, as good as dead in certain ways, the former Watcher twisted up into something Angel wouldn't have even recognized a couple of years ago. Cordy had something terrible rattling around in her mind that she couldn't even bring herself to talk about. And every night, Fred was waking up screaming.

The bastard hit a nerve.

Angel nodded. "Listening."

"You know what you're up against," Moesha P'athar said quickly. "You *can't* win, and I can't allow you to leave without some understanding between us. A pact, of sorts."

"Don't listen to him," Gunn said angrily. "Don't make any deals."

"Terms?" Angel said evenly, never taking his gaze off his enemy.

Moesha P'athar looked relieved. "Look the other way. Just this one time. I won't kill you. Do that and I'll owe you. I can help you take down Wolfram and Hart. Save a whole city full of innocents."

Angel had a good idea why the club owner was bothering to negotiate. He said it himself: Angel couldn't win this fight. He might survive it, he might be able to make a strategic withdrawal, but only if he was willing to sacrifice Gunn in the process, *and* if he was willing to abandon the babies to whatever laughing boy here had in mind.

Those weren't real options. Time to play detective, though time was running out.

"On a schedule?" Angel asked.

The club owner nodded. The fight would slow things down. He sighed as if the outcome was inevitable: Angel and Gunn would die. And even if the fate this *thing* had chosen for the children was interrupted, the infants would invariably be slaughtered. So there was no gain to fighting, and countless innocents whom Angel and Gunn might have been able to protect in the future would have no one to help them.

Angel frowned. "Sorry . . . *babies?* Come on, do you think I can turn my back on that?"

The club owner shrugged, jiggling obscenely. "Hey, it was worth a try."

The guardians of the altars left their posts and quickly surrounded the pair.

Lifting his sword, Gunn pressed his back against that of the vampire. "Angel, man, fill me in, here."

"He didn't have anything to do with the killings at his club."

"This is apparent to you *why*, exactly?"

"Look around you. This is big. Moesha P'athar's taking a lot of risks. He needs some big payout and he needs it now. Only reason could be that everything else has turned to crap for him."

The creatures came closer, all chattering and clicking limbs.

"Do you think he's worried about the club victims' loved ones looking for revenge?" Gunn offered.

"That and more, I'm sure."

The guardians were almost on them.

Gunn drew a deep breath and let it out, forcing himself to relax and ease into the fight. "So what do I need to know about these guys?"

"No time. Catch on as you go."

"By all that's unholy," Moesha P'athar roared, "kill them and be quick about it!"

His emissaries obeyed, a half dozen leaping at the fighters simultaneously. Angel and Gunn's "back-to-back to the finish" tactic was ruined instantly, as they had to leap out of the way and roll in separate directions to avoid the gnashing maws and rapierlike limbs of the creatures that collided in the space they had just occupied.

Gunn came up, sword at the ready, and quickly severed the limbs from two of the creatures, beheading a third before he'd even worked up a sweat. *These guys aren't so tough after all!*

He grabbed one of the severed limbs and decided to try a little experiment. "Hey, piñata-face. What's your problem?"

The creature stopped, angling its eyeless, earless head in what passed for confusion. Gunn had been right: If these things could hear and comprehend Moesha P'athar's commands, then they would be able to hear *him*.

The thing said nothing, but its evident confusion seemed to suggest: *Piñata-face? Please explain.*

Gunn accommodated the unspoken request, but eschewed words equally. With great satisfaction, he beat the monster until its head exploded, revealing a cornucopia of decidedly noncandylike gore. He smiled momentarily at his handiwork until four similar beasts advanced on him, one from every direction.

He hefted the club in one hand, the sword in the other. "One at a time," he muttered. "Don't you guys know you're supposed to come one at a time to make it easier for me?"

Apparently, they didn't know—or didn't care. Gunn had no way of knowing exactly what was happening with Angel because the stilt arm things had formed a kind of cage around him with all their limbs. They could stretch their appendages out to a good ten feet, keeping their bodies raised up high, though they allowed their hungry faces to dangle low enough for a good chopping off of their heads.

Suddenly, though, it all started to make sense . . . and Gunn almost wished it didn't: The creatures that now surrounded him were different from the first batch. Some had two heads instead of one. Others had anywhere from five to eight limbs.

Gunn now understood why Moesha P'athar said they couldn't win this fight, and why Angel had tacitly agreed. . . .

These weren't new creatures at all; they were the same ones he'd already slain, ready for round two. This wasn't good. It was as if these guys had taken a classic mythological figure and given it their own unique flavor. Cut off a limb, and two more grew back to take its place; same with heads. Slice them in half, you ended up with two regenerating enemies. Manage to kill one, really kill one, like . . . deep-fry it, Gunn imagined, and six more rose from the ashes to take its place.

This was why Angel had stopped to actually hear the club owner's offer. And the decision Angel had made . . . it included Gunn's life, only he, Charles Gunn, hadn't been consulted. Gunn knew that being the leader meant making tough decisions: He had run his own crew long enough to learn that lesson. But this was different. He and Angel were supposed to be partners—and partners didn't treat each other this way.

He didn't have any more time to think about it. Bogeys were flying in from every direction, and there was no longer any question in his mind: He and Angel were going to die here tonight.

For the first time since the decision to leave Fred behind had been made, Gunn no longer felt guilty about it.

Angel had been clinging to the foolish hope that tearing the creatures' bellies open and spilling their guts might slow them down long enough for him to get away from them and reach Moesha P'athar and "suggest" he call off his dogs. Or arm-thingies. Or whatever these creatures were. It made sense, they acted to protect their round torsos; but it didn't turn out to be true. Leaping high with his ax and tearing open the monsters in this way only ended up creating . . . more monsters.

He had been slashed half a dozen times, and the scent of his blood had drawn more than his share of the beasts to him, giving Gunn more time. And buying time was really all they could do.

Moesha P'athar was still on his throne, performing a rite of supplication to whatever demigod or ancient Power for whom the children had been intended. He chanted, blubbered, sweated, and panted as he read from some ancient text that he had produced from . . . where? Had he been sitting on it?

Meanwhile, the "sky" surrounding them was changing. Dark clouds were forming, and a gigantic, ever-changing shape with claws, tentacles, and what looked like an endless supply of shimmering *eyes* was taking shape, a dozen slavering maws opening near the boxes in which the babies wailed in terror.

Yet, so long as the fight went on, Moesha P'athar was distracted, his fear making him stumble as he attempted to recite the very precise mantras required, and the basic karmic disturbance of a battle in the midst of this evocation could be enough to tip the scales and keep the big, bad beastie in the "sky" from reaching this place and taking its prizes.

The strange thing was, with creatures like this to guard the club owner, what need did he really have of further protection?

Unless, of course, these regenerating monsters had been a previous boon from the incoming infant-eater, in which case, this might be a ceremony of renewal, and if he and Gunn could keep these things busy long enough, manage to disrupt Moesha P'athar's plans well enough, they might be withdrawn from him, and then it would just be the blubber guy versus a champion of the world and a very angry sword-wielding Charles Gunn.

Now *that* presented some possibilities. The problem was, time was running out, and not in a good way. These *things* were getting stronger, faster, and more ferocious as they whipped and slashed at him, and he was being wounded and worn down a hell of a lot faster than his own regenerative abilities could handle.

They simply wouldn't make it. Not like this. Not unless—

Angel felt an unexpected flicker of heat—and ducked instinctively. He fell back just in time to see a tightly focused cone of spiraling emerald flame tear through the center of one of the endlessly regenerating monsters, blasting it into a dozen or more ichor-covered pieces. Then a second blast of energy fell upon the gory chunks of the unkillable thing—a golden net of glowing mystical power that broke into exactly a dozen pieces itself, each falling upon the remains, sealing it within a yellow-white field from which it could not escape or morph into something bigger, meaner, and nastier.

Two more magical hits and two more of the creatures exploded and were contained.

"I'm out," a gravely voice called. "Need time to recharge."

"Yay!" a woman cried. "More for us!"

Angel knew that the battle had been joined, but not by *whom*.

The newcomers were fast, and their movements were difficult to track. Even with Angel's supernaturally enhanced senses it was easier to follow the trail of carnage and destruction left in their wake than to actually catch any one of them idle long enough to form more than a fleeting visual impression. He would see a flash of a pale, grinning, undeniably human face . . . or catch the darting motion of a long-fingered elegantly carved hand cloaked in a dark brown leather glove. The shimmer of a gauntlet greedily snatched up the low light. A silken cloak rustled, and he saw the haunting and sensuous expanse of a long, deeply tanned perfectly turned feminine leg as it whirled about, delivering a high kick and a six-inch spiked heel to one of the creatures.

Then the form that had leaped high enough to do the damage in the first place would fall, landing gracefully, and blur away.

"I normally don't object to foreplay, darlings," came a throaty, sensuous woman's voice. "But I've danced with partners like this before, and prolonging things with them simply doesn't lead to a satisfying conclusion."

"I agree," came a deep, elegantly refined voice. "Tell them all to be quick about it. They keep us from more pressing matters."

Angel could smell this last one's maniacally scrubbed flesh, marred only by the slightest trace of herbs and spices on his fingertips, most notably ground celery seed, of all things. Unlike the others, this one was standing still. Yet no matter how hard he tried, Angel couldn't force himself to look fully in the man's direction. He could only catch glimpses from the corner of his eye of a figure who seemed to be vibrating so violently that, even seemingly motionless, he was a blur.

"Angel, what've we got here?" Gunn called.

"Magic users," Angel said to him. He looked to the club owner. "Hey, jerk!"

Moesha P'athar looked up—and Angel threw his ax, *burying* it in the club owner's skull. Twitching, the bloated man dropped the text and fell from his throne, jiggling and waddling grotesquely the whole way down.

"Made you look," Angel said, grinning. But the elation faded as he saw the being that Moesha P'athar had been trying to raise start to take corporeal form—and reach for the closest of the children with a long, unwinding tentacle.

"That ain't happenin'," Gunn said determinedly as he raced past Angel, leaped onto the altar where the child was standing, and hacked a chunk off the end of the tentacle. The unseen walls of this place shuddered as a scream filled Moesha P'athar's private retreat, and a hissing spray of blue-white liquid—blood, perhaps—hit Charles full on, slapping him to the ground.

Ignoring the sounds of combat behind him, Angel darted ahead and made it to the throne, where Moesha P'athar had dropped his book. It had fallen closed and facedown, with no way of telling quickly what page he had been on. Or was there?

Angel looked to the book's spine, found a well-worn crack, and opened the text to a page highlighted by a drawing of the gigantic thing that was now reaching into this world to claim its tithe. On a hunch, he tore the page from the book and ripped it into shreds.

The screaming came again, this time even louder than before. Angel dropped to his knees, his hands clasped over his ears, but the terrible sound of the summoned *thing* seemed to reach right into his brain. Then, as quickly as it had started, the wailing stopped.

Angel looked around and saw that the room was now *just* a room, and all traces of the magics Moesha P'athar had called into being, including the regenerating beasts, were gone.

In their place stood a half-dozen supernatural warriors: five men, one woman. They were the sorcerers who had come to his rescue.

A single mage stood in the lead. He was heavily armored in the eastern style. He wore a black mask that looked like the traditional embodiment of a grinning demon, with narrow slits cut for eyes, nostrils, and teeth. A pair of large golden horns curled upward from the sides of the warrior's helmet. Fabric fanned out on either side of his head, bearing beautiful designs not unlike those found on the wings of rare butterflies. A strange cap adorned with straw-colored "hair" rose a foot above the top of the fighter's skull. His body was covered in layers of armor and fabric. Pads overlaid with steel and gold protected the shoulders and arms, and his hands were covered with gauntlets. Small lacquered iron plates laced together with silk and leather hung from the armors forming exquisite designs. Skirts reached down to the knees in the front, mid-calf in the back. His sword was black and gold.

The man just behind him and off to one side was

a supremely handsome African American with dark eyes and black hair. Shards of crimson swam in his eyes, and a single red streak rippled through his hair. His leathers were cut away to reveal his muscular arms and legs, and he wore a crimson sash around his waist.

The other four were clustered closely together. The woman wore dark silken robes that parted here and there to show cleavage or leg—both of which she had in copious supply, but her hood obscured her face, providing only shadowy glimpses of beautifully, perfectly symmetrical features, emerald eyes, and full, crimson lips. The man beside her had tightly curled salt-and-pepper hair, dark eyes, and skin that was deeply scarred, perhaps by some childhood disease. Half his skull was covered by a shiny metal plate, and his muscular chest was bare, his left arm lost in some battle and replaced by a low-tech construct of metallic bones and pulleys reminiscent of the Terminator. His silver left hand clenched and unclenched with tiny *whirs* and *clanks*. The rest of him was covered in loose vinyl pants and boots. Next to him stood a huge man with wild black dreadlocks beaded with silver. His arms and much of his chest were exposed, as well, but he had stylized brown leather plates that arced down from his mighty shoulders and reached up to cover his abdomen in stylish molded armor that continued down to his mid-thighs. He wore leather gloves and boots, and glared angrily at Angel and Gunn.

The last man also wore dark, impressive armor, including a helm with talonlike blades reaching out from its back. His shoulder plates were extravagant and molded to rise up like the sharp tips of wings. His long black cape, hooked to his elbows, also gave him a raven's appearance, and the soft blue ink tattooed all over his flesh made him look like a mythical bird of prey given human form.

They all carried weapons. Staffs, swords, cudgels, short axes, and more. Most had been tattooed in various ways: some with runes that were common enough, others with symbols Angel had never seen before.

Not one looked pleased by the sight of the dead club owner.

The mage dressed in the Eastern-style armor moved ahead, walking past Angel without saying a word. He knelt over the corpse, whispered something, and extracted a shimmering silver dragonfly from the man's body, which he absorbed into the flesh of his palm.

His soul, Angel thought. *That guy just stole his soul!*

"So what's the deal with y'all?" Gunn asked casually.

"We're fighting on the same side. Does anything else really matter at this point?" the African-American mage asked.

Gunn shrugged. "Can't argue with that."

Angel watched the leader of this pack move back to his minions.

The club owner was dead, his minions scattered, and the children were safe, but Angel's investigation into the nightclub murders was back at square one.

Or was it?

The sorcerers had *stolen* Moesha P'athar's soul at the moment of death. Now it was trapped where they could torture it for a thousand lifetimes if they so chose. . . .

Or use their magic to extract its secrets.

"The time has come for us to depart," the head mage in the Eastern armor declared.

Angel took a step toward him. "Not so fast."

The head mage stared long and hard at Angel. "I know who you are and, I will admit, I am impressed. Angel, you have no reason to challenge us . . . and no reason to think you could win if you did."

"Challenge? Me?" Angel did his best impression of a laugh and edged closer. "Nah, I just want to talk."

"We have pressing business."

"It's after you guys, isn't it?"

The mage whirled on Angel. "What do you know?"

"Just what you're telling me." Angel stopped just a few feet away from the mage, his hands open and dangling at his sides. "Thing is, I have a hard time believing you were here to save innocents. Look at you. I know those markings. All from different orders, yet working together."

The head mage removed his mask, revealing a wizened and chiseled face with sky blue eyes, a hawk's nose, and a gray goatee. "The children have been saved."

"Yeah, about that. Helping the helpless? My style, not yours. Not on this scale."

Silence was the mage's only reply.

"Angel, help me out here," Gunn said warily. "I thought you said what this Moesha P'athar guy was up to was something big. That's why it was worth us both dyin', *right?*"

Angel didn't notice the irritation in Gunn's voice. "This was big. And us dying to help a dozen innocents *not* get turned into those things?"—Angel nodded at the soldiers who had been killed by the mages—"Yeah, it was worth it."

Gunn was confused. "I thought they were gonna get eaten."

"That thing he was calling down was a Streghes. It feeds on children who have not yet reached puberty. Believe it or not, it's from a race of dark faeries."

"Still, with the eating . . . I don't get it."

"That's how it starts. In with the innocent souls . . . then, a few years later, these spider-limbed creatures with drooping heads claw their way out from the inside. Big monster dies, lots of little ones are born. If they live long enough, eventually they turn into the same kind of thing that ate them to start with. And they go hunting for food."

"A sick version of the circle of life."

"You could call it that," Angel said, pointing at the wizards. "But these guys . . . they don't get involved in stuff like this. A couple dozen worlds coming to an end, a couple of thousand, then maybe they do something. Maybe they join up, *if* there's something in it for them. But not for something like this. I'm not buying it."

The woman leaned against one of her fellow warriors and called, "We should tell him."

The head mage hissed, "Keep *quiet*. It is not our way to have outsiders know our business."

"I respect that," Angel said casually. "Won't stop me from nosing around, though. You're my only lead. I think you came here for the same reason I did. You thought he had something to do with the killings at his club. Even that wouldn't interest you, though, unless whatever got up to no good there was messing with you guys now."

Gunn smiled. "We *are* a detective agency, y'know."

The woman came forward, easing past the African-American sorcerer, who appeared annoyed at her impertinence but did nothing to stop her. She stood beside the head mage. "Hello, boys. Call me . . . Bliss."

"Why would I want to do that?" Angel asked flatly. "Is it your name?"

She smiled. "You're funny." Her head tilted to one side. "You've had experience with sorcerers before," she said softly. "I can tell just from the way you reacted to us. So you know how important it is that we protect our true names."

"Know someone's true name—" Angel began.

Gunn cut him off. "Yeah and you have absolute power over them if you know the right mumbo jumbo and stuff. Fine. You don't trust us, we don't trust you. No reason why things should be any different. But since we're not tryin' to kill each other, and we seem to have a common problem, maybe we should try to share. Y'know, play nice."

"Oh, now you want to share," Angel muttered. "Before, it was like, 'Get your hands off my joystick.'"

Bliss's eyes widened. "Yes, you may *both* come home with me." She appeared genuinely excited at the prospect.

Gunn addressed the head mage. "So . . . you feelin' shy? Not gonna tell us what you're really doin' here? I can understand that. Don't want anyone else gettin' up in your business. 'Cept, it's our business too."

This time, the African-American mage did not hold his counsel. "If we fight, you'll lose."

Gunn scraped his blade over the ground. "If we fight, we'll take a lot of you with us."

Angel took a step toward his companion in warning. "Gunn . . ."

The African-American mage with the crimson streak grinned maliciously. "It would be the work of a single gesture, or even calling to mind a single phrase, and your friend could be enveloped in an inferno of flames while the forces of gravity that bind you to the earth would be severed, leaving you to drift helplessly to the night sky, to die gasping for air, your body ultimately disintegrating in this world's upper stratosphere."

Gunn angled in toward his partner. "Angel, if we fight, we'll lose."

"I've been trying to tell you that," Angel whispered as he turned his attention to the sorcerers. "Look, we're here about the murders in the club. Somehow, I don't think that's why you're here. Whatever killed them is after you people, right? And that guy was the only lead any of us had."

The head mage shook his head. "Even if what you say is true, what of it? Our affairs have nothing to do with you."

The woman stepped forward. "Unless, of course, that offer about both of you at the same time—"

The head mage shouted, "Bliss, be *quiet*."

She laughed. Apparently, she enjoyed getting a rise out of him . . . teasing him, that is. "You are so easy."

"So are you," the head mage responded, and that shut her up, though Angel couldn't tell if it was because she was offended or simply surprised that he would respond on her level.

Angel broke it down: "We have a common enemy, the world's in danger, I'm imagining—"

"Team-up time," Gunn interrupted, not really relishing the idea.

"Our people have gotten nowhere," Bliss offered.

The African-American mage said, "Given time . . ."

The head mage shook his head. "We don't have time. We could use all the resources we can get our hands on."

This incensed the African-American mage. "Were the council to vote—"

"They would be overruled. For good or ill, this is my call." The older mage turned to Angel. "All right, vampire, we'll accept your help. But here are *our* terms . . ."

Fred drove Gunn's truck through busy downtown Los Angeles, on her way to the posh restaurant where she'd soon be meeting Alicia. Streetlights and neon streaked past. Glaring headlights wavered. Suddenly, Fred was cut off by a car that looked exactly like something out of an L.A. gang movie. Fred hung back, allowing the low-slung, orange four-door plenty of space. Rap music burst from the car's open windows, and the backseat was filled to bursting with wannabe gansta Caucasian college guys bobbing their heads to the beat and trying way too hard to look impressive. They moved off, and Fred settled into the drive.

She was feeling good again for the first time in a very long time. Just getting out and driving somewhere by herself was empowering. Sure, there was the typical traffic, all the L.A. maniacs risking life and limb on the roads just to cut their trips short by a few seconds or maybe even a minute if they were lucky. She'd caught up with every one of the tailgaters and lane changers as soon as a light came into view. Then they were off, going at it again, oblivious and dangerous. It suited Fred to ease back and let them have the road.

She was worried about Charles and Angel, there was no denying it. But they had shut her out of their lives tonight, and Alicia was inviting her back in. She knew that they had acted out of concern for her, but that really didn't help. It was like they simply didn't trust her after what had happened. After . . . well, Dr. Seidel's murder. And it was murder, there was no question about it. If he had so desired, Charles Gunn could have gained entrance to Club K. Blood on one's hands was all it took. Fred had planned to bring about Professor Seidel's demise, as well, but her plan called for a fitting form of justice: exiling the professor, alive, to Pylea. He would have died there, yes. But Charles had gone for something more immediate, snapping the man's throat, and leaving Fred with a tumult of conflicting emotions about the whole incident. Mainly, she had once again had control wrested from her, and it had been the man she loved who had betrayed her.

A red pickup suddenly changed lanes, erupting from her blind spot like a streak of blood, then cutting her off. Fred nailed the truck's brakes and narrowly avoided a collision. Fortunately, there was no one behind her.

"Look where you're going!" she screamed, but the pickup was out of her range, bearing down on the bumper of a station wagon in the next lane over. Fred drew a deep breath, let it out; looked at the steering wheel, afraid she had pulled it off the column. Everything was fine. She thought of Alicia, and a smile came across her face.

Twenty minutes later, Fred was closing in on the restaurant. Only . . . something was happening in the street up ahead. The night was bathed in flashing red and blue lights. Men and women in police uniforms were directing traffic away from the outside eatery.

Fred suddenly had a very, very bad feeling about this. She pulled the truck over to the side of the road and raced ahead to what she feared was a crime scene.

CHAPTER FOUR

As Fred got closer to the restaurant, she could see a couple of uniformed cops cordoning off a section of the outdoor restaurant with yellow crime-scene tape. Another couple of cops were putting up blue police barricades to block off the street in front of the restaurant for police and emergency vehicles. A crowd of people was starting to form behind the newly installed barricades. What was going on here? And where was Alicia?

Fred was already regretting her suggestion to meet at this restaurant. She had the sinking feeling that Alicia might have gotten mixed up in whatever was going on here. Fred shook her head; it was as if trouble just followed her around. They should have just met at her local diner.

Fred reached the barricade and could see a group of people being questioned by some plain-clothes detectives. She reasoned that they must have been restaurant patrons who had witnessed what had happened. Fred glanced over the heads of a few of the curious observers to see if Alicia was among the people being questioned, but she didn't see her friend. Fred *did* see a body covered by what had once been a white tablecloth but was now stained with blood. A police photographer was taking pictures of the corpse and the surrounding area of the outdoor eatery. From the little Fred could see, it looked like there had been a shooting. The front wall of the restaurant bore a hole and had spidery impact marks radiating out from it, probably from a bullet.

Fred jumped as she suddenly heard the sound of an ambulance's siren behind her. She turned and watched a cop open the barricade for the ambulance. The driver and another EMT got out, pulled out a stretcher from the back, and walked over to the body covered by the cloth. Fred looked again for Alicia. She circled the barricaded area but could see no sign of her friend.

Fred turned and watched, panic rising inside her, as the two EMTs asked one of the detectives if it was okay to move the body. The short, red-haired detective nodded, and they placed the body onto the stretcher. The man in question was Detective Moffat, the same guy she had gotten away from at the club earlier today. He sure got around L.A. This restaurant was nowhere near the club where all those people were killed. Just before the EMTs were about to move the stretcher, Moffat came over and took another look at the body.

He lifted up the cloth and said something to himself that Fred could not make out at that distance, looked out into the crowd of spectators, and spotted her, his impassive gaze instantly transforming into a glare of annoyance. The detective walked over to the police barricade where Fred was standing, his wide, fireplug physique blocking her view as the EMTs moved the stretcher over to where the ambulance was parked and loaded it into the back.

"You seem to be at *all* the criminal hot spots today, Miss Burkle."

Fred looked up in surprise. The detective knew her name. He hadn't asked it when they met at the crime scene earlier. That meant he either knew who she was at the time and had been toying with her, or he had made inquiries afterward. Either way, she didn't have time for his games . . . unfortunately, he was standing between her and the answers she sought.

"So do you, Detective," snapped Fred. She felt frustrated and desperately attempted to come up with a new plan to get around this guy.

"Tell me: Do you just drive around town looking for police lights and crime scenes?" asked the detective. "Because if that's what turns you on, I can just give you a roll of caution tape to play with and then I can get back to work."

Fred tried to see beyond him, but he didn't budge. "I'm meeting someone here," she explained.

"A male friend?" He sounded almost hopeful.

"No. A girlfriend."

He suddenly became cold. Distant. Now the look in his eyes was all business. "Name?"

"Alicia Austin."

Moffat closed his eyes and sighed.

"Please, come with me, Miss Burkle," the detective said as he opened the police barricade for her to pass through.

Moffat turned and called out to one of the uniformed cops, "Hey, tell that ambulance to stay put for a minute."

"Yes, sir," responded the young cop as he ran over to the ambulance.

"What? What happened?" Fred asked, her fear mounting. "Is Alicia all right?"

"No. No, I'm sorry, she's not."

"Was she wounded? I need to see her."

The detective said nothing.

"Where's Alicia?" asked Fred, panic reaching a crescendo in her voice.

As if in answer, Detective Moffat guided Fred over to the ambulance, where he opened the back doors to let her see the body inside. Fred and the detective climbed into the back of the ambulance.

"Let this woman see the face of the victim," said the detective to the EMT.

The EMT pulled back the cloth so that Fred could see the face of the corpse. It was a face that Fred had not seen in over five years. It was Alicia.

"Can you identify this woman as Alicia Austin?" Moffat asked.

Fred's world started to swim. Her skin felt as if needles were being stuck into it in a thousand places, and her head felt light. She reached out with trembling fingers that almost, but not quite, touched the waxy, still face of her friend. "Alicia . . ."

The detective gently guided her out of the back of the ambulance and helped her to a nearby chair at the outdoor eatery. Then he went back, closed the ambulance doors, and signaled the driver to go before turning to Fred.

"It looks like your friend was in the wrong place at the wrong time," said the detective, his tone soft, his demeanor entirely sympathetic. "There was an attempted drive-by shooting of a local crime lord. Your friend got the bullet that was meant for him. She died instantly."

Fred shook her head. This could not be real.

Fred could feel herself pulling away from what was going on, her mind retreating to the place it had resided for five years when she had been trapped in Pylea.

"Miss Burkle, I don't think we should be talking about this any further right now," Moffat said. "I'm going to ask for another ambulance. I think you may be in shock."

Fred didn't respond.

Moffat had his phone in hand when Fred's hand suddenly shot out, grabbing his wrist.

"I'm all right," Fred told him, the words coming out in a sharp, commanding hiss. She had mentally slapped herself out of it. She could *not* do *this* now. Alicia needed her. The guilty party must be brought to justice, and Fred *had* to be a part of it. This was no time to go back into the safe little cocoon in her mind, where only logic and math mattered. Her friend was dead, and someone was going to pay.

Fred's reverie was broken by the sound of Detective Moffat's voice. "I think you should at least go to the hospital and get yourself checked out. There are good trauma counselors we could recommend—," the detective offered.

"No."

Moffat wiped the sweat from his forehead. "Listen, I'd like you to come downtown for some questioning, but I don't think now is a good time for it."

"Yes, that's fine," Fred said mechanically, getting to her feet. "I need to go now. I'll come to the precinct tomorrow."

"You shouldn't be driving. Let me have one of my guys take you back." He nodded, and a uniformed officer approached. "The hotel, right?"

Fred dully wondered how the detective had known that. *Had* he been keeping track of Angel Investigations? She had too much on her mind to press the matter right now. "No. Somewhere else. A friend's place."

"All right, we'll take you there. What's this person's name?"

She told him, and somewhere across the city, the name she had spoken was echoed by something that also wanted the man she had been thinking of . . . but for very different reasons.

"Wesss-leyyy . . . ," the darkness itself seemed to call to him.

Wesley Wyndam-Pryce stood in an abandoned warehouse, a single shaft of blue-white moonlight reaching down to bathe his tousled hair and bare, lean-muscled chest. His dark pants were loosely fitting and tightly belted at the waist, the cuffs stuffed into his boots. He wasn't alone.

A half-dozen well-armed demons surrounded him. All six looked roughly the same: lime green skin, beady little eyes, huge, protruding noses, batlike ears, and ridges at the crowns of their skulls that reminded Wes of knotted rope. Their maws were wide, each possessing only a dozen long, curling, jagged teeth that were widely spaced apart, giving them a fairly simpleminded appearance. But their clan was known for hiring themselves out as skilled hunters, interrogators, and assassins. And they were usually successful in their line of work, largely due to their high intelligence—not to mention their muscular, armored bodies.

"Time to play, Wess-leyyy," the closest demon said with a leer.

Wes opened his palms, showing that he held no secret weapons. "Very well. Is something keeping you?"

Wes was anxious to get on with things—and the demons were more than accommodating. They raced at him, hissing angrily, the closest raising a spiked mace that he clearly intended to bring down on Wes's skull.

Wes's instincts took over. He dove out of the way of the weapon and kicked back at where he judged it would end up. His boot connected with the hand gripping the weapon. There was a grunt of pain, and the mace clattered to the ground as Wes rolled several times and sprang upward, turning in midair to land facing one of his opponents.

He saw another blade racing his way. The steel edge flowed in waves. He was dimly aware of the towering form wielding it. Wes ducked under the blade and gripped his assailant's arm. He fell to his back, planted both boots in his attacker's midsection, and used the figure's momentum to his advantage. With a strong kick, Wes sent his opponent flying overhead.

Wes didn't wait to see that one fall to the ground. He'd know from the sound exactly where he'd land.

The next one wasn't bothering with crude weapons. To Wes, he looked like a silhouette, lit from behind by a fiery crimson glow. He was holding something behind his back.

Something charged with magic.

"That's hardly sporting," Wes said, countering the underhanded move by employing one of his own. Wes delivered a swift kick to the demon's knee and heard a horrible crunching sound. It dropped the fireball, fell on it, and rolled around as mystical flames licked its armored body.

Wes decided it was time to end this. Lying within what looked like a simple crack in the floor was a staff he had hidden for just this purpose. With lightning speed, Wes snatched up the staff, tapped a release on its side, and a blade hissed into place. Arcing the staff upward, Wes slashed across the face of an attacker. A shrill cry came from the creature, and it stumbled back. Wes planted the dull end of the staff on the ground and used it to vault in another demon's direction. He delivered a powerful kick with both boots to the demon's chest. Something cracked in the attacker's breastplate, and his sword flew from his hand as he fell to the ground. Wes went down with him, spinning the staff and planting it against the demon's throat.

Yet another demon was coming his way.

He brought the staff around in a blinding arc, catching the final demon, who flew backward.

"All right, then," Wes said, spinning the staff. "I think this proves who's boss."

The demon lying at his feet laughed. "No problem, Wes. So long as you keep paying us, that couldn't possibly be an issue."

Wes reached out and helped the demon to his feet. Withdrawing a thick roll of bills from his back pocket, he thanked the demon for the workout in the creature's own language.

The last demon whom Wesley had nailed with the staff stumbled by, nodding appreciatively as he held his throbbing skull. "You're inhuman, buddy!"

Wes smiled thinly. "I try."

The demons departed, and Wes went to the small table near the back, where he had a towel and a fresh white shirt waiting.

Someone clapped from the darkness. Long, slow, sarcastic clapping.

Clap.

Clap.

Clap.

Wes sighed. He heard the telltale heel *clacks* of his appreciative audience member as she wandered near, but didn't bother to face her. For some time now, Wes and Lilah had been involved in something approximating a relationship. Wes had no desire to be unkind to the woman, despite her affiliations, but he was intent on breaking things off with her. And, unfortunately, subtlety was often lost on Lilah.

"What is it you want, Lilah?"

"Now isn't *that* a loaded question?" Lilah Morgan asked as she placed her carefully manicured hands on his sweaty, scarred back, then reached around to the front.

Wes slid out of her grasp and strode purposefully to a chair where he could sit and face her. She wore a light gray business suit and the imported white stockings he liked so much. Flipping her long, straight brown hair away from her beautifully sculpted features, Lilah caressed the shirt Wes had left on the table.

"That was an impressive little display," Lilah mused.

"Well, impressive little displays are something you would know about, now aren't they?" Wes asked, taking the time to work on the technique he had learned from another clan of demons to slow his heart rate after major exertions. Despite his desire to go gently with Lilah, Wes could not completely erase his memories of the very nasty enterprises in which Lilah had recently been involved. She had even tried to use information he had gathered to further her own dark plans. "Oh no, wait. Little displays aren't much your style, are they?

Working for Wolfram and Hart, that is. You're more of the 'setting cataclysms and apocalypses into motion' mindset, yes?"

Lilah shrugged, but looked pleased. "Flattery will get you everywhere." She bent over the desk, resting on her elbows, easing her perfectly rounded backside into view. "Come on, Wes. I've been a very bad girl today. Don't you want to punish me?"

Wes leaned back and allowed himself a distracted grin at the possibility. Odd as it might sound, this was what passed for flirting between the two of them. And while Wes did not wish to encourage Lilah, it was simply all too easy to slip into old comfortable rhythms when chatting with her. "I've already had my workout. And this batch is quite likely to teach me some new tricks. What do you have to offer?"

"Like you don't already know," she said in a husky, seductive voice.

"Well, that's just it. I do know"—he shook his head—"and I'm afraid it needs to stop."

Flinching, Lilah straightened up. From the start of her company's "little game" with Angel and his cohorts, she and Wes had been playing on opposite teams. Lately, pesky little things like the black-and-white lines between good and evil had blurred, placing the two of them in each other's arms. The comfort they felt was more often rooted in cruelty . . . which was equally pleasurable, in her experience.

"Gee, we could go on like this all night," Lilah observed. "But I'd rather we do it someplace"—she took in the filthy, rat-infested warehouse—"someplace *seedier*."

The distinctive ring tones of a cell phone suddenly came from the travel bag Wes had left on the table. While Lilah was double-checking to make sure it wasn't her phone, Wes crossed the distance between them, took out the phone, and answered it.

He avoided Lilah as he identified himself and listened to the voice on the other end of the phone, his expression turning grave. "Right. I understand. I'll be there directly."

Wes hung up, quickly toweled off, and hurriedly slipped on his shirt. "Sorry, Lilah. I know this is normally the point at which my resolve falters and I end up exploring whole new levels of depravity with you, but it turns out I am truly needed elsewhere."

Lilah shrugged. "Really? Duty calls? Some new bad guy in town?"

"No. But thank you for asking, considering you or your firm is usually behind the worst that happens in this city. This is personal business."

"And what we do isn't personal?"

He hesitated. "Somehow, I don't think you really want me to answer that. I know that I don't want to." He grabbed his bag and walked briskly to the door. There was a spring in his step that Lilah recognized.

"Something up with the Kewpie? Little Miss Muffet? Skin 'n' Bones?" Lilah taunted. "If you tell Lilah about it, I promise I won't send any more evil into the world until at least"—she checked her watch—"how's an hour sound?"

"No time, sorry."

Lilah waved her hand dismissively. "Well, give her a hug for me. Oh no, wait. You might bust the wishbone or something if you squeeze her too tight. I wonder how that big, black stud she's sleeping with manages?"

Wes sighed. "Come now, Lilah. This is beneath even you."

"Nothing's beneath me, haven't you gotten that yet?" she asked. Grinning lasciviously, she added, "Except you, maybe, on a good day."

"It's not a good day. And I don't see any good days arriving anytime soon. I have to go."

Lilah contained her fury. She had come here seeking release, and Wes had denied her even that. She knew his feelings for the little chopstick, but she didn't pretend to understand them.

"I'm just going to have to find some other way to amuse myself, Wesley," she said, crushing glass beneath her heels as she walked away with a chilling calm. "Somehow, though, I don't think you'll like what I have in mind."

• • •

Angel and Gunn were back at the hotel, telling Lorne and Cordy the story of what they had been through tonight.

Charles couldn't stop bounding from one spot to another. "There is nothing in this life that makes a healthy young man like myself work up more of an appetite for an authentic Pink's chili dog than looking death right in the face and saying—"

"'Hello, death—yes, I really am a big enough dumbass to be talking about you like this'?" Cordy offered.

Gunn frowned. "Why you gotta be like that?"

"I don't know," Cordelia said honestly. "I just feel more like my old self when I do."

"She's got a point there," Angel observed.

Lorne sighed. "So let me get this straight: The club owner's not the guy we're after, but you met a bunch o' funky magical monks who said, 'Come on board, join the party, we're under siege too,' and naturally, that was too good an offer to turn down."

"Mixed metaphors aside, yeah," Angel agreed.

"So what, now you're going to be . . . ?" Cordelia asked, shaking her head, "undercover monks or something?"

"It breaks down pretty easy," Gunn assured her. "Just outside of Los Angeles there's this mystical abbey, and—"

"An abbey," Cordelia echoed.

"Right," Gunn said, opening his mouth to speak again and immediately getting cut off.

"Oh yeah, there are lots of those in the Los Angeles area," Cordy went on. "I mean, that's where they used to record those 'Chant' CDs, right?"

"The monks' magic keeps anyone from seeing the abbey or even getting too close," Gunn explained. "Satellite surveillance systems can't even get a bead on it."

"And it's all kinds of magic types from all over the world?" Cordelia asked. "Like one of those geeky science fiction conventions? Do they host panels and sign autographs?"

"Don't know why they're gathering, exactly," Angel interjected. "We'll find that out in the morning. My guess is that it's something major."

Cordy leaned back on the couch. "Did they give you any details about the thing doing the killing?"

Angel nodded. "They confirmed that the deaths were exactly the same. It looked like natural causes, but it couldn't have been from natural causes. There were too many at one time."

"Yeah," Gunn jumped in, "and the thing must have taken down some of their own kind or they wouldn't have left the abbey in search of the killer—that's not their MO."

Cordy angled her head and said, "You two really think this is such a hot idea? You're both lightweights as far as magic is concerned."

Angel set the glass of blood he had been sipping down on the counter, his determination evident. "I could smell that thing on them. Same thing I smelled at the nightclub. If we've got any chance of finding out what it wants and how to stop it before it gets into the city again, this is it."

"Okay. Well, I'm sitting this one out. Need any Internet research or whatever, give me a holler. Otherwise, forget about it." Cordy shrugged. "What about Fred?"

Angel responded quickly. "Absolutely *not*. Um . . . not that this is a boys' club deal. They have ladies. Lady monks." He swallowed and quickly pointed at Gunn. "He got hit good by one."

"Hey!" Gunn protested. "Did not."

"Sure, of course that's what you'd say . . ."

Cordy rolled her eyes. "No, nimrods. I didn't mean, 'Is Fred a part of the undercover deal.' I meant, 'Where is she?' I thought she would have been home by now."

Gunn looked surprised. "She's not upstairs?"

"The woman's got a life outside all this, poopsie," Lorne reminded him. "One of her old pals from college looked her up. They went out to dinner."

"Guy pal?" Gunn asked warily.

"Girl pal, snookums. A fellow braniac, apparently. Don't be paranoid."

Gunn shook his head. He and Angel had been out risking their lives, trying to follow the lead on a mass killer, and Fred . . . went out for pasta. If their situations had been reversed, he would have been so tense worrying about her that he never could have just up and left. They were having trouble, yes, and it wasn't just because Fred was upset at being left behind tonight. Their problems ran deeper than that. He simply hadn't expected it to come to this. Not so quickly.

Cordy smiled. "Well, I hope she's at least having a good time."

The racking sobs wouldn't end.

Fred was in tears. She was also in Wesley's arms.

He comforted her as best he could, trying the entire time to stay in control, but it was difficult. He had changed. Where once he would have only felt compassion and not had a single thought in his head other than how he might help his dear friend—who was so much more to him in his heart—he now had to fight off notions of opportunity and turning this scenario to his advantage.

The situation between Fred and Charles was already strained, and here, in her moment of need, she had once again come to him instead of her lover.

Her tears eventually ran their course, and soon they were seated at his kitchen table, stream still wafting up from the two untouched cups of mint tea before them. Fred stared into the surface of the tea as if it held great wisdom.

She talked about Alicia, shared stories of their time together, and tasted the tea with a blank expression on her face as if in a state of shock.

"Maybe I should stay here tonight," Fred whispered.

Wes let out a deep, troubled breath.

"Or not," Fred recovered quickly. "I don't want to be a nuisance. I should probably get going soon, anyway. . . ."

"Please," Wes said softly, touching her hand and calming her once more. He had no way of telling her the true reason for his reaction to the idea of her staying overnight: He worried about whether he would be able to control himself. Not that he would ever harm her, or force his attentions where they weren't wanted—heavens no, it was simply that if she came to him, desperate, needing release, forgetfulness, escape from this tragedy and other recent events, he would have to be inhuman to turn her away. And he was not. Not yet, despite what the demon had told him tonight, and despite what he had been doing with Lilah.

"You need to talk to them," Wes counseled. "I can understand why going back to the hotel and facing Angel and Gunn might not seem like an appealing prospect, how seeing their faces when you tell them what happened, how just talking about it more, might feel like you're reliving it, endlessly. But . . . it shouldn't be like that. These are the people who care about you. You should be with them now."

"You care about me," Fred whispered.

"Yes. Yes, I do. And that's why I'm giving you this advice."

"I don't know. I don't think it's going to do any good."

Wes wasn't quite sure he followed. "In what regard?"

"She was murdered."

"I understand that."

"Angel Investigations. We're a detective agency. We should get involved. Find the shooter." Fred nodded purposefully, the idea coming together fully in her mind.

Wes touched the side of her face and directed her gaze toward his. "Fred, please listen to me. As you know, I have very little reason to sing Angel's praises these days. But, from the beginning, his stated mission has been to help the helpless. Well . . . who could be more helpless than someone killed like this? She had no rights, no power, no control. Everything she ever was or ever could be was taken from her. I agree. He should do something."

Fred nodded, something close to a smile forming on her lovely face. To Wes, it was like seeing the sun breaking through the clouds on an otherwise stormy day.

And it was a sight he longed to see for the rest of

his days. "I'll drive you over there," Wes offered. "But I hope you'll forgive me if I don't come inside. I think, under the circumstances, it would be better if Gunn didn't know we'd been together."

Fred entered the hotel as Wes pulled away. She thought of what he had said about Gunn and the man's jealousies, and decided that maybe Wes was right. On top of everything else she was dealing with, that was one thing she really didn't need right now.

The whole group was gathered by the reception desk. They turned practically as one as she dragged herself inside, wondering how much of a mess she'd made of herself with all the crying.

She didn't have long to wait and wonder.

"Hey, you're back," Cordy said, her cheer instantly fading as she took in the sight of the bereaved young woman. "And . . . I don't need to have visions any more to know something's not right. What happened?"

Fred crossed the lobby and stopped a half-dozen feet from the others. She told them just about the whole story, changing only the single detail of who dropped her off.

"The police didn't think I should be driving. I have to go back tomorrow to get your truck," Fred told Gunn.

Each one was sympathetic, understanding, and

consoling—at least until Fred made her suggestion that Angel Investigations take the case.

"Fred, I can't," Angel said immediately. "We can't. It's not what we do. The last thing in the world that I want is to say this to you—"

"Then don't."

Gunn came closer. "Fred, the police have this one. Finding out what or who killed those people in the nightclub, stopping it before it moves on to a lot of really innocent people—that's for us. We turned up a lead at this mystical abbey that we need to check out."

Fred slowly closed her eyes, barely restraining her emotions. "So . . . if I was shot, you wouldn't look into it?"

"What?" Angel said. "No, wait, that's different—"

"Or if it was Charles, or Cordy, or Connor?"

"Baby girl, come on," Gunn whispered.

"Hey, no magic bullet. No creepy-looking guy with blue skin or a tail or three eyes pulling the trigger. Let the cops handle it. What do we care?"

"We protect our own," Angel said.

"That's what I'm trying to do," Fred said. "Alicia was my friend. This wasn't an accident."

"How do you know that?"

"I just do. Tell me we haven't gone off to hell or places just like it because you've got a hunch or you just feel like doing something is right."

"Hoo-boy," Cordy whispered. "Storm-of-the-century alert."

"Yeah, and it's not blowing over without a fight!" Fred bellowed. "You people are my friends, my family. How can you turn away from me like this?"

"We're not."

"Call it whatever you want. You're leaving, I'm staying, and you won't help me."

"I'm sorry, Fred. Listen, maybe when we get back, if the police haven't turned anything up . . ."

"It'll be too late by then."

Gunn looked edgy. "Too late for what? What are you thinking?"

"Whoever did this will have gotten away."

"Let's say they don't. What if the police find whoever did this and that person gets arrested. Is that enough for you?"

"Sure," Fred said, looking away swiftly. "Why wouldn't it be?"

No one spoke, but recent memories hung in the air like ghosts. In them, Fred, Angel, and Gunn were gathered near the weapons cabinet. It had just become known that Professor Seidel was the dirtbag who sent Fred to Pylea.

"We're gonna get this guy," Angel had vowed.

Gunn's eyes burned with anger. "Count on it. He's gonna pay."

"No," Fred said, stopping them both in their tracks with her eerie stillness and determination. "He's gonna die."

Soon an ax was in Fred's hands, and she had been talking "crazy," rattling off all the reasons she should take bloody revenge on the man she had idolized who had betrayed her.

Now . . .

They were in the same place again, and Fred seemed to want something other than justice.

She stared at the group. "I said, why wouldn't seeing the s.o.b. who shot my friend being arrested and sent to jail be enough for me? I'm not ignoring what happened a little while ago. But I'm talking about the here and now. It's justice I'm looking for, not vengeance. And I guess . . . well, all things considered, I don't have the faith in the police that maybe I should."

"I could make some calls," Gunn offered. "See if I can get any of my old crew out asking questions."

"I can talk to Connor," Cordy said swiftly. "He's been a little mixed up lately, but he can track people just as well as Angel. I'm pretty sure he'd do it if I asked."

"I'd be willing to, ah, charge up my credit limit with the muses," Lorne added. "Maybe they'd have some ideas. It'd be a sacrifice on my part, sure, but hey, what are friends for?"

Finally, it came to Angel to make a contribution. "I could, um . . . call Giles."

Fred looked at all of them and couldn't have been any more surprised at the words that came from her. "No, you're right. I'm being selfish."

"No one said that," Angel protested.

"No way," Gunn agreed. "Selfish, naw, that's—"

"Let me finish," Fred said, cutting in. "What I'm saying is that I'm . . . I'm messed up. I recognize that. My friend's gone, and all I want to do is treat it like a case so I can keep myself at arm's distance somehow. So that I won't feel so bad. And the worst thing is, there was nothing stopping me from calling her a month ago. Two months ago. I could have called as soon as I got back. But I didn't. I keep trying to reconnect with the past, with the person I was before I got sent to Pylea, but there's that thing they say . . . let the dead past stay dead."

"Fred . . ."

"I write a paper and I end up finding out my old professor was trying to kill me. I make a dinner date with a college friend and she ends up dead. If I had just picked another place, any other place . . . I mean, I *know* it was an accident, but it was an accident that might not have happened if I had done something differently. She wouldn't have been there. She wouldn't have been sitting in that place, in the line of fire, if it wasn't for me."

"It's not your fault, Fred," Gunn said seriously.

Fred wasn't listening. Her thoughts drifted back to the moment she had lost it over her old professor; the moment she handed over the ax and promised that she was going to go lie down. The second everyone's back was turned, she was out the door, heading for Wes's place.

Fred seemed to pick up on those memory ghosts, and how they were invading everyone's thoughts at once.

"I have to see Detective Moffat in the morning. Cordy, if you want to come with me or whatever, fine."

"Why would I want to do that?" Cordelia asked. "I hate police stations."

Gunn and Angel both glared at her.

"Oh!" Cordy said. "You mean like being there to make sure Fred doesn't blow it off and go all Charles Bronsony trying to find the shooter. Right, the little fink who rats out the other kids when they're doing something wrong. Nope, sorry, got me confused with someone else."

"I'll still go see the muses," Lorne said. "You never know what they might come up with."

"The muses, Connor, the Initiative, Gunn's old crew . . . there are better things they could be doing with their time. Lives they could be out there saving. It's like Angel said: If the police don't turn up anything, and we're just sitting around doing nothing after this whole thing at the abbey gets wrapped up, then, fine. We'll do some checking. In the meantime, no." Fred looked to Angel. "Promise me one thing?"

"Yes."

"If you end up in a position where having an

advanced physicist on the team would help, you'll call me in?"

"Who else would I call?" Angel asked.

Fred shot him a smile. "I'm going to get some sleep. And I really mean that. I'm exhausted."

"Be up in a little bit," Gunn called.

Fred nodded as she went up the stairs, but didn't look back.

Once she was out of sight, Gunn turned to Angel. "So, what do you think?" he asked. "We get someone to follow her. Just for backup, in case she runs into trouble?"

"No," Angel said.

"Come again?"

"Trust. She needs us to trust her. She needs to feel she can trust us in return. If she needs help, she'll call. Same with us."

Gunn wasn't happy about it, but he knew Angel was right.

CHAPTER FIVE

Angel and Gunn stood in a desolate field outside of the city beside a towering tree with long, skeletal arms that reached across the distance separating them from the gathering of sorcerers. The tree's branches strove upward, too, toward the starry night sky, which would soon lose its dominion. Sunrise was still a good half hour away, and Angel wanted to be safely within the abbey the mages had talked about before it struck. Unfortunately, there was no abbey—or so it seemed. Every now and then, one of the mages would look back at that sprawling empty area with something approaching reverence, which indicated to Angel that the abbey was in that spot, but mystically shielded from their view.

Gunn was the one to break the silence between the two groups. "So y'all are the grand high muckity-mucks, that right?"

The mage dressed in the Asian-style armor cleared his throat. "We are."

Gunn smiled. "Hey, Angel, we got the whole Jedi Council here."

Sighing, Angel did his best to shoot Gunn a look of warning, but Charles was on a roll.

"I'm kind of surprised at the number of brothers here," Gunn commented, sweeping his hand in the direction of the African mage he had seen last night and at least five more Africans among the fourteen wizards assembled there. "Figured this would be another one of those Society of Pasty Face White Dudes Who Don't Get Out Much deals."

"Standing right here," Angel said in a harsh whisper.

"We have not been properly introduced," the head mage said. "I am Shanower." He motioned toward the African man with the crimson streak in his hair. "This is Marekai."

"I couldn't be any happier to see the two of you again," Marekai said stiffly, his lips curled in displeasure or distaste.

Shanower gestured, and a magnificent edifice suddenly appeared; or rather, it had been there the whole time but the spells preventing others from seeing it had now been lifted. The darksome abbey was a black stone building that consumed the equivalent of a city block, its gold-trimmed spires reaching higher than those of any other building in Los Angeles, threatening to impale the clouds. The design was a simple square, each plane interrupted at its center by protruding towers, topped by a dome covered with dagger-shaped observation towers. The doors and outer walls bore intricately sculpted faces and figures of soldiers and saviors. The materials that had been used in the construction of its beautiful facades were gold, silver, steel, and stone; at its core, however, the citadel had been forged by ancient magic.

"And there you see it," Shanower said, his breath catching, as if the sight of this majestic abbey filled him with emotion even though he had probably viewed it in all its glory many times before.

"Not bad," Gunn said, raising an eyebrow and delivering a slight shrug. "A little *Name of the Rose*-y, but definitely impressive."

"Your high opinion of our accomplishments warms us to no end." Marekai's voice was sharp and venomous.

"I do what I can," Gunn said, smiling broadly, pleased that he had gotten to the mystics. They were *way* too full of themselves.

Still, the high watchtowers drew Gunn's attention. Was the abbey expecting some kind of attack?

"They serve a purpose, yes," Shanower said, noticing Gunn's interest. "Or they will, once we get closer to the event horizon."

"Event horizon? That's a scientific term," Angel said. "I've heard Fred use it—something to do with black holes?"

Shanower nodded. "There's an undeniable relationship between science and magic. Many such occurrences of the two mixing are simply a result of synchronicity or simultaneous creation, but yes, the relationship exists. And we wizards are open to all possibilities."

"So give it to me again from the top," Angel said. "What's the nature of the problem we're looking at, and what do you hope to accomplish?"

"Yes, go slowly and use small words," Marekai muttered. He was silenced from any further commentary by a displeased look from Shanower.

"The walls between worlds are both remarkably resilient and startlingly fragile," the head mage explained. "A paradox, I admit, but so is most of existence. There are certain worlds, certain *dimensions,* in point of fact, that are so deadly, such a contaminant to the fabric of all existence, that reality itself attempts to reject them, to ferret them out and destroy them whenever possible. Sometimes that cannot be done. And with such a host of viruses, if you will, living in the body of all reality, the only other solution is quarantine. Barriers are erected that are very difficult if not impossible to breech, at least under normal circumstances."

"Which these aren't," Gunn jumped in.

"Correct," Shanower said. "Everything ages. Systems break down. Things fall apart. Every so often, cracks form in the walls, the barriers weaken, and some threaten to fall completely."

"Unless something is done about it," Angel ventured.

The head mage nodded. "Yes."

Angel crossed his arms over his chest. "So you've got some big ceremony to perform that'll strengthen the walls to make things safe again."

"For this world and a thousand like it, yes," Shanower told him.

"But something's not making that easy for you," Gunn suggested. "The same *something* that killed those people at the nightclub."

"Two of our members have fallen," Shanower admitted guardedly.

"Fallen," Gunn said derisively. "I love how none of you people can just—"

"Call a spade a spade?" said Marekai, the most highly ranking of the African mages.

Gunn was startled. "Did you really just say that to me?"

Marekai wore his contempt openly. "You really shouldn't be surprised by how many 'brothers' are among our number. Civilization in this world began in mother Africa. And magic was there long before that."

"Yeah, thanks for the history lesson," Gunn said to Marekai.

The mage brushed at the crimson streak in his hair. His body was suddenly covered in sweat, and there was a warmth in the air that hadn't existed only a second earlier.

Marekai smiled contemptuously. "That aside, I would, if I were you, do away with the notion that a similarity in skin pigmentation makes you, one of the lower caste, a brother in any sense of the word to any of us."

"The lower caste," Gunn repeated slowly, not believing this guy.

"Mundanes," Angel said under his breath, "non magic users."

Another hooded mage looked to Angel and Gunn uneasily. "We are all concerned that our abbey was infiltrated. That means we are all at risk."

Marekai shrugged. "True. But I still think we're going to be *more* at risk as a result of having fools such as these underfoot."

Gunn had heard about enough. He turned to the vampire. "Any chance we could just let this thing whack the bunch of these guys and find someone else to do the spell?"

"Nope, looks like we don't have a choice," Angel said with a shrug.

"Y'know?" Gunn said wearily. "Somehow, I just *knew* you were going to tell me that."

Marekai laughed. "Well, you can read each

other's minds. Maybe that makes the two of *you* brothers."

Gunn started forward. "Maybe that makes *you* in need of an ass-whuppin'."

The mage smiled, and suddenly the air directly in front of Gunn's face grew even more heated. It crackled, and a terrifyingly beautiful form of a firefly forged from flame manifested itself—and attacked!

"Gah!" Gunn yelled, leaping back as a shower of sparkling light and ionized particles of air harmlessly descended on him, the firefly disintegrating before it could reach him. Gunn took a moment to regain his composure, his heart thundering. "Oh, that was mature."

"I *am* mature," Marekai angrily assured him. "For three hundred and seventy-three years I have walked this earth."

"Three hundred and seventy-three," Angel mused. "Not bad."

"Who's side are you on?" Gunn demanded. "And besides, I can fight my own battles."

"Listen, you're not the only one feeling a little offended right now," Angel replied as he turned to the head mage. "This is how you keep order?"

Shanower bristled and looked to Marekai. "He's right. That vulgar display is hardly worthy of the one whom I have named as my successor."

Marekai hung his head. "I'm sorry."

"No more than I am," Shanower informed him.

"You have walked this planet for four centuries and you still cannot control your passions."

Marekai's shoulders bunched. A nimbus of crimson fire winked into existence around him. "I said—"

"And I heard you," Shanower said, gesturing and causing Marekai's rising flames to instantly dissipate.

"Whoa," Gunn said. "I'm sensing some tension here."

"You're not the only one," Angel told him. "Hey guys, let's get back to business, shall we? We're here risking our lives because we want to stop these killings. Y'know, the whole 'help the helpless, protect the innocent' thing. What's your story?"

Shanower drew a deep breath and let it out before continuing. "If the walls fail, everything we've built over the centuries, the millennium, will be swept away."

"So you're just covering your assets," Gunn observed.

This time, anger flashed in Shanower's eyes as well as in those of Marekai. "Enough," the head mage said commandingly. "We should talk about the creature."

"Fine," Angel agreed. "What do you have?"

"We believe it comes from one of the worlds that is forbidden congress with our own," Shanower told him.

"Mean and nasty," Gunn said. "Got that. Anything specific?"

Shanower opened his hands beseechingly. "Because these worlds—and the dimensions they inhabit—are kept isolated, we know very little about them."

"So we can't just jump to 'What does it want?' and 'How do we kill it?', huh?" Angel asked.

"Unfortunately, no. We know what it looks like, and our greatest scholars are attempting to find any references to similar beasts from the ancient texts."

"There ya go, it wouldn't be an abbey without ancient texts, now would it?" Gunn quipped.

Angel ignored him. "You know what it looks like? That means you have a witness."

"Of sorts, yes," the head mage said cryptically. "And we will take you to see that witness at the proper time, should that prove to be the consensus of our members—"

That was it. "Let's just cut to the chase," Angel said. "If I'm reading this right, I'd say you guys are just about split down the middle on whether to combine resources and let us in—emphasis on the 'just about.' And the fact that you're on the fence about letting me even see this witness makes me think I'm going to have a hell of a time doing my job once I'm in there."

"It's true," the huge mage with dreadlocks said.

"Many of us do not want outsiders gaining knowledge of our private affairs."

"Your love lives are the last thing we're interested in, dawg," Gunn said.

"He means—," Angel began.

"I *know* what the man meant," Gunn interrupted. "I'm just having some fun, is all."

"Well, don't. That's not why we're here."

"Oh. Yessir, bossman. What was I thinking?"

"If the two of *you* have an internal dispute you wish to settle, we could give you some time . . . ," Shanower offered.

"No need," Angel assured him. "Listen, I understand that a lot of you don't want us here. But I get the feeling there's more to it than what you said. You're either going to have to decide, right now, to let us in and give us what we need to find this killer, including a meeting with the witness, or we should forget the whole thing. What's it gonna be?"

Angel was bluffing, of course. He couldn't walk away now. But he hoped this tactic would help him get what he needed.

The eldest mage nodded. "Things are not so simple. There is . . . some *division* among our ranks that existed long before we met you."

"What he's trying to say is that we're living in a selfish age," the mage with the skullcap and artificial arm said. "It used to be that no one gave a passing thought to what was in it for them when they were called to duty. When we were summoned because the need for all our strength had arrived, no one ever questioned the need for unity. Now we have to hire business consultants and deal with managers; we have to enter contracts that guarantee individual rewards rather than just calling upon the wizards to perform their sworn moral duty."

"Please understand," said Shanower, "it is imperative while you are here that everyone outside our inner circle—the mages standing before you now—believes that you, Angel, are one of us, a recalcitrant member who has reconsidered our offer and decided to join us after all."

"Understood. Any special reason for the secrecy?" Angel asked.

"We need to avoid a panic," the beautiful female mage in the billowing cloak explained. "If the ceremony does not take place in three days time, countless worlds will suffer, including this one."

"There are other reasons for our caution, which you will soon come to understand," added Shanower.

"And what about the witness?" Angel asked.

The head mage turned to the others, then nodded and looked back to the vampire. "We will take you to the witness once you have been made to look like one of us. And we will grant whatever other requests you have, provided they are within reason and it is within our power to do so."

"I guess that'll have to do," Angel muttered, realizing this was the best he would get from the mages at this point.

With that, he turned and headed in the direction of the abbey. The other mages followed him, as Angel and Gunn exchanged significant looks and headed inside.

The first fiery rays of dawn licked the horizon as they reached the main entrance. The facade resembled a skull, jutting out from the main building that was two stories high. The doorway itself was a tall rectangle with stairs leading up to it. On the second floor there were two large ovoid windows, each nearly the same size as the doorway below, with a small strip of bonelike cartilage in the center. There were indentations on either side of the doorway, giving the illusion of cheekbones just below the two great eyes peering down on the darkness.

The entrance was guarded by female sentries wearing shining black armor and carrying short swords. Mesh skullcaps concealed the women's hair, and plates with steel grills obscured their faces, leaving only their heavily shadowed eyes in view. The woman on the left had deep blue eyes; the one on the right, soft brown. Both women were very tall, with trim, athletic builds.

They kind of reminded Gunn of the Amazons from *Wonder Woman*.

"Hey, ladies, what's happenin'?" he asked.

He noticed them adjust their grips on their weapons, and he raised his hands and held out his palms as he laughed. "Come on, now, just makin' conversation."

"Don't," Shanower said sternly. "They belong to an ancient sacred warrior caste and possess powers that few of us fully comprehend. Offend one of them and there is no telling what you might be transformed into." He nodded at Blue-Eyes. "Cockroaches seem to be that one's specialty, though."

"So they're not in it for any reason except to do what's right," Angel said admiringly.

"With any luck at all, yes," Shanower noted with a deep sigh. "But I cannot comment on our negotiations with them."

As Angel approached, the blue-eyed protector drew her short sword, carved an invisible rune in the air, and aimed the tip in his direction. Suddenly, a thick wall of fog surrounded them, cutting off all sight and sound outside of its tight perimeter.

"What are you doing?" Shanower asked angrily.

"We cannot let you pass," the guard said to Angel. "You are an unclean being. Undead."

"I bathe," Angel said, easing away from the sword. "The dead thing I can't do much about."

"This is the one you were told about," Shanower said sternly. "The champion we asked to join us."

"There is great evil inside him," Blue-Eyes whispered. "It would take very little to release it. There are far too many temptations within this keep, both of the flesh and of the spirit, for one such as this. The safety of this venture cannot be assured if one such as he is allowed within."

"You are absolved of all responsibility or blame," Shanower said flatly. "Your contract will be unaffected. So I have declared."

She stepped back. "Then we shall let him pass. But our eyes will always be on him."

They walked past the guards. "See?" Gunn observed, his elbow brushing Angel's arm. "They won't be taking their eyes off you. And you think you aren't pretty."

"Shut up," Angel urged.

Gunn fell silent, but his wide smile spoke volumes.

Torches lit the corridor ahead of them. Great stone pillars rose on either side of him, a dozen such pillars lining each side of the hallway. Archways were carved between each set of columns, and behind the archways were small receiving areas in front of a series of locked doors. Statues, paintings, and glass display cases with remnants of the mages' past triumphs were positioned outside the chambers. The ceiling was also curved, a golden honeycomb reaching down to the high observation level on the second floor. Although he appeared to be alone in the north wing of the grand hall, several guards patrolled above.

"We have much to accomplish over the next three days," Shanower explained. He gestured, and the man with the artificial arm came forward. "This is Archiel. He will make you ready to receive visitors and be your guide for as long as you stay with us. The rest of us must leave you now."

The group continued down the hallway. Marekai shot Gunn a nasty look, while the woman who called herself Bliss glanced back at Angel appraisingly, then turned away with an enigmatic smile.

Angel, Gunn, and Archiel entered a small barren room, and the door shut itself behind them. The room had three cots and three windows, all of which had been tinted to filter the early morning light. There was a table, several chairs, and an area where blankets and other supplies had been piled.

It looked exactly like a monk's cell should look, all dusty and awash with earth tones.

A penitent's cell, Angel thought. *Only . . . why three cots?*

"Are you staying with us?" Angel asked the mage.

"Not in the way you mean," Archiel replied enigmatically. "This room was already in use, so you will have a roommate. He was among those gathered outside just now, though he was uncharacteristically silent. I doubt you'll even notice that he's here—he likes to wander most of the time."

Archiel tapped a wall, and a section of it disappeared, revealing a bathroom fully equipped with all the modern conveniences.

"Nice!" Gunn said approvingly. "Can you throw in some white bathrobes and slippers too?"

Angel shook his head. "Let's move on, shall we?" he said, and then turned to face the mage. "You know what I'm interested in—the witness."

"You will be taken to him shortly."

"For now, what can you tell me about him? What information was he able to give you?"

"The witness is a young lad, the only one spared in the slaughter . . . though none of us is quite sure why his life wasn't taken as well," Archiel admitted. "He described the killer as a living shadow, with energies of some kind sparking within it."

"And you think it came here by accident through one of those rifts that you're all so worried about," Angel said. "How did it get *here*, though?"

"There may be a very simple answer to that question," Archiel answered. "As you've probably gathered by now, we are not a closely knit tribe by any means. Some among our numbers are more talented than others, some more scrupulous and wise. We believe that one of our members had . . . relations . . . with a woman who was in the club on the night of the killings. We think he may have even brought her here before the sentries arrived, and bragged of what we were doing."

"That doesn't track," Gunn pointed out. "The killings took place too quickly. There wasn't any time for this thing to walk around and interview everyone."

Archiel raised an eyebrow. "It didn't have to. We have reason to believe that it takes the memories of its victims, and perhaps their abilities, as well. It is a parasite of some type, feeding off the life energies and experiences of those it kills."

"No wonder you guys haven't been able to just round it up and crush it like a bug. It can just blend into any shadow?" Gunn asked.

"Possibly—we don't know," Archiel told him.

"I picked up a scent at the crime scene," Angel revealed. "Not a scent, exactly," he amended. "Just something I've never experienced before. But I haven't felt it here. Not yet."

"Back to this witness of yours—I'm surprised the kid was able to handle seeing a thing like that without going haywire in the head," Gunn said.

Archiel refused to meet Gunn's gaze. "There is much to be done before—"

"Hold up," Angel said sharply. "This boy *came forward* with what he saw, right?"

"He was deeply disturbed by the incident . . . understandably so," Archiel told them. "Certain means *were* employed to help release his memories of the event."

Angel didn't like the sound of that. "You're telling me you've been using magic to drill holes in his head and look inside?"

"Not . . . in the literal, graphic sense that you describe," the mage said distastefully, "though that would certainly be possible, if somewhat pointless."

"You've been reading his mind," Gunn said dully.

"With his consent," Archiel asserted. "The process is painful, I admit. But he has shown great courage—"

"Right," Angel said, "like he's going to say 'no' to the people he idolizes."

The mage looked taken aback, as if the thought that the boy had been coerced in any way simply hadn't occurred to him—until now. "You don't understand our faith in our beliefs, the devotion of our young acolytes."

"Guess not. I'm still hung up on the 'Let's stick a magical drill bit in the skull of an innocent kid and see how much we can drag out of him' part."

"We are not so selfish and we are not so cruel," Archiel said, offended. "His sacrifice will be remembered and rewarded."

"Save it," Angel said flatly. "I really don't want to hear it."

"Fine." Archiel got up. "You'll see him soon enough and judge for yourself, then, if he's been mistreated. In the meantime, you must be made ready."

Archiel gestured, and an array of medieval-looking leathers, vests, boots, and robes appeared on the closest cot. "Choose your garments."

Both Angel and Gunn decided to keep it simple: black leather pants and boots, white shirts, gray belted tunics. Angel elected to keep his duster, as it gave him places to hide weapons.

"What do you guys do when disputes come up within these walls?" Angel asked. "Do those women we saw outside come running if there's a fistfight or stabbing or whatever?"

"We have a mechanism in place for such contingencies," Archiel assured them. "You'll come to understand all of this, in time. As we discussed, you must blend in, and making that happen will not be easy. Obviously, this is not just a matter of your outward appearance, but of your actions and demeanor when you are here."

"Right," Angel said. "We have to pretend we're heavy-duty wizards though we have no clue about spellcasting."

Gunn nodded. "I've been wondering about how we're going to pull that off."

The mage cleared his throat. "I will be close by at all times, though you will not see me. When you need to perform some bit of magic, simply announce what you would like to do so that I am prepared, then gesture a little. I will provide the actual sorcery."

"That's a'right," Gunn said, "but doesn't that mean you'll also be watching us the whole time?"

"It does."

Gunn crossed his arms over his chest. "Okay, scratch *Name of the Rose* and add *Big Brother.*"

"How do we know we can trust you?" Angel asked.

Archiel laughed. "How do you know you can trust *any* of us? You know where the door is. No one's forcing you to be here. If you want to go, then go."

"So you're one of those who doesn't want us here," Angel said. "You figure you've got this whole thing covered just fine."

"Not at all," Archiel said, his metallic hand absently scratching an itch on his other arm. "Pride is the crutch of the insecure. *You* asked about trust. My honest response is that I would feel better knowing that you and your partner regarded each of us with equal suspicion until this matter is resolved."

Gunn nodded. "He's right. Shanower could have his own agenda for bringing us in. Maybe he's doing it right now to draw attention away from whatever part he's playing in these killings."

"Or maybe you're trying to draw attention away from yourself," Angel said casually.

Archiel laughed. "See, you're already learning

our customs. There is a reason why the phrase 'healthy paranoia' came into being."

"Got that right," Gunn muttered.

"So we have to fit in. You're covering the magic. What else do we have to worry about?" Angel asked.

Archiel leaned against a nearby wall. "I'll spend some time with the two of you teaching you the standard greetings and the like. None of it is difficult to learn. We're a solitary and suspicious lot. We keep things simple and universal as a way of obscuring our actual pursuits."

"You make it sound like corporate espionage," Gunn told the mage.

"You're not wrong," Archiel revealed. "We all have secrets, and many would go to practically any lengths to keep those secrets private."

"You think that *thing* might have been brought here to help steal the secrets of your mystical pursuits?" Angel asked.

"I don't know," Archiel said. "Anything's possible. It certainly is displaying knowledge that it could only have acquired from its victims, so on that level, it makes sense."

"What bothers me is why it left that one kid alive," Angel said.

Archiel nodded. "Puzzling, I agree. Either it wanted to be seen, and thus send some kind of message to the elders, or it didn't have the strength to take another life. We must believe that it is not all powerful, that it has limitations, and probably, a specific agenda and timetable. Otherwise, why not just kill us all as it slaughtered those people in the club?"

"Wizards are harder to kill," Angel ventured.

"Yeah, and all that mojo might weigh him down, make him feel kinda bloated and stuff," Gunn suggested.

Angel and the mage looked at Gunn strangely.

"Hey, it would explain why the thing takes its time between feedings!" Gunn said, defending his position.

Angel grunted and turned back to Archiel. "Like I asked, what else do we have to deal with while we're here?"

"The ceremony is in three days' time, and preparations are underway for the event," Archiel explained. "You should not have to deal with either. Your ranking—or, I should say, the ranking of the mage you are impersonating—exempts you from such menial tasks. And you will be gone from this place, one way or another, before the ceremony itself begins."

"One way or another?" Angel asked suspiciously.

"You'll either succeed or fail. Survive or perish. I don't know how to make it any more plain than that." Archiel went to the window, where the sun was steadily rising. He basked in the light filtering through the tinted glass as Angel drew away from it. "However, there is the matter of the acolytes who have been assigned to your classes. They may prove tricky."

"Wait a second. Kids? *Teaching?*" Angel asked with alarm. "No one said anything about teaching. I'm really not cut out for it. How about we just skip the whole acolyte thing."

"No," Archiel said firmly. "It's custom. Defy custom and you'll arouse suspicion. To your students and the other mages, you will be known as 'Kano.' That is the name of the mage whose role you are assuming."

"Okay," Gunn said quickly, "what's my fake name?"

"You don't need one," the wizard told him. "You are going to assume the role of a lowly assistant."

"Forget that noise," Gunn said, annoyed. "Angel and I are partners."

"Not here. If we present you as a fellow practitioner of magic, then we have to double our efforts in maintaining this ruse. Even if you were an acolyte, a student, you would have to know some magic. We would have to magically invest ourselves in you as well as Angel. That is beyond our resources at this time. Besides, as a servant, you may blend into the background more easily, and thus be able to unobtrusively observe all that goes on around us with unbiased eyes."

"Yeah, I guess that works. . . ."

"But you must be prepared to play the role to the fullest. And that may mean long stretches of doing, well . . . nothing. Mages like the one Angel is impersonating do not always walk around with servants, and when a servant is not being called upon, he or she must stay out of sight and out of the way."

"Naw, dawg, that's just not me," Gunn said, shaking his head.

Angel nodded to the door and sniffed. Someone was right outside the door. Angel had that person's scent. "We'll talk about this later. We've got company."

Without so much as a knock, another mage entered the chamber. This one was a male albino wearing luminous white robes that did nothing to contain his inner light; his body *seethed* with power. "I am Xax," he said. "Disrobe, please."

Angel was surprised. "Come again?"

"Take off your clothing." The mage didn't seem to understand what part of his command was confusing.

"I'm assuming you have some reason for asking me," Angel said warily.

"And doing it so nicely, too." Gunn waved a hand in the air. "We just got dressed, man!"

The newcomer shot a look of annoyance in Archiel's direction and then turned his attention back to Angel and Gunn.

"An inordinate amount of mystical energy is being used to make your presence appear natural in this environment," Xax explained wearily. "That type of expenditure is bound to draw attention before long. It can't be maintained the entire time you're here. For that reason, magic that is more localized and less likely to be noticed by those we are attempting to keep in the dark about your true nature, including the shadow-thing, is needed. I will apply arcane symbols directly upon your flesh that will be activated to replicate the effects of the nonlocalized magic currently at work in and around you."

"Well, that explains everything," Gunn said sarcastically.

Xax ignored him. "You're both getting some magical tattoos. Don't worry, they're not permanent. Okay?"

Angel slipped off his duster and began to disrobe. "Uh . . . right. Just down to the waist, or what?"

"That will be fine." Strange runes burned themselves into the air as the albino gestured. "These mystical signs will keep your thoughts private, except, perhaps, to those most powerful in the psychic arena. Think of them as mystical fire walls. There are two or three mages here who might be able to break through them, but that's it."

Gunn followed suit. Both men gasped as the albino hurled the mystical symbols at them, searing the magics into their flesh. When it was over,

Angel's torso and arms were almost completely covered; Gunn only had a handful of sigils on his skin.

"Why'd he get more?" Gunn asked.

Xax settled back into a chair Archiel brought for him. The albino looked drained. "The additional spells used on Angel will allow him to do certain necessary things while he's within the limits of the abbey and its protected area."

"Like what?" Angel asked curiously.

"For one thing, they will allow you to walk in sunlight," Xax told him.

Angel froze. The last time he'd been able to do that was in Pylea.

"Are we actually still on Earth?" Angel asked. "Or did we pass through to some other dimension?"

"So long as no one attempts a crossing into our environs, we are between worlds," Archiel told him.

Gunn drew out his cell phone and tried to get a dial tone. It was dead. "And if someone does?"

"Then we settle in one spot, be it Earth or elsewhere," Archiel answered. "If we end up on Earth, Angel would be vulnerable to sunlight. Hence the signs of protection."

"Okay, what else do these things do?" Angel wanted to know.

"Your flesh will be warm to the touch," Xax said. "You will seem to have a heartbeat. And the curse that binds your soul to your undead form will be rendered undetectable to the magic of even the most powerful sorcerer."

Gunn chimed in. "Hey, what about one of those brain whammies where you dump a whole ton of learnin' in someone's head in like five seconds flat?"

"There *are* such spells," the mage said warily.

"I think it'd be good if my man Angel here got a whole encyclopedia of magic dropped in there under all that product. And I was thinking along the lines of theoretical and applied physics myself." Gunn bounced around excitedly.

"'Under all that product?'" Angel repeated. "You're talking about my *hair*?"

"Your brains gotta be in there somewhere," Gunn said. He looked to the albino. "So, dude, what do you say?"

"No whammies to the brain," Angel said firmly. "Things always go wrong with that stuff. We're still coming off that memory spell of Lorne's."

"You're no fun," Gunn said, as the mage "painted" a few more signs upon Angel's bare flesh. Each shimmered a bright emerald before dulling and branding itself into his flesh. Then Xax and Archiel left them while they finished dressing.

"You okay?" Angel asked, slipping his shirt back on.

Gunn shrugged. "Worried about Fred, I guess."

"Yeah, me too," said Angel quietly.

Gunn paused for a moment, deep in thought, and then shook his head, as if clearing his mind of Fred's image. He reached for one of the robes Archiel had laid out, and tried it on. Upon the elegant robe were images that moved, among which was a comet racing across a starry sky. Gunn could feel the heat of the comet as it streaked from his collarbone to his hip, wrapped itself around his body, and then descended again. The tiny stars blinked and filled him with warmth. "Man, this is *tight!*"

"Come on," Angel said, smiling. "Let's go see the witness."

CHAPTER SIX

Archiel led them to a cell that was considerably larger but equally austere as the one Angel and Gunn had been assigned. A single, shadow-laden room with one high window from which a single shaft of light filtered down. Its golden glow fell upon the matted black hair of the thirteen-year-old boy who sat cross-legged in the corner facing the wall. He wore a simple brown tunic and sandals and he had something clutched in his hands that Angel couldn't see from his angle. There was a dagger lying carelessly beside him, its sharp blade and emerald-encrusted hilt glinting in the light. The boy didn't turn when they entered the room. He just rocked back and forth, back and forth.

The air here was as pure and refined as it was throughout the abbey, the temperature remaining constant wherever they went. Even so, Angel felt chilled. The shadow-thing had been here. Angel could feel it.

He wondered if he would be able to sense the creature when it was actually present, or if it was only the strange energies it released during a kill that Angel was detecting.

"They call him Rabbit," Archiel informed them, gesturing toward the boy.

"Any particular reason for the nickname?" Gunn asked.

"He seems to like the name. It is the only one he would ever respond to."

Angel found that interesting. "You mean he wasn't born into this life?"

"No," Archiel said patiently. "He wandered into the keep of one of our least sociable members some five years ago and simply refused to leave. Dagort, the mage whose life he entered, didn't have the heart to turn the child back out into the cold. This surprised us, as we didn't believe Dagort had a heart at all."

"Can we speak with this Dagort later?" Gunn wanted to know.

Archiel shook his head. "Dagort was the mage whom Rabbit saw killed in this very room."

"Okay," Angel said, considering the situation. It was no wonder that this child showed all the classic signs of psychological trauma. Not only had he been a witness to an act of violence, but the victim had been like a father to him. The fact that Rabbit had sought out this existence at such an early age suggested that he had either been abandoned or had run away from some unpleasant situation.

The fact that he was so withdrawn now, that he refused to leave this room where the murder had taken place, indicated to Angel that Rabbit needed the kind of help that these sorcerers weren't equipped to provide. Rabbit needed counseling and round-the-clock care. When this was over, Angel swore inwardly that he would make sure the boy received just that.

Angel reached for the blade, wanting to make sure it was not anywhere within the boy's reach as he approached. "Rabbit—," he began, and that was as far as he got. The boy spun the moment the vampire's hand brushed the dagger. He dropped a small brown teddy bear, and was suddenly screaming and clawing at Angel like a wild animal.

"Nemesis!" Rabbit hollered. "Nemesis is coming! It'll get me! Let go!"

Angel held the boy off easily, and Gunn and Archiel helped calm him down.

"He refuses to be separated from the dagger," Archiel observed. "It must be a keepsake from Dagort."

"And Nemesis must be what this thing is called," Angel said. "I have no idea how Rabbit here knows that. Maybe Rabbit made up the name himself. Or this thing could be one of those big bads that likes to refer to itself in the third person."

Gunn nodded. "It could have left the kid alive to send a message: 'Tell them Nemesis is coming,' something like that."

They sat together in silence for several minutes until Rabbit seemed himself again.

"What do you remember?" Angel asked. "What do you think happened? What did you see?"

"This is unnecessary. We already told you—"

"I want to hear it from him," Angel said quickly. He needed to know that the boy had not been harmed, that he had not been coerced into allowing these people to use him in their quest to preserve the power they had each devoted themselves to attaining.

If they had, then once this beast was stopped, and the ceremony to strengthen the walls between worlds had been accomplished, there would be a reckoning.

"What can you tell me about the night the bad thing came?" Angel asked.

The boy stared at him blankly.

"This is pointless," Archiel said. "Without magic to help—"

"Enough," Angel snarled. "Either he was like this when you people found him and you're lying about his giving consent, or what you did made him like this. I want to know which it is."

Suddenly a dim awareness came into the youth's eyes . . . and he told Angel everything he could remember about that night and the shadow-thing called Nemesis.

"Well, you got your answers," Gunn said as he and Angel were guided down another hallway by Archiel, who left them for a moment to go deal with some "pressing business."

Angel nodded. The boy had been traumatized, yes, but it had been by the experience, not the actions of the mages. Without the sorcerers' energies that had been used upon him, *with* his consent, Rabbit may never have been able to recall the details of Nemesis's vicious attack.

Rabbit had been in that cell with Dagort and several of his assistants and acolytes when the creature had melted out of a patch of shadow in the corner and struck down the young woman who was closest. It was all talons and teeth, its egg-shaped head that stretched obscenely as it consumed her, momentarily assuming her shape. Virginia had been Dagort's most promising student. She knew hundreds of lower-level spells that the creature promptly used to disorient and disable his victims. Sentient winds howled loud enough to destroy the hearing of one victim, while mists came alive and sucked the air from the lungs of other victims.

Dagort himself had been the last to die. Nemesis

wearing Virginia's form struck him with a barrage of savage physical blows while its newly acquired spells kept the man's metaphysical barriers of defense from ever fully engaging. It giggled as it consumed him, then dropped Virginia's dead body from within its shadow form and tiptoed to the terrified Rabbit.

"Don't tell," it whispered. "Or I'll be back for you."

"What are you?" Rabbit had asked.

The thing laughed. "I am Nemesis."

Nemesis then brushed his face, burying the boy's memories of what he had just witnessed deeply, and then sank into the darkness and was seen no more.

Rabbit kept Dagort's knife within reach at all times. He *had* told what he had seen, and he feared that Nemesis would make good on its promise and come back for him. The mages had cast spells on the blade of the knife to make it harmless to the boy, and he was being watched constantly on the off chance that the shadow creature might return.

"The thing is, nobody's suspicious of anything," Angel said quietly, peering either way down the hall. "Two of these guys have disappeared and no one's paying any attention. Could they all be so self-involved that they don't notice anything *unless* it affects them directly?"

"Could be, man," Gunn answered.

"Are we all so ruthless and cold?" a whispering voice said beside them.

Angel and Gunn both started, as Archiel materialized in the spot from which the voice had come.

"I wanted you to see firsthand that I am with you, even when you think I am not," Archiel explained.

Angel hadn't smelled or sensed a *thing*. They walked the halls of the abbey for a time, greeting other mages, until they reached a courtyard where a battle was underway.

Bliss, the female sorceress who had come to their aid the night before, was fighting an abomination that had already struck down a mage with blue tattoos covering his flesh. Dozens of students and other sorcerers watched the fight, jaws agape.

The creature's body resembled a gluttonous, red- and purple-veined flower. Its quivering layers of flesh pulsated with clear sacs containing shiny black pearls the size of a man's fist. A half dozen tentacles rose from its base like the limbs of a starfish. At the core of the monster was a wormlike, gelatinous trunk from which long, thin stalks protruded. At the end of each tiny stalk sat a human head. Some appeared to be alive, their eyes darting back and forth with madness and fear, their mouths uttering silent screams. There were close to a dozen heads in all, but not all were alive.

The necks of those that were dead seemed to be shrinking, as if the lifeless head would be ground into the sickening mass of the creature where the bones of humans were clearly visible. A shattered vertebra poked out of its mass.

The sorceress made a wide arc with her brilliantly glowing hand, forcing several of the creature's grasping appendages back, then she plunged the glowing sword she held in her other hand through another tentacle, making the creature convulse.

"We've got to help her!" Angel shouted, but Archiel placed a warning hand on the vampire's chest. "The line between reality and illusion is stretched very thin in this place. Watch and learn."

Ahead, Bliss saw that the monster was now poised to crush the blue-fleshed mage with another heavy, misshapen tentacle. She screamed a curse and then leaped at the pulsating core of the horrifying creature, releasing a torrent of blue-white magical energies into the beast's face. Then she landed, dropping her sword and punching a fist through the wailing creature's maw. The tentacle that was poised to swat the second mage twitched and fell to the side as the beast shuddered and died quickly.

Bliss rose, stepped back, and gestured. Suddenly, the courtyard was empty except for her and the spectators. "And that was how I saved Ord and felled the beast called Onslaught. Any questions?"

There were dozens, and she answered them gracefully and with a knowing patience.

Angel and Gunn stood speechless, and were unaware that they were once again "alone" until the woman ended class for the day and approached them. Nothing either man had seen at the abbey, not the spiraling worlds captured in a bottle or any of the dozens of other beautiful and strange sights they had beheld, compared to the elegant beauty of the cloaked and cowled woman.

"Did you both enjoy that?" Bliss asked.

"Yuh-*huh*," Gunn said, totally blown away.

Angel rewarded her with a thin smile. "Do that kind of thing a lot?"

"What do you mean?"

"Showing off."

She laughed. "I like your candor. And yes, I do. Every chance I get. Shall we walk together?"

They crossed the courtyard in silence until Angel spoke again. "I have some questions," he admitted.

Bliss laughed. "I'm sure you do, my dear. But the real question is whether this is really the best place for you to be. Given what I know about you, I can't help but wonder."

"Did someone forward my bio?" Angel asked. "It seems like everyone here knows the story of my life."

"It was related to all of us in the council," Bliss

explained. "This monastery is filled with enchantments, Angel. I myself am quite talented at casting happiness spells."

"I'll bet you are," Angel said uneasily.

Gunn walked behind them, half-listening as he took in the strange sights they passed. Crystalline doves burst to life and flew through corridors; the walls themselves breathed as they transformed themselves into kaleidoscopic collages better suited to Impressionist art.

Bliss went on. "With you, Angel, I am certain I could induce perfect happiness without the need for any spell. It is not that hard to come by."

Angel removed her hand from his arm. "Is that a threat?"

"One moment of perfect happiness and Angel would revert to Angelus," she cautioned. "The beast would be loose. I'm saying, for all of our sakes, that you should be on your guard. On the other hand, there is no reason to completely wall yourself off, to live like a penitent. It is more than yourself you deny."

She strutted off, the folds of her cloak dangerously opening and closing, exposing hints of luscious, pale flesh.

Gunn shook his head. "Man, she may be a bit of a weirdo, but she sure is hot."

Angel raised his eyebrows and looked at him sideways.

"What?" Gunn asked, defensively.

"You're in a magical abbey. For all you know, beneath the perfect exterior she could look like that many-headed squid she was fighting back there."

Wincing inwardly, Gunn got Angel's point. The woman was a mage, after all. She might have been using enchantments to make herself more desirable and to cloud his mind.

Archiel suddenly appeared.

"What's her deal?" Gunn asked. "Y'know, Bliss?"

"Sex magic," he said with a yawn. "Not everyone believes in the results."

"This is twice I've seen her fight," Angel said. "I don't see how anyone could *not* take her seriously."

Archiel went on. "There are practitioners here who achieve their magical arts through painting, poetry, music. Some use complex mathematics; others great displays of strength or stamina—by pushing the physical limitations of the flesh either by what you might call self-improvement or self-deprivation. They go beyond the borders of normalcy. They break the bonds of what is real and cross over into the unreal—or what normal people would consider real and unreal," Archiel explained.

"You seem pretty grounded," Gunn told the mage.

"It's an act."

Gunn looked at him strangely.

"Seriously, I'm not even in the same room with

you. What you are addressing right now is called a sending."

"You mean like a hologram? 'Obi-wan, you're my only hope?'" Gunn reached out and tapped the man's shoulder. He felt solid enough. "So am I just thinking that I touched something when I tapped you?"

"Oh no, the sending is three-dimensional, solid. The same basic illusion can be achieved by the simple bending of light, but that's so easy to detect."

"Weird."

"You've entered the world of weird, Charles Gunn. But you know that. You stepped boldly into that realm when you acknowledged the existence of vampires. You accepted that the world was very different from what most people would expect. This place takes that guiding principle by which you've chosen to live your life and turns it up a notch. Sendings are as real as what you see before you. And I may or may not be one of them. That's what you have to come to expect in this place."

They traveled on, passing crystal mirrors where each shimmering pane of glass was alive with its own separate personality. Some pulsed with colors that were impossibly beyond the known spectrum; there were no words to describe them.

Angel looked into one of the mirrors as they passed, startled that he could see his own reflection in one of them. But he downplayed his surprise as much as possible. Still . . . his hair, if he could just get it a little more under control. . . .

Thudding footsteps came from the end of the hall.

"This can't be good," Gunn said, tensing up.

"Wait and see," the mage advised.

A figure turned the corner and came into view. Glaring at them with dully glowing eyes that conveyed absolute menace, the nine-foot-tall, seemingly stone-carved creature lumbered toward them. It lurched from side to side as the light fell upon the large, flat planes of its gray-skinned body, highlighting its otherworldly form in broad strokes. Thinner beams of light caught the rises where its white and green veins were etched and radiated a low luminescence. A brown tunic belted at the waist gave it an odd sense of modesty, despite the cold, dead look it gave them with its unreadable eyes and its wide gash of a frowning mouth.

The stone giant's three-fingered hands clenched and unclenched, and its head nearly brushed the ceiling as it stopped before the group. Angling its skull to the left, then the right, its stony bones crackled as it looked to be preparing for a fight.

"Hello, Rocky," Archiel said serenely.

The stone golem's expression softened. It reached into its pocket and offered a closed fist to the newcomers. "Wanna see my turtle?"

"You must be very careful with him now," Archiel advised. "Don't squish, remember? Even if he gets away and you have to go after him, be gentle."

"I know." The golem opened his hand. A jade turtle was revealed. It had tiny crimson-jeweled eyes, and it looked like it was made of wax, but it was alive.

"He's a good turtle," Archiel said with genuine enthusiasm. "Have you named him yet?"

"Uh-uh," the golem said.

"Keep trying."

"'Kay." Without a second glance, the golem slipped the turtle back in his tunic and thumped off in search of a fresh audience.

The small group passed a silver platter mounted on the wall in which horrifying demonic forms blew raspberries and hissed derisively with their snakelike tongues.

Gunn raised his hand to one side of his face and used it like a blinder to keep him from seeing these weird shapes in his peripheral vision.

Archiel explained about the golem. "We can create beings . . . but these creatures lack creativity. It's an age-old problem. We always get the same result—an imitation of life, nothing more."

An imitation of life, Angel thought. *Does that sum up my existence? Are Gunn, Fred, Cordelia, and the others just my source material? Am I that empty inside?*

They moved on. "Many of the more showy things you will see here, like Rocky the Golem, the polo-playing lizard people, the pixies trapped like fireflies in old bottles," Archiel explained, "are either the work of the acolytes or they are provided for them."

"Rocky's yours?" Angel asked.

"Yes," the mage told him. "I have an affinity for earth and stone."

A group of teens came running down the hall—and froze when they saw Angel, Gunn, and Archiel. They bowed their heads, averted their gazes, then broke into a run again the moment they had passed their elders.

Archiel sighed. "As sorcerers-in-training get older and, let's hope, more mature, such magical displays as these are considered vulgar and, frankly, signs of insecurity. The more you have to show off what you can do, the less likely it is that you have true power."

Gunn couldn't help but think of the display Marekai had made with the dragonfly. No wonder his actions had been considered such a breach of etiquette. Gunn wondered if his business with that mage was over . . . or only just beginning.

Brushing the thought aside, he hurried to keep pace with his companions. There were wonders ahead, endless wonders . . . and endless terrors, too.

Fred approached the cluttered desk of Detective Moffat, her purse in her hands. It had been gone through thoroughly when she had arrived, and she had also been made to step through a metal detector. The experience had left her a little rattled.

"Hello, Detective," she said as he looked up, nodded, and pointed at a chair across from his desk. Fred smiled so hard, she thought her jaw would begin to ache any moment. "I'm . . . I'm better today."

Moffat leaned back and focused his laser-sharp gaze on Fred. "Not by much, I imagine. I wouldn't be if I were in your shoes."

Fred kept her smile plastered firmly in place. "Don't think they would fit you too well. And the heels would kill your arches."

Moffat's brow furrowed, then a thin smile etched itself on his egg-shaped face. "Oh, that's right," he said, almost to himself. "I forgot that you guys do that—use humorous banter to deal with stress. I can respect that. We do it too."

You guys? she thought. *What did he mean by that?*

And how on earth did this guy know so much about them?

The detective met her gaze and held it firmly. "I get where your suspicions are coming from. No one likes being spied on. But you know that there have been officers who have taken an interest in Angel Investigations over the years. We keep tabs, simple as that."

"Simple as that," Fred repeated distantly.

"I could be dramatic about this. Take out one of our many files on Angel Investigations, run each of your profiles, but let's not and say we did, 'kay? The bottom line is, I know who you are, Winifred Burkle. I know about your disappearance, your return, and the presence of yourself, Charles Gunn, and this Angel guy on campus the night Professor Seidel disappeared."

Fred was thrown completely off-balance by the detective's statements. If her earlier assessment of him was correct, that was exactly what he wanted.

"But I'm not assigned to that case," the detective said, leaning back and tilting his head from side to side, creating tiny bone-crunching sounds.

"There's a case?" Fred asked automatically.

"It's closed at the moment. That's the word that came from above. But if you work here, and you pay attention to gossip, which you should because you just never know what little kernels of truth might be buried in it, you folks over at Angel Investigations have someone very powerful watching over you, cleaning up your messes. That might be good, that might be bad. Personally, I'm not a big fan of people pulling the strings that affect my everyday life."

"Right," Fred said, taking it all in, and already feeling on the verge of overload.

"I'm telling you all this because you annoyed me yesterday—you and your boyfriend. I'm looking for some change in the status quo between us. It's not too late to start developing a trusting relationship, but lies like the ones you and Mr. Gunn hit me with yesterday aren't going to help in that pursuit. Do you understand?"

"You're looking for the truth and nothing but the truth, so help you God?" Fred ventured, a tense titter of laughter punctuating her words. She swallowed and sat up straight when she noticed the detective still wasn't smiling.

"I know there are details you're not going to want to share. And, frankly, it's probably the kind of thing that I don't want to know, anyway. There are detectives who have worked in this department who were branded with a kind of scarlet letter on their permanent records for believing in the weird crap you folks deal with every day . . . well, believing in it and broadcasting to everyone who'll listen that they believe."

His stoic expression melted away as he leaned forward, setting his hands on the desk before him, a look of unexpected compassion replacing it. "I asked you here to take your statement in regard to the accidental shooting death of your friend, Alicia Austin. Before I take that statement, however, I want us both on the same page about a couple of things. Are you with me?"

"I'm right here," Fred said anxiously.

"Hmph," he muttered. "All right. First, although it's too early for an official verdict to come in, I can tell you right now, off the record, that her death *will* be listed as accidental. No one here is going to be chasing down leads on this, because no one *officially* believes the shooting is anything other than what it appears to be. Vittorio Otakun has more enemies who truly want to see him dead than practically any other figure in the Los Angeles crime world today. He's an arrogant son of a bitch, he thinks he's untouchable, and he couldn't stop laughing for an hour yesterday after he realized what happened."

"He thought it was funny?" Fred asked, chilled.

"He did. You don't have to believe in monsters and demons to know that there is true evil in this world."

Fred nodded slowly. Professor Seidel had taught her that lesson all too well.

"So that brings me to my second point. Otakun is a very dangerous man. . . ." He nodded at the wooden chair in which Fred was uncomfortably perched. "If I had someone sitting there whom I thought might, even hypothetically, feel the official ruling of accidental death wasn't correct and was going to do a Nancy Drew number on me, I would want her to know that Vittorio Otakun wouldn't take kindly to a visit from someone he doesn't know, someone who doesn't at least have a badge to make him think before just hauling out a nine millimeter and blasting away. On top of that, this guy's got real 'mommy' issues. He just can't handle strong women. So I would suggest to this Nancy Drew type that if there's something she wants to know about Otakun, she comes to me first."

"Okay," Fred said quietly. "I understand."

"So, that brings me to my third and final bit of business." Moffat yanked a file marked CONFIDEN-TIAL from a stack of paperwork on his cluttered desk and left it within Fred's reach. "I'll be back in about five minutes," he said, rising from his chair. "*Don't* take off. Remember what I was saying about building trust."

"Okay," Fred said softly as he rounded the desk. She looked up as he gently set his hand on her shoulder.

"I am sorry about your friend," he said, once again looking like a loving, favorite uncle. "I've lost people too. I know how it feels to just need to make sense out of it, even when it doesn't make any sense at all."

Then he was gone. Fred looked around the room, waiting to ensure that no one else was watching her.

With trembling hands, she took the file that had

been left for her and read it as thoroughly as time allowed.

When Angel and Gunn returned to their cell, three teenage boys were already waiting. Two of them had long, coarse, blond hair and rough, cruel features. They introduced themselves as Logan and Marco. The third boy, who sat some distance from the others, had short-cropped brown hair and bright jade eyes. He was Daniel.

"So," Angel said uncomfortably, fully understanding the necessity of this function as part of his cover, but hating it nevertheless. "My name is Kano."

"We know who you are," Logan said, his scowl deepening.

Marco chimed in: "You don't look like a Kano."

"I get that a lot," Angel said, reminding himself that he was this age once too. Granted that was a couple of centuries ago, but their surly behavior reminded him simultaneously of himself as a teenager and of Connor, who pretty much defined "bad attitude."

"Can we go now?" Logan demanded.

Gunn stepped forward. "Hold on. Let me see if I've got this straight. All three of you want to be mages."

Logan didn't even look at Gunn. "We *are* mages. No one treats us with any respect because of our age."

"Yeah, they act like we don't know anything," Daniel said softly.

"So . . . my trying to teach you would be pointless?" Angel asked.

"You've got that right," Logan snarled.

"Great," Angel exclaimed. "My job here is finished. You can all leave now."

The teenagers exchanged confused looks.

"What, do I have to call down an incantation for you to get the hint?" Angel asked. "Go, scram, get outta here, you bother me."

Still, the boys did not get up and leave.

"We're . . . we're supposed to get training," Daniel muttered.

Marco rose to his feet. "You can't kick us out. I'll tell my father!"

"Like that would do any good. I'll tell *my* father," Logan said, crossing his arms over his chest imperiously.

So they aren't related, Angel noted.

Angel shrugged. "You're all short-sighted and arrogant. That's a good start. Tell you what: You prove to me why I should waste my time. Show me your stuff. Do some magic."

"Is this guy for real?" Marco asked.

Daniel glanced over. "I heard he doesn't get out much."

"Tick-tock, tick-tock, bored now, come on . . . ," Angel told them.

One by one, the boys rose and looked about the room. And one by one, they ended up focusing their attentions on Gunn.

"I say that I can destroy the servant with a single fireball," Marco announced.

"Excuse me?" Gunn asked in alarm.

"I can turn him to ashes, the bones ground to dust, with a gesture," Logan said, one-upping his companion.

"Hold on," Angel commanded.

"Second that," Gunn added worriedly.

The boys ignored them. Daniel, succumbing to peer pressure, added, "I can make it so he was never born *just by looking at him*. I'll blot him out of the book of life."

"That's it," Angel said firmly. "No burning. No grinding. No erasing."

"But you wanted to see," Logan said, confused.

Angel scratched his head. "*This* is what they teach you? How to *kill*?"

Not one of the teenagers met his gaze.

"No, I get it," Angel observed. "This is the 'fun' stuff you try to learn when no one's looking."

"No burning, no nothin', you heard the man," Gunn said nervously.

"I don't see what the problem is," Logan declared as he pointed at Gunn. "He's just a simulacrum, isn't he? You can make another one. And you said you wanted to see—"

"No!" Angel said firmly. "And he's not a—"

"Simulacrum," Daniel offered. "An artificial life-form brought into being by magic."

"I was born in the hood, you little punk!" Gunn roared. "I'm gonna come over there and school your asses in a way you never—"

"*Anyway*," Angel interrupted. "No, Charles is a person, like you or me. What made you think he wasn't?"

Logan shrugged. "You just keep him standing there, not doing anything. Figured he was just a prop."

Gunn shook his head. "I am a patient and kind man," he repeated under his breath, over and over.

"You guys can really do all that stuff?" Angel asked. "Fireballs, all that."

"With a magical construct, sure," Daniel offered. "It's just different ways of undoing the bonds that sorcery put together."

"Untying knots," Angel said. "But not with people?"

"It'd probably scorch 'em pretty bad," Daniel admitted. "Magic's in *everything*."

"Yeah, you know that, *Master* Kano," Logan said in a challenging tone.

"This isn't about what I know. It's about respect."

Logan turned to Marco. "I want to see him *do* something."

Gunn shoved off from the wall. "Respect your elders."

"Give me a reason," Logan said with a laugh.

The door opened, and Angel half-expected to see Archiel coming to their rescue. This was getting out of control!

Instead, Bliss entered.

"Ho, fellow practitioners," she said, grinning ear to ear. "I heard the challenge all the way down the hall, and I was drawn by the notion of watching the great Kano in action. I *so* want to see this too."

Great, Angel thought. *Just what I need.* He drew a deep breath. *Archiel said to just announce what I was planning, then gesture a little. Should be easy enough.*

"I've got a test for the three of you," Angel explained.

All three students groaned, the universal mantra for such revelations.

"First off, some 'props,' as you called them," Angel said. "A barrel half as high as me filled with water, and a smaller vessel, maybe a quarter the size, sitting beside it."

He gestured—and nothing happened.

The students looked at one another. Bliss and Gunn also exchanged surprised glances.

Angel gestured again—and again. Still nothing.

Aw, crap, Angel thought. *Now what? Archiel, where are you?*

The boys were laughing now, and Logan was suggesting "Kano" wasn't even a real mage, just some loon, like "the other one" who shared this cell. Angel didn't know exactly what that was about, but he wasn't pleased.

Neither, apparently, was Bliss. She raised her chin, blinked twice, and the barrel and the smaller vessel winked into existence in a rush of swirling ruby-colored energies.

The boys hushed.

Angel did his best to hide his relief. "Well, the first test was patience, and all three of you failed," Angel announced, making it up as he went along. "The second test is simple." He went to the smaller vessel, kicked a hole in it near the base, and pointed to it. "Fill this to the top—*without* using magic."

Hesitantly, the teenagers gathered around the barrel and the broken vessel.

"That can't be done," Logan said firmly.

"Gee, and I wouldn't have pegged you as a quitter," Gunn ventured. "Heck, I could do it. What's your problem?"

Logan and Marco worked on the dilemma for close to ten minutes, pouring water into the vessel, attempting to stop up the gap with their hands, a shoe, anything at hand. Daniel didn't even bother. He just sat, waited, and looked deep in concentration.

"Look at him," Logan said, breaking into a sweat. "What a loser. At least we're trying."

"Fill it to the top, right?" Daniel asked.

Angel nodded.

Without another word, Daniel crossed to the vessel, snatched it from Logan and Marco, and submerged it almost to the rim *within* the larger barrel of water.

"There," Daniel said. "It's filled."

"Cheater!" Logan hollered, shoving at the other boy.

Angel moved in fast and separated them. "Daniel solved the problem. The lesson is that if you end up depending on magic for everything, you're going to end up screwed. You have a brain; use it."

The vampire ended class with that one, and dismissed the boys. Bliss sauntered over to Angel and Gunn. "Archiel isn't here," she announced.

"Kinda figured that," Angel said.

"Then it was you," Gunn added. "He was out of the picture, so you stepped in."

"That's right," Bliss told them. "Angel, I may not *want* you here—"

"I don't think there's any question about that," the vampire said.

"Fine. I *don't* want you here," Bliss admitted. "But I'm not about to ignore Shanower's ruling, and I'm not going to let your cover be blown just to get my jollies. Not when this deception that the council has perpetrated could blow up in all our faces if it was uncovered."

"So I should trust you because you're serving your own interests," Angel said.

Bliss smiled. "I could care *less* if you trust me. We should go find Archiel."

It turned out that the mage was unconscious in the hallway. Bliss used a spell to locate him, another to turn him visible. Someone had clubbed him hard on the back of his head.

He slowly came around. "I don't understand," he said after he had been told what occurred. "I saw no one, detected no one anywhere near me, and no one *should* have been able to even know I was there."

Except someone with powers like Bliss, Angel considered. She could have clubbed the other mage unconscious and then stepped in at the last moment just to save the day for exactly that reason.

Healthy paranoia. For now, Angel would hold on to that. Or was it simply that someone didn't want them there *and* was willing to go to some lengths to make them leave, no matter the cost to the overall mission the wizards had undertaken?

Who had struck down the mage in the corridor? And did that act have anything to do with the nightclub killer? Had it now moved on to this place as a feeding ground?

Angel had no idea. All he was certain of was that he would have to learn the answer, and quickly . . . before time ran out.

CHAPTER SEVEN

An hour later, Fred was knocking on the door to Alicia's apartment. It was in a fairly expensive part of town, and had security out front. She'd had to be buzzed up by Sharon Roets, Alicia's roommate. When Sharon opened the door, Fred was surprised. Sharon was small, cute, in her late twenties, and had a kind of Lisa Loeb thing going on with her brown, thick-rimmed glasses and pageboy cut. Her clothes were, well, remarkably unremarkable for someone who lived with Alicia: Fred fully expected to find a walk-in closet worthy of *Sex and the City*, the kinds of clothes Cordelia would have once gone insane to possess. But, Sharon . . . she wore a pantsuit that was brown on brown on brown, and not in a good way.

Sharon let her in and was pleasant enough, but the woman really didn't seem to be in the mood for company. That was understandable, considering the loss she had just suffered. Yet . . . Fred had the idea that wasn't it at all. Sharon came off as distracted, not grieved, as she gave Fred the quick tour and let her into Alicia's bedroom.

"The cops have been all through here," Sharon said wearily. "I don't think there's much of anything to find, honestly."

Fred was startled by Alicia's room. It was as generic as the rest of the apartment, a showroom piece that had not been personalized in the least.

"Alicia lived here?" Fred asked, expecting to have felt a connection to what Alicia left behind on some level, and finding *nothing*. There were a few business suits in the closet, an all-purpose little black dress, some nice shoes, and that was about it. A small jewelry box sat open before the mirror across from the bed. The earrings, necklaces, and rings within looked more like costume jewelry than anything Alicia would have picked out.

"It's a company apartment, and she wasn't here all that much," Sharon said, suddenly applying some of that phony, forced brightness that Fred had called upon enough times to recognize at a glance. It was like Fred had hit on something that Sharon didn't want explored too closely. "She's got these big storage closets near her places in New York and Dallas with all her stuff. Well, she—she *had* them."

Sharon turned and went to her own bedroom.

Fred followed, and saw that Sharon had her luggage open and was about half-packed up for what looked like a pretty long trip. Taped-up moving boxes were piled in the corners, presumably to be shipped on after her later.

"I'm just curious about how she'd been acting lately," Fred explained. "Did anything seem to be bothering her?"

Sharon wouldn't meet her gaze. "Nothing she talked to me about."

"So she didn't seem like her normal self?" Fred waited for a reply, but Sharon busied herself with her packing. "Please, I need your help."

Sharon set down an armful of blouses and turned. "Listen, I don't know anything, and it's better for me that way. It'd be better for you, too."

A laminated ID badge was still clipped to one of the blouses. Fred read the company information off the top.

"You and Alicia worked at the same place," Fred realized aloud.

Sharon went back to packing, snatching the badge from the blouse and tossing it to the corner of the bed. "Different departments."

"You didn't like working there? I mean, you seem to be in an awful hurry to get out of here. I'm just wondering why."

"Family crisis back home."

Fred nodded, already fully aware from the file

she had read that Sharon had no family. "That sounds pretty rough."

"I'll manage. But—thanks."

Sharon was looking the other way as Fred snatched the badge. Making fake IDs was easy, but you needed something to work with.

"Guess I'll be going now," Fred said, backing away and depositing the badge in her purse.

Sharon said nothing. She didn't even look at Fred.

Hiding much? Fred wondered as she let herself out of the apartment.

Soon, Fred was back on the street. She'd been forced to park a little ways off and was heading down the oddly deserted sidewalk—strange, considering the number of cars parked everywhere. As she passed a vacant section of sidewalk by a fire hydrant, she heard the startling shriek of squealing tires.

A black sports car turned in from the road, drove up on the sidewalk, and skidded to a stop before her, rocking violently as three men in dark suits got out. Fred turned only to see a second identical vehicle racing her way. It, too, jumped the sidewalk and came to a screeching halt mere inches away from connecting with the building wall before it. As more goons got out of that car, a third skidded to a stop, tires squealing, to block her only possible way out.

A young, muscular Asian-American guy with silken black hair exited the fanciest of the cars. He sauntered like a gangster in one of those Hong Kong action films that Charles was always renting. His clothing probably cost more than she had made in her entire life; he wore a slick black suit with a thin tie, and a long coat that looked like it came from the wardrobe of *The Matrix*, along with designer sunglasses.

Fred recognized him as Vittorio Otakun from the file she had seen hours earlier.

"So, do you fellas see what I see?" Otakun asked, chewing gum and grinning. He was a handsome devil, Fred had to give him that. But, from all she had read in the file, the devil part was no exaggeration. He was into guns, extortion, murder, and about to make a move into drugs.

"You know, being parked like this is bound to draw attention, and fast," Fred said, smiling in an attempt to mask her terror.

Otakun made a pouty face. "I guess we won't be able to take our time, unless we take you with us. Do you want to come with us?"

Fred shook her head so fast and so hard, she thought it might come off. She recalled the detective's advice.

"Like I was saying, everyone," Otakun called, jovial and energetic, "what we have here is a genuine detective. A lady detective. A poor lost little woman trying to make it in a man's world. Hey, we can all sympathize with feeling oppressed, can't we?"

Fred had been a slave in a hell dimension; she was pretty sure that meant she had them all beat on that score. She had no idea how Okatun knew so much about her. Did he have contacts within the police department? Or do some of his people follow everyone the police spoke with? Anything was possible, and she certainly wasn't going to get a straight answer from the man. What was important was surviving this encounter.

"You read the police report, yes?" Otakun asked.

"Uh—no, why would I—"

He moved on her, backing her up toward the wall.

"Okay, okay, *yes*," she admitted. "I read it."

"And you've got one of those Mensa club brains, the kind it'd be a shame to splatter all over the walls here, right?"

"I think a lot, yeah."

"So think about this: The shot that killed your friend came from a weapon that professional snipers and soldiers use—perfect, dead on, right through the heart."

Yeah, Fred thought, *one of the reasons I keep thinking they hit what they were aiming at.*

"At that velocity and that angle, that shot was supposed to go through her and take me down," Otakun said, tapping his forehead where the shot would have taken him. "She was standing up, I was sitting down, see? Except, when the shooter fired, I sneezed, so my head wasn't quite where it would have been. The wall right behind where I was sitting caught the bullet on the exit. It's fate. It wasn't my time. That's up to me to decide. When I die, it will be my choice, no one else's."

"Wow, must be nice having the option," Fred said softly, her anger emboldening her. "Most of the rest of us are just in a waiting game."

He slammed her against the wall. "You making fun of me?"

Fred's terror was back, full force. "No."

"You get one warning, *Stick*. That bullet was meant for me. That means whoever fired it is mine to deal with, not yours. Get in my business and me and my boys will end up eating you with a spoon. And not in a good way."

There is a good way? Fred thought.

Fred felt her heart rise with hope as a police cruiser approached and slowed down. Then it resumed normal speed, heading off down the street and taking with it what little hope for rescue that she had allowed herself.

Otakun slapped his open palm against the wall next to her head, making her jump and cry out. He smiled at that. "Good," he said confidently. "You should be scared."

Fred was silent. She didn't look him in the eye.

"Good," he repeated, pushing off from the wall, his long coat whipping up and snapping at her as he walked off. His guys went back to their cars, grunting in amusement.

Fred didn't think it was funny at all. The fact that Otakun had followed her to Sharon and Alicia's place to deliver his warning meant that he would probably still have people watching her, checking on her every movement. And that meant she had to be a lot more careful from now on. But she fully intended to take the detective's advice and steer clear of Otakun and his associates and enemies.

If her vague suspicions about Alicia's killing had any merit, then, strange as it was to contemplate, Otakun was a victim of sorts, as well. He was being played, convinced that someone had meant that shot for him.

Fine, let him think that. Let him go after his enemies looking for the shooter and maybe get his own head blown off in the process, what did it matter to her?

Her thundering heart finally returned to a normal pace. It did matter. She would make a call, let the detective know what had happened. What else could she do? If the department was convinced that Alicia's death was accidental—or if they were determined to proceed under that belief, anyway—then they, too, would be in the position of either "getting in" Otakun's "business" or letting him handle things as he saw fit.

Who knows, he might just turn up the truth.

In the meantime, though, Fred's investigation would keep going. The gangster had tried to take control away from her. But, after what had happened with Professor Seidel, Fred wasn't about to let anyone do that to her again.

She walked down the street, more determined than ever to find out what had really happened.

Three stories above, a solitary figure peered down at Fred through a high-powered telescopic lens. The watcher had considered intervening when the minor attack on Fred had been staged, but the risk of exposure had been too great. If Fred knew for certain that she was being followed, her every movement cataloged, then everything she did from this moment out would be tainted by that knowledge.

It was interesting to watch her, to see what she might do—fascinating, actually. There was much to be learned from observing Fred's choices and actions in the wake of her friend's murder. One's true character emerged during times of greatest stress.

The watcher had reasons for wishing to know about Fred's true character.

Many reasons.

"So what's next?" the watcher whispered, observing Fred shakily heading to the truck she had borrowed from Charles Gunn.

In truth, a fairly well-educated guess had already been made. Setting down the telescopic lens, the watcher gathered up the gear that had been acquired for this task. There was no worry about Fred getting away. A small briefcase next to the watcher's foot held a laptop equipped with GTS tracking software keyed to a small device that had been placed beneath the truck's chassis some time earlier.

Unless Fred did something completely spontaneous and, well, un-Fred-like, such as abandoning Gunn's truck and taking a cab to her next stop, the watcher would have no problem following.

A sinking feeling dropped down into the pit of the watcher's stomach. Rising swiftly, the observer scanned the street below and cursed.

Gunn's truck was still there, Fred was nowhere in sight, and a yellow cab was turning a corner several blocks away. The watcher raised the lens quickly, but was not able to get the cab's license plate.

She was gone.

"Fine, play it like that," the watcher said. "I'll find you again."

The only question was whether the target would be found in time, because the observer had plans, big plans, for Winifred Burkle, and would be very vexed indeed if those plans were ruined.

And if the watcher became vexed . . . there would be hell to pay.

Literally.

Gunn sat near the small table. He and Angel were alone in the cell, or so it seemed. Archiel may—or may not—have been with them. He sometimes responded to direct inquiries and, for reasons unknown, sometimes did not. Angel stood before the window, basking in the filtered sunlight.

"So let's recap," Gunn suggested. "We're in freak central, there are about three hundred folks crawlin' around this place along with a supernatural killer, and only fifteen people who know who we really are and why we're here—"

"Not including the guards."

"Right," Gunn said. "And no one's going to tell us a single thing they don't have to."

"Tough case," Angel observed. He seemed distracted, like he was working something out in his head, or trying to do so.

"We have suspects, motives, and at least a few mages who don't want us here but aren't worried about blowin' this whole deal to drive us out."

"Seems like it, yeah." Angel shook his head. "You have no idea how badly I want to run out there and play some Frisbee."

"Frisbee? What, are you kidding me?"

"The sun. I want to be out in the sun."

"Somehow I don't think it would be smart to ignore the pretty efforts of the parties looking to blow your cover wide open."

Angel stood away from the window and looked at his friend. "Yeah, that's the thing, this sabotage just doesn't make sense. Does whoever's screwing with us think they're going to scare me off? They're not gonna scare me off. And if, like you said, they blow my cover, then the council's plan comes to light and it's bad for everyone. But if they didn't want to be a part of this ceremony, they wouldn't have come here."

"I don't know about that," Gunn said. "Maybe this oozing shadow didn't come here by accident. Maybe someone brought this Nemesis character here to keep this whole ceremony from happening. And now that someone's trying to use you to blow the whole thing wide open. This gathering is being held together by a very thin thread as it is. It wouldn't take much to make a lot of these guys run off."

"Well, there'll be a pretty nasty apocalypse if the walls fail."

"So what's the plan?" Gunn asked.

"I'm gonna go check some things out," Angel told him.

"Right, then I'm coming with you."

Angel shook his head. "You saw the way those kids acted. I'm supposed to be this big-deal 'Kano' guy."

"Right. So?"

"So I've been paying attention while Archiel was giving us the tour. Bliss doesn't walk around with assistants or acolytes. None of them do."

Gunn was taken aback. "Oh. So I'm not one of the cool kids to hang around with?"

"Don't be stupid. I'm just saying that I get the feeling no one's gonna open up to me unless I'm on my own. Having a—whaddaya call it—posse, in this place, only works at certain times and under certain circumstances."

Partner, not posse, Gunn thought, but he kept his annoyance to himself.

"Fine, we split up. What should I be doing?"

Angel moved toward the door. "Be ready."

"That's it?"

"In a place like this, that's enough."

Suddenly, the door burst open, and the mage with the wild eyes and the blue-tattooed flesh bounded into the room.

"Ord, Ord, my name is Ord, don't wear it out!" he cried, grabbing Angel's hand and shaking it maniacally. "You must be the roommates. Good, good! Just make sure you understand how things work."

Ord dashed wildly from one side of the room to another. "My side, your side, my side, your side!"

Archiel's whisper sounded behind Angel and Gunn. *"He may be insane, but his control over magic*

179

is astonishing. You will learn much from him."

"The bunnies flutter in the trees like butterflies," Ord said. "Listen hard and you can hear them conspiring against us."

Angel nodded and forced himself to smile. "Okay, well—"

"I know you are, but what am I?" Ord asked, then went into a dance that made the jigs in Pylea look positively restrained.

"You get the feeling this is the one room assignment no one else wanted?" Gunn asked.

"Getting that," Angel said with a deepening frown. "Getting that *big-time*."

"So, I can't help but notice . . . you're here. Why is that?" Lilah Morgan sat behind her desk, her feet up, the long, supple, and elegantly stockinged expanse of her legs leading up to her short navy blue skirt, which drew the attention of the cretin she had hired to shadow Wesley—exactly the result she wanted to achieve. Even the vague promise of sex tended to keep most male creatures docile, even those that weren't human.

"I have been . . . unable . . . to track the target with the efficiency and consistency you requested," the goon admitted. "I believe that I should be replaced in this assignment. All funds transferred to my account will be refunded."

"One formerly poofy British ex-Watcher is too

much for you?" Lilah asked, baiting him a little.

The goon stood up straight, literally getting his back up. "He's not the man he was."

"Agreed. Thank God." Lilah wasn't sure that she would classify the Wesley Wyndam-Pryce who had shown up on Angel's doorstep a couple of years back as much of a man at all. Now he was scarred on the outside and the inside, and he had so much darkness in him, so much rage, so much intense energy all tightly bottled up . . . until she got it to explode, that is. One way or another. This little game between them may have started out as just another assignment from her superiors, but it had quickly evolved into her hobby, her favorite pastime. Some might call it an obsession.

Lilah listened intently as the tracker gave his report. He had not seen Wesley following Fred, but there were several "unaccounted for" periods.

"Okay, so, let's just deal with this morning," Lilah suggested. "Wes and a couple of these muscle-bound meat-puppets he sometimes hires for backup enter the warehouse where at least nineteen vampires were reported to have made their nest. An hour and a half later, Wes and his little soldiers leave, a loot of soot and ash on their clothing. It doesn't take a genius to figure out that he dusted the vamps. And then what happened?"

"He got away."

"Specifically," Lilah coaxed.

"He got into one car, his companions loaded into a van. They went in separate directions. I followed the mark. But when he stopped for doughnuts—"

"Doughnuts?" Lilah said, barely keeping herself from bursting out laughing.

"It should have been my first clue. In any case, he went inside to place his order. When he came out . . . well, it wasn't he who came out. It was one of the fighters."

"You maintained visual contact at all times?"

The goon shrugged. "Except for a millisecond when the door to the doughnut shop opened and I caught a nasty glare. It cleared, and he was . . . different."

"You were checking for spells of glamour, illusion, false appearances?"

"Always. There was no stink of sorcery on him."

"But it wasn't he," Lilah said. "It had never been he. The switch must have been made in the warehouse."

"Correct."

"You were back to square one. Eventually, you caught up with him. Then what?"

The underling hesitated.

"Come on, time is money," Lilah said. "Spit it out."

"He got away again."

She shrugged, her smile set perfectly in place, though inwardly she was seething. She had hired this fool because he had a reputation of being able to track *anyone*. "He can be slippery. Details?"

He related them. This time, Wesley had been on the street, heading toward an antiquarian bookstore rumored to sell old mystical tomes on the side, and he had stepped into a deep black shadow beneath a street awning—and had never come out. The tracker checked it out, but Wesley was gone; he'd vanished, like a ghost.

"He *knew* someone was following him," the tracker pressed. "Why else would he act this way?"

"Because he's paranoid and takes precautions like that all the time?" Lilah said absently.

The tracker paled. Lilah realized that she was tipping her hand, so she recrossed her legs, drawing the man's attention exactly where she wanted it once again. "Well, don't worry about it."

The goon let out a deep breath he'd been holding. "I'm so glad you understand. Very relieved."

"I understand completely. Basically what you're telling me is that, for all intents and purposes, you've proven to be utterly useless."

"I . . . I wouldn't say that."

"Of course you wouldn't. I'm saving you the trouble." Smiling, she leaned back, allowing her blouse to part slightly, giving him a tiny glimpse of bra and cleavage. It was an old trick, one she had learned early on in this game: Send 'em out happy. "Did you happen to read the fine print in your contract about our early retirement benefits?"

"Re-retirement?"

There was a hiss of air as someone, or something, advanced on the tracker from behind. The blade that separated the tracker's head from its shoulders, and the blade's wielder, were both invisible and tidy. The sword instantly—and mystically—cauterized the headless stump of the neck leading down to the body *and* the bodiless stump of neck leading up to the head. No blood spray, no muss, no fuss.

It was the attention to little details like this that made working for Wolfram and Hart such a pleasure.

"Um . . . Ms. Morgan?" asked a voice out of thin air.

"Yes?" Lilah asked pleasantly, addressing a spot approximately six feet above where the invisible assassin's heavy feet left a discernible crushing of the pile.

"Is there really fine print in the contract about early retirement?"

Lilah cocked her head to one side. "Come on, now. Lesson one: Always read every word of any legal document before you sign it. I don't really have to remind you of that, do I?"

"Nothing in . . . invisible ink or anything like that?"

"If there was, you, of all people, should be able to read it, don'tcha think?"

Sighing, the assassin picked up the two pieces of

Lilah's former errand boy and dragged them to the door. She waited until he was gone—she had a magical sensor installed to let her know if she was alone in the room or not, a small stone affixed to the underside of her desk that gave off a slight warmth when any creature that was invisible or intangible was present.

Standing up and straightening out her skirt, Lilah leaned against her desk and called up a number on her private and untraceable speed-dial.

The phone rang three times before a man answered. "Hello?"

"Hello, yes. Remember me? The *money*?"

"Lilah!" He sounded positively exuberant. "What can I do for you today? Are you looking for a status report on the current project?"

"No. I have a little job for you."

"A job?" he asked, suspiciously. "I *have* a job. You know what a critical time this is, and how I'm already having to stretch myself to cover all my responsibilities—"

Lilah ignored the whining white noise on the other end of the call. "It's actually quite simple, and right up your alley."

"We're on a schedule. A very tight one, at that."

"I know," Lilah said warmly. She'd been practicing. "And this doesn't mean that I'm looking for you to step up the timetable, so relax. I'm all about patience, and I know when things are preordained and how

bad timing can ruin any plan. But it serves your purposes to make me happy, and there's something you
can do that would make me tickled pink."

"I'm listening."

"If anything, what I'd like you to do should help
protect both our interests. There are some people
who might be onto you unless we do something to
distract them. If you're exposed and stopped, if
you don't get what you want, then I lose too. I've
sunk a ton of cash into your operation and I want
to see that investment protected."

"What kind of people?" the man asked warily.

"The help-the-helpless kind. Not your kind of
people, or mine."

"So, it's like that."

"Yes," Lilah said. "Yes, it's like that. I'm glad to
see we're on the same page with this." She rattled
off the exact details of what she had in mind. "I'll
call you back to let you know where and when."
She rolled her eyes as he rambled on with a few
more objections. She quieted him. "I understand
about the instabilities—that's the *whole point*."

Lilah hung up. Some of what she'd said had
been true—enough to make the lies surrounding
those statements seem reasonable. Wes had not
yet taken an active interest in the club murders
and the nightmare creature who had committed
them, but he was *very* interested in Fred's
movements, and the twig was just about to poke

her nose right into the middle of things.

Lilah had been reading a little bit about physics. There were all kinds of wacky ideas the brainiacs were tossing around out there, some hitting much closer to home than anyone without a firm grasp of the magical and metaphysical might possibly recognize. One of the notions that stuck in Lilah's head had to do with the interconnectedness of all things. In one of the critical experiments on this topic, scientists had taken the smallest of all particles of matter and had given it a clockwise rotation. Then they had split it in two, and sent one of the halved portions halfway around the world to another lab. Each half continued to follow the clockwise rotation until one day, one of the scientists took half of the particle and reversed its rotation, setting it counterclockwise. Halfway across the world, with nothing whatsoever that human science could quantify serving to connect the two halves, the second particle suddenly, and at the exact same moment as the first, also reversed its rotation.

So, the eggheads were catching on. Sooner or later, if you let yourself think three-dimensionally enough, you could connect the dots between any one thing or person and another and see that there was no such thing as coincidence or chance or fate. Everything was a matter of action and reaction. And everything that happened informed every other thing, no matter how seemingly unrelated it might be at first.

That was the lesson Fred would learn eventually . . . provided she didn't get herself killed in the process.

Lilah was well aware of Fred's latest misery. Boo-hoo, her pal got popped.

Lilah had suffered worse losses and had been party to more horrifying acts of pain and cruelty by the time she was *ten* than Fred was likely to glimpse in her entire life, even with the dream vacation in Pylea factored into the mix.

Sympathy? Not likely. Lilah would have more sympathy for the devil, if they were ever to meet up . . . and, she wagered, they'd have a whole lot more in common.

Wes stepped out of the bookstore and glanced around to see if his latest "shadow" was around. After mentally checking every possible hiding spot for someone following him, Wes was forced to admit that he seemed to be all alone. Strange. He had been tailed by one entity or another for weeks.

Ah, well. Maybe his watchers were between shifts.

Glancing at his watch, Wes saw that it was 12:10 p.m. and decided to check up on Fred. He was worried about how she was coping with her friend's death last night.

Wes pulled his cell phone out of his pocket and dialed Fred's number. Strangely, she didn't pick up, and neither did her voice mail.

I don't like this, thought Wes. *It's not like Fred to be out of contact.*

He dialed the hotel, and Lorne answered on the second ring.

"Angel Investigations, we help the helpless, and we do it with *style*."

"Lorne, it's Wes. Is Fred there? I've been trying to reach her, but she isn't answering her cell phone." Wesley couldn't mask the concern in his voice.

"Oh hey, Wes," Lorne said. "Yeah, Fred . . . poor thing hoofed it over to the police station to talk to that detective about her buddy's death. Probably turned off the phone so she wouldn't be disturbed during her little tête-à-tête. Maybe she took my advice and went for a nice drive after the meet-and-greet. Probably nothing to worry about, sweet cheeks. And may I just say, dark looks good on you, but don't overdo it."

Wes cleared his throat. "Ah—thank you. And you're probably right where Fred is concerned, but I wish I knew for sure. She was very upset last night."

"Ah, so sweetpea was with you."

"Briefly, yes. Do you have a problem with that?"

"I'm just surprised she didn't beeline her *toochis* back here."

"Frankly, so was I. But she's a friend, and I don't turn away friends in need."

"I hear ya, cuddlemuffin. For the record, I think you did the right thing by not coming in with her. Things are kinda tense where you're concerned at the moment."

"Understandably. But there is the greater good to consider."

"Don't I know it," Lorne commiserated. "Hey, I've been known to lose my head over this stuff. But enough about me. We're worried about Fred, too. Sometimes, you just have to give a person their distance, though. *Comprende?*"

"Yes," Wes agreed. He was about to ask about Angel and Gunn's investigation when, suddenly, Wes heard people screaming and spun to catch sight of a couple racing from a nearby alley. The woman's hair was being blown forward into her face, as if a terrible wind was striking her back, and sections of newspapers and other bits of trash billowed up and out of the alley.

"I'll call back later," Wes said, disconnecting the call and sliding the cell phone into his pocket. Wondering what on earth was going on, Wes entered the mouth of the alley and immediately encountered a thickset giant. The ogre's towering, gray-green, eleven-foot form was clothed in something like a burlap sack with holes cut out for his tree-trunk legs. His head was bald and lumpy, his ears big and pointy. A shimmering vortex was closing behind him, and he appeared confused.

"And just what are you?" Wes asked.

"Hungry," the creature said.

Wes nodded. "Yes, you have that inter-dimensional jet-lag look about you. No decent in-flight movies? No snacks along the way?"

"Food . . . ," the creature said, sounding ravenous . . . and deadly.

"I don't suppose it would interest you to know that there's a *sensational* bistro just down the street? The food's not alive, kicking, screaming, and begging for its life, but it is rather tasty."

"You . . . are . . . food."

Wes sighed. "Thought as much. Had to ask, though. Only polite thing to do."

Wes extended his right arm out to the side and activated the release mechanism for the fold-away sword that he carried for these kinds of occasions. It *snikted* into place, and with the sword fully extended, Wes rushed the ogre with a take-no-prisoners look in his eyes.

CHAPTER EIGHT

The offices of Norris Aeronautical Industries were located on the waterfront, housed in a three-story building. The first floor consisted mainly of the lobby and security areas. The second floor was research and development, and the third floor was administration. The building's designer had taken the concept of sterility to new heights. Fred glanced around the enormous lobby. It was all glass and steel. There was not a piece of greenery or even a splash of color in the place. Even the security guard's uniforms were black and gray. Fred approached the receptionist at the information desk, who was also wearing black.

"Norris Aeronautical Industries, please hold," she said into the phone.

Fred smiled pleasantly. "I'd like to schedule an appointment with someone in Human Resources? I'm interested in a job here."

"That would be a good reason for a non-employee to ask for Human Resources," the receptionist said with a healthy serving of attitude and a side order of snide. She looked Fred up and down, taking careful inventory of the young woman's less than expensive-looking clothes. "Janitorial, I presume?"

Fred was left sputtering as she tried to come up with a decent comeback, knowing full well that the best ones would come to her after she had left the place. Then a hand touched her shoulder and a warm male voice intoned, "You'd presume wrong. And, by the way? You're fired."

The receptionist froze. Fred spun to see the man who had come to her aid and was shocked to recognize Mitchell Grant, another old friend from college. Just looking at his rugged, handsome, yet kind and open face, slightly lined now, prematurely aged by his obsession with the sun, brought it all back to Fred. The mask of detachment that she'd been keeping in place fell, and she started gasping, tears welling in her eyes, the incredible expanse of the reception area spinning.

"Whoa, whoa, whoa," Mitchell said as he took hold of her and led her to a plush couch a half dozen feet away.

"Should I send for the resident physician?" the receptionist asked, her tone completely servile, a stark contrast to the evil bitch mode she had been operating in just a few moments before.

"I don't think so," Mitchell said, taking Fred into his arms and gently rocking her back and forth.

"I could—"

"You could have your job back if you stop talking to me and start answering the phones."

"Yes sir, thank you, sir," the receptionist said swiftly, and without a single trace of sarcasm.

Suddenly, Fred found herself bursting into sobs as the image of Alicia's cold, dead face stole across her thoughts. Fred couldn't believe it. She was falling apart—*again*.

"It's okay, let it out," Mitchell said, caressing her back. "I may not look it, but I'm right there with you."

Finally, through her sobs, Fred whispered, "Not gonna fire the evil lady?"

"No."

"'Cause . . . she *is* evil."

"Oh, I know. But if I fire her, then how can I make her life a living hell the next couple of months before I make her run screaming and *then* I fire her?"

Fred pulled away from him, smiling at that. "You haven't changed."

"Don't be so sure. I am just a stooge of 'The Man' these days. You should see the defense contracts this place has."

"Bread and butter, right?"

"Still feels weird. The custom-tailored clothes,

the German import, the fully paid-for beach house . . . it sucks, really."

Fred laughed so suddenly, and so hard, that she thought a little of the tuna sandwich she had scarfed down for lunch on the drive over would come out of her nose. She took a moment to compose herself, then asked Mitchell what he knew about the tragic events of the previous night.

It turned out that he knew practically as much as she did.

"I'm answering questions for the coroner's inquest," Mitchell explained, "and I'm the point man over here for funeral arrangements."

Fred was surprised. Mitchell's name hadn't come up once in the detective's report. "I thought her family would want her—"

"This is about what Alicia wanted. Her will makes it perfectly clear. She loved the water, and wants her ashes scattered on the waves."

Fred was confused. "Mitchell, I know we all went to college together, but why are you so involved in all of this? Were you and Alicia . . . close?"

He nodded. "For a long time, yes."

"Wow, I didn't know . . ."

"We broke up about a year ago and decided to try the 'Let's stay friends' thing."

"That never works, you know."

"I know! But that's the thing, busting up statistical

probabilities. It worked for us. We got even closer."

"Can we go somewhere and talk?"

"Absolutely."

The hotel restaurant was dimly lit, and the lunch crowd had thinned considerably. A glass of white wine sat before Mitchell. He stared into it absently, as if trying to lose himself in its sparkling depths. As Fred touched his hand, he looked up suddenly, a broad smile crossing his handsome, tanned face.

"Wow, so you're all Mr. Corporate now," Fred marveled.

Mitchell actually blushed. "You know what it's like. We used to talk about it. You sell your soul for a couple of years, get all the things you've ever wanted, then go off and do what you want the rest of the time."

"Yeah, if you can claw your way back out again."

He couldn't seem to argue with that one. "I don't have a life. That was one of the reasons it didn't work for Alicia and me. We loved each other, but making time for a relationship, having the work take a backseat to whatever was happening with each of us . . . it just wasn't something either of us was ready to do. We rushed into things."

"What if you could do it over?" Fred asked. "Knowing . . ."

"That she'd be gone?"

Fred nodded.

"I'd do everything differently. But it's a moot point. There isn't any way to bring her back."

Fred thought of a dozen ways she knew to raise someone from the dead, but she held her tongue. Every one of them came with too high a price.

A strange look came into Mitchell's eyes. "You know, back in the day, I always thought it was going to be the two of us."

"You're *kidding*," Fred said, incredulous.

"Oh, okay," Mitchell said in evident embarrassment. "I didn't realize you felt that way. Sorry. I guess I'm just—"

"No! I mean . . . I had, like, the *biggest* crush on you. I mean, my God. But I didn't even think you noticed me. Not like that."

"You're pretty hard to miss."

"Yeah, one *not* so sexy beanpole tomboy, made to order. Just right for the man who has everything."

"That's how you see yourself?"

"Um . . . no, not really. Not anymore." She hesitated. "I'm with someone. His name is Charles. You'd—you'd like him."

"Another physics geek like us?"

"Ummm . . . no. I kinda went the other way."

"Really? How far?"

"How far is far?" she asked. "Charles is a good man. A good heart, a good soul . . . I guess."

"Now that's committing yourself."

197

Fred didn't want to get into the problems she'd been having with Charles. In truth, she barely wished to recognize them herself.

"This is pretty interesting. I had a thing for you, and here you were crushing on the Mitch-Man."

"Uh, not when he was referring to himself in the third person," Fred said firmly.

"Point taken. I don't know. Just sitting here with you, I feel nineteen again."

Fred's eyes widened. "You were nineteen? We were in graduate school."

Mitchell smiled sheepishly. "Yeah. I kind of did the whole Doogie Howser thing."

"How did I not know this?"

"I shot up fast when I was a kid. I never looked my age."

Fred's brow furrowed. "So that would make you—"

"Come on, don't ruin the moment. Don't do the math."

"Doing the math is part of my DNA. And that whole, you know, crush thing. Crush is a stupid word for it. It's like, oh, I like you. I have feelings for you. So I want to *crush* you with my feelings. And that sounds appealing, right?"

"Not when you put it that way."

She looked at him. "We're not going to do something stupid, are we? I mean, we're in the lobby of a hotel—an expensive hotel. Not far from where you work. For all I know, your company probably keeps rooms here." She laughed nervously.

"Huh?" Mitchell said. "No! No, actually the thought hadn't even occurred to me. It's not a bad thought. But you said you were with someone."

"And I am. So totally am."

"Right. I just like the penne here."

"Sure, what's not to like," she said.

"I don't know. You're not having it." He took a few bites, then captured her attention with his penetrating gaze. "So what were you coming to Norris for? Clearly it wasn't to see me."

"Why do you say that?" Fred asked.

"Oh, I don't know. Your jaw dropping when you turned around and, hey, it's Mitch. Plus, you were, ah, asking about a job. Alicia told me that you *had* a job."

"She did? When was that?"

"Couple of months back. I told her we should call you. You know, set something up, get together. But, I don't know. She was always so busy. And she always insisted that she be the one to make contact first. You know what she was like. She made up her mind about something like that, you didn't mess with her on it. I wanted to"—he pulled back with a distasteful expression—"you weren't . . . I mean . . . you weren't there to put your hat in the ring for her job?"

Fred was stunned. It was a ghoulish notion. Yet

she could see that he might think that. After all, she had just disappeared without a trace for five years. Flaky Fred taking off at the drop of a hat. That's how it might seem to people. Especially when she came back and didn't look up her old friends. A lot can change in five years—people, especially.

"No, nothing like that," Fred said hurriedly. "I just . . ."

"I'm getting it."

The pieces seemed to be coming together in his mind. He scratched his left ear, something he always used to do when he was working out a problem. "Yeah . . . you're thinking it wasn't an accident."

"I never said that."

"You're looking around, trying to find probable cause or whatever you'd call it. Someone with a motive, right?"

"I just . . ." Fred shook her head.

"Eliminate the obvious, run through the probabilities, whatever remains, however unlikely, has gotta be true."

She rubbed at her temples. "I want it to be an accident," she said. "I don't want to find out that someone had her killed. Even if it means that it was my fault because I suggested that place. I could still live with that easier than the thought that it was intentional and that whoever did it is

just going to get away with it. That's not something
I can live with."

"You saw Sharon?"

"Yes."

"And she made some noise about things being
weird at Norris?"

"She didn't have to. She was packing up, making
out like she's next."

Mitchell was impressed. "So you actually are an
investigator? With a license and all of that?"

"I work for a bigger agency. We handle some
pretty tough stuff."

"You know I would love to hear the whole story.
I mean what really went on. The way it came to
us was real foggy. But now is not the time. You're
right. Everything hasn't been exactly right over at
Norris. I tried, but I couldn't get a bead on it.
Alicia was upset about something. In the
beginning, I thought it was me, I thought I had
done something. I'd see her at her desk, in the
lab, when she didn't think anyone else was
around. She figured no one was watching her, and
it wasn't me."

"We can try to get into her private files," Fred
suggested.

"I've never been much of a hacker," he said.

"I can do it," Fred said. "But I need access to the
mainframe, the live system."

"I can make that happen. I mean, it would have

to be when there are not a lot of people around," Mitchell advised.

"You could lose your job if we got caught."

"Have to make sure not to get caught. We have to have plausible denial."

"I've got another idea," Fred pulled out her cell phone. "We're going to need someone else."

"A wheel man?"

"And a lookout." She dialed Wesley's number. As it rang, she said, "This is totally crazy. You know this, right?"

"I'd rather risk everything I have to find out the truth. I owe Alicia that much."

"And you like me."

"Yeah, how strange is that?"

"Well," she said, "I do have my charms."

Wesley's number just rang and rang. She didn't even get his voice mail. "That's weird," she said, putting the phone back. "I guess I'll try again later."

Mitchell drove her back to Norris, dropping her off near the rental car she indicated. Fred had a sense that she was being followed, so she used one of the many fake IDs she had taken with her from the office to secure the rental car and to hire a guy to get Charles's truck and take it back to the hotel. Fred was confident that she had left no trail with these transactions. After all, she had done all the computer work herself.

"So we'll meet back here?" he asked. "In the visitor's parking lot? Around eleven tonight?"

She nodded, having to restrain herself from actually saying "It's a date." They exchanged a few more pleasantries, and Fred smiled back at him as if she wasn't worried, but that wasn't at all true. With the exception of how it might impact Mitchell's life if they were caught, she wasn't bothered in the least about the subterfuge. The cloak-and-dagger stuff had gotten pretty easy for her. Nor was she concerned that Mitchell would make a mistake or freak out and blow the whole deal for her.

She wasn't even bothered by the idea that Mitchell could be in on "it," whatever "it" was, provided there even *was* an "it." She had considered the possibility, naturally; that's how she had been trained. Treat everyone like a suspect. Safer that way. She had her guard up, but that was just being reasonable, not paranoid.

Yet it made her sad to have such thoughts at all.

She was digging into her purse, looking for the car keys, when she saw a burly man in an old suit approach.

It was Detective Moffat.

"Hi," she said, trying and failing to mask her sudden nervousness. "What are you doing here?"

"I might ask the same thing. But I've got no reason to keep you in the dark about things. Just the opposite, in fact." The detective nodded in the direction of the handsome man entering the Norris building. "The Powers-That-Be have me running around like an errand boy, getting papers signed, closing this thing down as fast as possible. Did your friend Mitchell tell you he's part of the official inquest?"

Fred nodded briskly. "Um . . . the Powers That Be?"

"You know. The mayor's office, the police commissioner . . ."

"Oh, right."

"I'm here to get Mitchell to sign his statement. I need you to do the same, but I wasn't expecting to run into you. Drop by later?"

"Of course."

"But I do have some news, and I'll only need a couple of minutes of your time, Ms. Burkle."

Fred hugged herself nervously. "Okay . . ."

"We found the shooter."

Grabbing Moffat's arm, Fred cried, "What did he say? Did he say who hired him?"

"He didn't say anything at all, I'm afraid," Detective Moffat said, removing her hand. "He was dead before we got to him. So, unless you know someone who can get the dead to give up their secrets . . ."

Fred had a feeling she could find someone to fit the bill on her Rolodex.

As if he had sensed her thoughts, Detective Moffat quickly recovered. "Let me rephrase that. I *really* don't want to know if you can or not. The bottom line is that it's over. The shooter was a male, approximately forty years of age, carrying no less than six sets of identification. It seemed that he was getting ready to bolt when Otakun caught up with him."

"Otakun killed him."

"They killed each other, from what the crime scene investigators have been able to put together so far. It took a while, it was bloody, and it looks like they both suffered a lot before it was over. Normally I wouldn't tell people things like that, but I had the feeling you'd want to know."

"I wonder what that says about me," Fred mumbled, trying to assimilate these new facts, trying to stay *calm*.

"It says, if I'm right about this, that you're someone who's been hurt very badly and needs closure. I'm hoping this will give that to you."

"You want me off the case?" Fred asked.

"There is no case. That's the point." The detective looked to the Norris building, then back at Fred. "The thing is, I wouldn't know that, looking at you."

Fred would not meet his gaze.

"Just promise me you'll be careful, okay, Miss Burkle?" Moffat asked as he walked away. "Sometimes when you start digging around in one of these, well . . . I just want you to know I was serious about my offer."

"What offer?" Fred asked.

Moffat looked her right in the eyes. "I guess I wasn't being direct enough. I let you know about the files my office has on Angel Investigations because I'm hoping to earn your trust. I'd like more cooperation, even if it is unofficial, between my office and yours. And I'm hoping that the two of us can make that happen."

Fred was surprised—and pleased. But she knew she would have to proceed cautiously.

"I think we could all serve this city a lot better by cooperating," Moffat said. "Think it over."

Feeling guilty that she had once again not trusted the detective, Fred found the keys, then got in the car and drove away.

She thought about Charles, and wondered what he was doing right now. . . .

Gunn waited alone in the chamber for close to an hour, but Angel did not return. He had nowhere to go, nothing to do. As the supposed servant of the great sorcerer Kano, he could walk about freely and make inquiries into the many mysteries facing them. But any attempt to do so would have been met with scorn.

He checked the time and saw that it was nearly four in the afternoon. He had no idea where their acolytes were. After all, it wasn't his job to keep track of their every movement. And luckily their new roommate Ord was rarely around. At least their being gone made it easier for Angel to concentrate on the real reason he was here.

The reason we're both here, Gunn corrected himself.

He settled back on his cot, thinking about the life he had chosen. This was what it was always like: long stretches of nearly unendurable boredom punctuated with brief violent bursts of life-or-death action. Strangely, the thing Gunn kept coming back to in his mind was not details of the case, few and far between as they were, but that comic book about Angel . . . and what Lorne had said.

Was Gunn angry because he hadn't been included? In the story, there had been a one-line mention of him and all the others who had joined up with Angel. Apparently, the writer thought he could come up with a better supporting cast, an edgier crew. The first issue ended with Angel— the fictional version—actually hooking up with a killer succubus he had been tracking, deciding her victims maybe deserved what they got, and that he should "get" some too.

Sheesh.

They didn't know Angel at all.

Admittedly, Angel's curse was all about perfect happiness, not sex. There were other ways he could be made to feel the bliss necessary to turn him into a monster once more, and he'd made love with Darla and fathered a son, impossible as that seemed, without losing his soul. In fact, the act had been one of such perfect despair that it had allowed him to hit rock bottom, see the light, and start treating people decently again. And Connor, mixed bag that he had turned out to be, had come of the union through no real fault of his own.

Gunn thought of the comic book . . . and couldn't help but wonder what it might have been like if they had done it *right*. If they had given some respect where respect was due.

Sitting there, Gunn noticed some sheets of parchment and quill pens and ink sitting on a nearby table. From another room he could hear the lulling sounds of an endless succession of chants in some language he couldn't even begin to follow, and he knew he had to be doing something or else those sounds might lure him to sleep, despite the early hour. In truth, he had barely gotten any rest the night before as he tossed and turned, worrying about Fred, about this mission . . . about everything.

Putting pen to paper, Gunn allowed his thoughts to fly free.

On the page, the following words took shape:

GUNN:
SCOURGE OF THE UNDEAD
ISSUE ONE

PAGE ONE

Open with a full-page splash of Gunn pointing angrily at the camera. It is night, and he stands in a dark alley behind a club, the shadows of a dozen misshapen demonlike vampires rising up on the walls to either side of the monster hunter. He wears a long, black leather duster that is tricked out with two brown leather straps over his kevlar-protected chest, small wooden stakes filling the slots in the straps like bullets on an old-fashioned gunslinger. Gunn's bald head has mystical-looking tats (it could be that they just look good or help to scare the bad guys) that extend down around to the sides of his face and neck. We get a sense that his body is covered with them. He wears mirror shades and carries a crossbow in one hand, a shining blade in the other. There is a garbage Dumpster pressed up against the wall off to Gunn's left, the lid down. This is important. It will come into play very soon.

One more thing: Gunn is smiling, and the smile is practically demonic.

GUNN
Come on, fools. You think I'm gonna risk getting a

tear in this jacket just for the sake of finishing off two dozen vampires? You guys are so small-minded. . . .

PAGES TWO AND THREE
Double-page spread. A wider view from a different angle showing huge UV lamps shining deadly light on the vampires from every angle. We can see all of the bloodsuckers now, and they are throwing their heads and arms back, hissing and screaming as the deadly light starts to bake them—a bunch of Lestat wannabes. It is like high noon, only at midnight, and Gunn is laughing his head off.

GUNN
. . .I'm a *lot* more than just the muscle.

PAGE FOUR
Several images of the vampires bursting into flame, muttering curses and vain threats. Then Gunn hits a remote control, fading the killer lights, and walks over to the Dumpster, knocking three times.

GUNN
Yo! Anybody home in there?

PAGE FIVE
The Dumpster's lid rises, but only a crack. A pair of beady eyes come into view, along with a head of spiky, product-ridden hair. Angel is inside the

Dumpster, peering out fearfully. Even though we don't see much of him, keep in mind that he wears a dorky-looking Hawaiian shirt, blue jeans, and open-toed sandals. He's a beach bum vamp. Comic relief. What else would you expect?

ANGEL
Light. So *bright*. Is it safe now? Can I come out?

GUNN
Yeah, come on.

Angel timidly opens the lid and awkwardly climbs out of the Dumpster. Gunn stares at the vampire, the hunter's arms crossed impatiently over his impressive chest.

GUNN
Man, when are you gonna grow a spine? I gave you 750 spf sunblock to keep you from bursting into flames with the rest of them.

Angel looks away, embarrassed.

ANGEL
It wasn't that. It's just . . . I dunno, those guys creep me out. They're scary lookin'.

GUNN
You *do* realize you're a vamp yourself, right? I

just keep you around to sniff out other vamps in their lairs.

ANGEL

What's that got to do with anything?

GUNN
(rolling his eyes)
Fine. We'll get back to the hotel and I'll get you your—

ANGEL

Plasma! Um . . . nutrient supply. Don't say the "B" word. Please? I can't even watch *CSI* or *E.R.*

GUNN

I swear, some days I'm just *embarrassed* to be seen with you.

Gunn set down the quill pen, realizing hours had passed. He looked over at what he had written and thought, on one hand, that he had been kind of harsh, that he was taking out his dismay on Angel. What kind of partner would just leave him alone, doing nothing, for so long?

No kind of partner, just a bossman.

If only he could talk to Fred about this, but they had been told that communication with the outside world had to be limited to absolute emergencies, and

Gunn's feelings hardly qualified. He was worried about her, though, but there was nothing he could do from here. Instead, he lit a lantern, hid the scrolls, then settled back to do the only thing he could do:

Wait.

Angel had been nosing around, desperate to uncover any lead about the case that he could find, but the mages were not exactly forthcoming. Whenever he made inquiries about the two slain sorcerers—whom everyone except council members believed were alive and well thanks to the "sendings" the other mages had created to cover their absences—he was treated with suspicion and personal concern. Whatever he wanted with Dagort and Symes, the fallen mages, he could simply take up with them, couldn't he? Unless he was plotting against them, and that was why he wanted information. And if he was plotting against Dagort and Symes, he could be plotting against the very people he was directing his questions at.

Angel didn't know if Archiel was with him or not; the sorcerer did not respond to direct questions, and Angel could not detect his scent or any other trace of him when the man was right in front of him, so managing to locate him when he was invisible was impossible.

Walking down a narrow hallway, Angel saw a woman dressed in a cloak just like the one worn by Bliss duck into a shadow-laden room. Maybe she

could give him the answers he so desperately needed. He entered the room after her, finding her standing in the darkness just beyond a small window. His
boots crunched broken glass as he approached her.

"Bliss?" Angel said. The woman ahead wore
robes like hers, and carried her scent. Yet she
had her back turned and looked deeply troubled,
which was odd for the lovely and powerful mage.

He reached out and touched her shoulder: The
woman spun, brandishing a double-bladed dagger
she had drawn. It glistened in the dim light, and
the woman said, "Holy water, vampire. That
should kill you, don't you think?"

She brought the weapon up toward his chest.
Only the touch of his hand upon her shoulder had
saved him. He had known in that single, startling
instant that this was not Bliss and had been
shocked into total awareness. Throwing his hands
back and over his head, Angel executed a perfect
back flip, bringing up his legs in a fluid motion that
kicked the weapon out of his assailant's hands.

He twisted his body so that he came up in a crouch
and drew his sword. The assassin had retrieved her
weapon and was advancing toward him. Her face was
twisted in a mask of rage as she attacked. Instinct
took over, and Angel brought the sword up in a
blocking motion, slamming it into the space between
the still dripping wet double blades. He twisted the
weapon suddenly in a move that he hoped would dis-

arm his opponent. She held on, and he saw her face clearly for the first time. She was the blue-eyed guard he'd met this morning. Only . . . her face had changed. Her flesh was amber and marked with strange ridges. She was part demon, and must have been terrified that he would learn her secret.

Angel felt a sudden pain at the base of his skull and nearly dropped the sword. The blue-eyed woman planted her boot on his chest and kicked hard, sending him sprawling back as she yanked her weapon away from the sword. Angel's sword sliced at her lower leg, but she darted back and away from the blade.

The killer was fast approaching. Angel rose to his knees and dug his hand into the pile of glass fragments on the rug. Ignoring the sudden, lancing sting of his own cut flesh, Angel came up with a handful of crimson shards. He met the assassin, knocking her thrusting dagger away with one hand as he swatted at her face with the razor-sharp fragments. She slipped on a patch of wetness on the rug caused by the holy water dripping from her blade and went off balance, falling toward him. The blow connected with a sickening tearing sound, and the woman screamed as several small clouds of blood exploded from her face, sending her into the far left wall. "Bastard!" she screamed, holding one hand over her ruined face.

Angel stared at her in shock. He had only meant to use the glass to keep her at bay. He had not anticipated that she would slip and fall into the path of his blow like that. The assassin grimaced and threw her head back, her eyes rolling into their sockets to expose their whites.

Angel suddenly felt a searing pain in his head, as if long, steel claws were piercing the base of his skull. The psychic knives drove themselves deep into his brain, raking his consciousness, affecting his ability to think and to reason.

The demon assassin was also a sorceress, he realized through the bloodred cloud of pain that had become his world. That was how she had convinced him that she was Bliss and had blinded him to all else.

The assassin leaped at Angel, hoping that her psychic assault had weakened him sufficiently to make him easy prey; Angel met her assault, countering her every knife thrust with a clean, effective style that he had spent years perfecting.

The assassin's mental abilities, advanced as they were, had no lasting effect on Angel. The time he had spent aiding the surviving members of a coven of witches, who were being unfairly stalked by a madman several months ago, had resulted in a friendship with Chastain, a witch who had strengthened his tolerance to attacks of the mind by engaging him regularly in punishing sessions that were augmented to withstand such assaults.

"Give it up," Angel snarled as he drove the assassin back. "You won't get out of here alive otherwise, and you know it. It's over."

"No!" she screamed, feinting to the right as she brought her dual blades forward, aiming them at Angel's unprotected eyes. The dark-haired man swept upward with his sword, attempting to parry the thrust by slamming the flat of the sword against her wrist.

He missed. The killer cried out in victory as the glittering double blades of the holy-water-drenched dagger approached his eyes.

The assassin grunted suddenly, her mouth forming a wide circle as her body rocketed away from Angel, her dagger missing his face completely. She fell to the floor, eyes wide, and Angel suddenly noticed the crossbow shaft buried in her forehead. He had not noticed that the light in the hallway had changed, growing brighter: He looked up and saw Bliss standing there, a crossbow in her hands.

"You always have to be the center of attention, don't you?" she asked.

"It's my curse," Angel said, his smile faltering as he caught a glimpse of the body lying at his feet. "One of them, anyway."

"I think we found your saboteur. My guess is that if we consult the duty logs, we'll find out that she was not working when Archiel was attacked. She had motive, too, and she was abusing her sacred vows to keep all she knew to herself and to protect at any cost. I heard her talking to another of her order about the threat you posed, and that is why I tracked her and was able to intervene when I did."

"Lucky for me," Angel said. "For her . . . not so much. I mean, being dead and not being able to really explain herself and everything."

Bliss's face reddened. "You still don't trust me."

"Since when do you care whether I trust you?" he asked as she averted her eyes. "Besides, I don't see how I can trust anyone here. This is two times Archiel wasn't where he should have been, and two times when you conveniently stepped in with a last-minute save."

"Trust is one of the things that makes us human, Angel . . . despite all our other differences."

"I'll keep that in mind," the vampire said stonily. He looked down at the body. "This is going to be covered up, too, I imagine."

"It must be. The chaos that could result if the council's deception is uncovered could mean an end to everything."

Convenient again, Angel thought. *Or maybe this is really just how things have to be.* "What can you tell me about Dagort and Symes?" Angel asked.

"A great deal, I imagine," Bliss said in an icy voice. "But I see no reason in hell or heaven why I would bother sharing with you now, after the way you have treated me. Return to your cell, Penitent. Perhaps you will find the answers you seek through meditation . . . or perhaps not. But I think it's worth a try."

He stared at her in silence and knew this was all he would get from her on the subject.

CHAPTER NINE

Angel returned to his chamber, where he found Gunn waiting . . . with a distraught Archiel. The mage was holding his head and appeared lost, disoriented. Gunn explained that Archiel had stumbled into their room only a short time earlier, panicked and quite ill. It didn't take long to get from Archiel that some magic had been worked on him that made him abandon his post and wander, unseen, unknowing, until the fog began to clear from his brain and he thought enough to come back to this place, for whatever reason.

As they waited, Archiel withdrew a healing potion from a satchel he carried, and drank from it deeply. The effects were almost instantaneous. The sorcerer looked up at Angel with clear, horrified eyes.

"Was there another attempt to expose you as a fraud?" Archiel asked, his voice trembling.

"If an attempt on my life falls into that category . . . then, yeah." Angel told the sorcerer and Gunn about the attack he had just faced, and its grim aftermath.

"Bliss is an unusual woman with powers similar to the one who tried to kill you. In fact, she once belonged to that order of protectors," Archiel informed them. "You must not trust her."

"And tell me again why I should trust *you*?" Angel demanded. "I kinda lost that bit while I was fighting for my life."

Archiel hung his head. "I understand that I've done much to lose your trust."

Gunn, who had listened to about as much as he could take, surged forward, stopping just short and putting his hands on the mage. "Man, it's what you *haven't* done that's the problem." He turned around and pointed at his spine. "Look! Here are our backs! Who's getting 'em? No one!" Gunn's chest rose and fell heavily. "It's one thing to make it so we can't see you. It's something else altogether to not be there at all."

Archiel flinched. He did not take his gaze off Angel. Archiel asked, "This *is* between the two of us, is it not?"

Gunn waited to see how Angel would respond to that. *Come on, dawg, don't tell me you're gonna roll on me now,* he thought anxiously as he awaited Angel's reaction.

"I'm here," Angel said flatly. "I'm listening. I'm not getting any answers."

Archiel looked greatly pained. "I don't suppose you are, nor will you, I'm afraid. I have no answers to give. You must either continue to trust me, though you have no reason to, or we should make other arrangements."

Gunn couldn't believe this. Angel had let this magic-using motherless piece of crap diss him. This guy should have been schooled, and Angel was just letting it go.

"All right, you stay on," Angel decided.

"What?" Gunn said, outraged.

Angel stood firm. "The immediate threat seems to be taken care of—"

"Unless Bliss was behind it all," Archiel cautioned. "Few of us trust her, despite her status as a member of the council."

"So I'm giving you the benefit of the doubt," he told the sorcerer. "I need all the help I can get."

Then what about me? Gunn wondered. *Why leave me on the sidelines? Screw this "cover" crap, let me help!*

Angel pointed a single finger at the mage. "You want me to trust you? Then you have to earn it. You can start by telling me about Dagort and Symes."

Archiel rubbed at his temple. "I would if I could. The effects of the witch's magics addled my mind somewhat. I know the information you seek is within me, but I cannot call it forth. Not yet. Please have patience, and I will help you in any way that I can."

"Fine," Angel said, though it clearly wasn't. "Step outside, and I'll join you there. I need to talk with Charles for a second."

The mage complied, and soon, Angel was alone with Gunn.

"What's the problem?" Angel asked, confused by the searing glare Gunn was delivering.

"You really have to ask?"

"Apparently."

"With Archiel, man," Gunn said angrily. "Why didn't you say somethin'? He dissed me, and you just let it go."

Now it was Angel's turn to rub his temples. "Hold on. Aren't you the one who said 'I can fight my own battles' and 'Stay out of it' back with Marekai?"

"Totally different situation. I can't understand how you can't see that."

"Seemed exactly the same to me."

Gunn couldn't believe he was hearing this. "You're gonna leave this guy in place to do more damage?"

"I don't think he's lying," Angel said simply.

"Well, I *do*. Doesn't my opinion count for anything?"

Angel looked utterly confounded. "You know—"

"I don't want to hear it. Not one word about chain of command and how we act outside the office. Not any of that."

"Charles . . ."

"You got your position, I got mine," Gunn said. "I think we understand each other."

Angel sighed heavily. "Yeah, like that could ever happen."

Great, Gunn thought, *now he's going for the "Hey, leave the thinking to those who can handle the weight" business.*

"Fine, man," Gunn spat. "Whatever."

"We'll deal with this another time."

Gunn nodded. "Damn right we will."

Angel left the chamber, seeing no sign of Archiel.

"I'm here," a voice whispered beside him.

"Then let's go." Angel had struggled with the idea of trusting Archiel and realized, of course, that he couldn't. Leaving the man in place, however, was a separate issue. Angel was telling the truth when he said he believed everything Archiel was telling. But he wasn't at all certain that Archiel had been entirely forthcoming. It was possible that Archiel was being manipulated, or was, in some tacit way, complicit with whoever was attempting to wreak havoc on his mission. Someone might still be attempting to seed further dissension among the wizard's ranks. All they would have to do is expose the council's duplicity in bringing Angel into their midst, while hiding the very real threat of the killing machine that was hiding somewhere in this place. Angel felt he had a better chance of learning the truth if he kept Archiel nearby.

And there was always Bliss, who had picked up the slack twice now. Could she be trusted? Or was she behind the sabotage? It seemed there was only one way he could find out, and that was to try to get close to her . . . while hoping that he wasn't playing right into her hands.

Back inside their room, Gunn continued to fume. If only he had Fred to talk to, but that wasn't possible. Not now.

Soon, he found himself going back to the scrolls he had been working on—and furiously creating another chapter of his private epic, in which *he* was firmly in charge.

PAGE SIX

Cut to the exterior of the hotel, the lights on bright, indicators of loud bass music flowing out from its confines. Inside, the first floor has been converted into a happenin' joint, with hard-working vamp- and demon-killing brothers kickin' it after a hard night's work helping the helpless. Gunn sits at a table with a couple of amazingly hot sisters, raising a drink and smiling, while 50 Cent plays in the background. Standing off to one side is the out-of-place Angel, who sheepishly examines his shoes while a green-faced demony guy mixes him up something that looks like a Bloody Mary but really isn't.

GUNN

Yeah, now that's what I'm talkin' about, right there.

Go in tight on the pale and elegant hand of WINIFRED BURKLE, Gunn's lady love, as she touches his shoulder from behind.

FRED

What's the matter, big man? Feeling lonely and forget my number?

Widen out to show Gunn shooing off the sexy babes as FRED steps around the table. She looks, well . . . *damn*. Think Jennifer Garner's outfit from the *Daredevil* movie: lots of leather, lots of skin, heels, lowriders, ancient runes, hair down and wild and free.

GUNN

Don't suppose there's anything I can do to make it up to you, is there?

Fred puts one foot up on the table, allowing Gunn to take in the amazing length of her leg as she "daintily" rubs at a little spot on her thigh-high boot. The monster hunter may be cool as ice when facing the undead, but someone with a pulse, someone he loves like this woman, and he's *so* ready to play delinquent student and detention madam. Oh, yeah.

FRED

Well, now that you mention it . . .

Close in on Fred as her eyes widen and it becomes clear that we can actually *see through her.*

FRED

You can come get me before these lunatics cut me open and serve me to their demon wolves!

Reverse angle of a very startled Charles Gunn.

GUNN

Huh? Not really here . . . ?

PAGE SEVEN

Wider, as the mystical hologram of Fred fades completely and Gunn reaches for the image in alarm.

GUNN

Fred!

Gunn's cry has drawn the attention of everyone in the club. Angel is now at his side.

ANGEL
Hey, what's happening?

Close-up of Gunn, who looks intense, filled with a murderous fury.

GUNN
Someone took my woman. And I won't *rest* until I get her back . . . and cut whoever did this up into a thousand pieces!

Angel shrinks away, raising a hand like a kid in school looking for permission to go to the bathroom. You can almost *hear* his voice crack.

ANGEL
Um, can I sit this one out?

In his chamber, Gunn smiled and scribbled away.

Archiel helped guide Angel to Bliss's private chamber. Shafts of murky moonlight burst from these rooms, intersecting like crossed swords. A long patch of darkness stretched between the light at the end of the corridor and the dull luminescence from the nearby doorway, where, within, Bliss sat alone, working on her own meditative katras.

At first her expression was hard when she greeted him, but it quickly softened and she allowed him inside—shutting the door so quickly, there was no way Archiel could have gotten in with Angel unless he moved like the wind, or could walk through walls.

That was all right. Angel was fairly certain that, even if Bliss meant him harm, she would do nothing, in her own chamber with a witness either present or just outside the room.

And the room itself! One moment, Angel was standing in a hall lined with golden mirrors. But when he looked away, then shifted his gaze back again, the furnishings were totally different. The mirrors were gone, and the walls, floors, and ceilings bore intricate patterns of carved ivory.

Angel noted that the place didn't change while it was being observed. One second, it was a chamber filled with blue and gray clouds that bore faces fixed in pure ecstasy, then it was a great room lined with windows that all looked out upon a different view of the abbey and the cloud of fog without. She led Angel to a jasper terrace. The wall behind him had the appearance of melted wax. They looked out on the city of Los Angeles.

"I didn't think we could see it from here," Angel said, unable to suppress his wonder.

"We see it because you want to see it," Bliss responded.

"Then it's an illusion?"

"Everything is an illusion. The only things that are real are what we think and feel. Trusting anything else is madness." She took his hand in hers. There was so much warmth in her, he immediately felt as if he might burn to pieces, but in an exquisitely pleasant way.

"There's no reason to fight your attraction to me," Bliss whispered. "I think you are beautiful beyond compare, but I have no intention of seducing you or allowing myself to be seduced by you. You are safe with me, whether you can admit that to yourself or not."

"You can make me see anything?" Angel asked.

"I'm not making you do anything. We stand before a mirror that reflects the things we love."

"So," he said, eyeing the glittering city skyline, "you love L.A. too?"

She shrugged. "It has its charms, your presence chief among them. But no, I have the experience, power, and control to keep the mirror from reflecting anything I do not wish others to see. I can, however, help to guide you in its use. I find it valuable to remind myself as often as I can of what it is we are truly fighting to preserve, the things we truly care about."

"What makes you think I want to share any of that with you?" Angel asked.

"If you wish, I'll close my eyes," she offered.

"Remember, there is a difference between happiness and *perfect* happiness. In your condition, denying yourself the second is imperative. Denying yourself the first hurts you and all those around you."

"You know a lot about me, and I don't know anything about you," Angel said warily.

"I know, but this isn't about me. I have my role to fulfill and I am at peace with that. You, on the other hand, are greatly troubled. If those troubles could be eased, then I believe you will be much more efficient at your given task."

"And you want this thing stopped."

"I do. For all I know, I'm its next intended victim."

Nodding, Angel relaxed and looked into the "mirror." It took several minutes before the image of the city of Los Angeles shimmered and changed, but once it re-formed, Angel found himself looking out on the streets of Sunnydale, and into the face of Buffy Summers, the Slayer to whom he had given his heart.

Yes . . . yes, she was part of the reason he did what he did. There was a prophecy that if he survived the many trials ahead of him, he would receive the reward of being made human once more. If that happened, then perhaps he and Buffy could be together.

Her image shimmered, and became that of Cordelia, another woman he had come to love deeply. Following her, there were so many others he had come to care about, including his son Connor, Gunn, Fred, Lorne . . . then Wesley appeared, and he saw the former Watcher carrying off his child. Images of Darla, Spike, Drusilla, then a parade of his helpless victims appeared, intercut with images of Doyle, who had been the first to die for his cause.

Withdrawing, Angel turned from the mirror with a feral shout, his face transforming with the rage seething inside him as he ran to the door.

"What?" Bliss asked, racing to cover the distance between them. "What did you see?"

Angel squeezed his eyes shut and forced the change away. "Terrible things."

"Look again," she urged.

He shook his head.

"Please," she said fervently. "I promise, you will see only what you must see."

Turning slowly, Angel looked back to the window . . . and saw the faces of people whose lives he had saved, grateful people who were now leading normal, happy lives, all because he had taken up the cause of helping the helpless.

He smiled, unable to hold on to his anger any longer.

"She was right," Bliss said softly. "That *is* something you should do more often."

"What are you talking about?" Angel asked.

"The one you're in love with—Cordelia. You

smiled, and she said it was something you should do more often. It was also one of the first times she told you she loved you, though it was not necessarily in the romantic context you might have liked."

Angel twitched. "Don't go crawling around in my head. There are things in there that bite."

"Think about it, though. You know a thousand ways to inflict pain and suffering."

"At least. I've had a lot of practice."

"My Penitent . . . the cell you dwell in is one of your own making," Bliss said, once again taking his hand and nodding toward the mirror, causing its surface to cloud over and show nothing but the night and fog holding the abbey in its grasp. "You surround yourself with people who love you, but you deny yourself happiness of any kind. Is it because you fear that any happiness at all will lead to perfect happiness? To the reversion of your curse?"

"Maybe."

"Angel, it seems to me that with so many years behind you, you should be equally skilled in giving and receiving pleasure."

"I do okay."

Bliss rolled her eyes, which were only barely visible beneath her cowl. "I'm not talking about rutting. How can I communicate this to you? Hmmm . . ."

Drawing a deep breath, Bliss let it out and ran the tips of her fingers over his knuckles. Angel shuddered, a sensation of pure, relaxing energy surging through him. He jerked away from her. "Don't do that," he demanded.

Bliss grinned wildly. She had him, now. "Do what? *This?*"

She touched him again, and this time, his every nerve ending came to life. He backed away from her, trembling with pleasure, his enhanced senses tumbling into overdrive.

"It's all about give and take," Bliss explained. "You've just taken a fraction of the experience I've given you. Do you have the courage to return the favor?"

Angel hesitated. "I need to know about . . ." He broke off, feeling dazed. "Sorry, trying to think here. Doing my best. It's hard."

Bliss looked down at his robes. "I imagine so."

Gasping, Angel sidled behind a desk. "Not that I meant . . . um, don't want to go there."

"*You* may not. But don't worry, I'm not proposing that the only way to defeat a temptation is to give in to it. Moderation is key."

Angel looked away from her, studying her ever-changing walls and furnishings. "I thought there were no limits with you, that you're all about pushing the frontiers."

"Oh, believe me, I'm as mercenary as the next mage. It's just that I have almost everything I want."

"Almost," Angel noted.

She sighed. "As I said, Angel, I'm not after *you.*"

Huh. So Bliss has a thing for one of the other mages, Angel realized. *Which one?*

She adjusted her own cloak, generous amounts of flesh easing into view, then disappearing again. "Getting back to what we were discussing . . . mindless excess, sheer limitless sensuality, the satiating of the senses for no purpose other than transitory gratification . . . this is not what I am all about. There are energies in every living thing. Those energies can be focused and directed for healing and rejuvenation, for gently easing humankind forward, toward greater physical and spiritual awareness. But it is a gradual process."

"So you're all about the common good?" Angel asked.

She set her catlike grin upon him. "Perhaps . . . or it could be that I'm working in the service of a greater and more selfish goal. I'm not about to tell you everything."

"So let's say I believe you. Why are you trying to help me?"

"I have my reasons," Bliss said, looking away toward the misty area where her mirror resided. A man's figure slowly took shape—then vanished. "And . . . there's quite a bit that I get out of it. Now, let's talk about the victims, shall we?"

Angel nodded, and soon he had more information about the deceased mages than he knew what to do with.

• • •

The tunnels were silent, and the slight splashing of his boots in the murky water seemed to become louder to Wes as he followed the sewer route to the Hyperion. He understood that traveling through all this muck and filth might have been an unnecessary precaution, but he also knew that people—and *things*—had been following him lately, and this means of egress would make it harder on either who tried to track him. He had been hearing rumors on the street, grumblings among the lowest of the lowlifes, that something *big* was happening, something he couldn't possibly handle on his own, something that sounded related to the case Angel and Gunn were on, according to Fred's report, anyway.

A rumbling sounded in the distance, a staccato, echoing roar like thunder, only—it wasn't raining above, and the noise was coming from somewhere inside the catacomblike sewer tunnels. Wes moved forward into the darkness, his hand on the hot, drumming stone wall to steady him with the constant twists and turns of the labyrinth before him. An impossible wind picked up, and he heard the sound of his own breath become intensified, turning into sharp, ragged gasps as the winds grew heavier and started to push at him.

He pressed on, and the wind became bearable. Swinging his flashlight ahead, he saw the distinctive forms of three underground workers lying face-down on the ground. They had been savaged.

Running his hand along the neck of each victim, he verified that the first two were dead. The bones beneath the flesh of their throats had been crushed, and bites had been taken out of them. Something had started eating them, then changed its mind.

Wonderful. Another flesh-eater, like the ogre from earlier today, Wes thought.

The last victim was alive, but barely hanging on.

"What did this?" Wes asked.

"Big, blue-skinned, ugly . . . eyes like my sister's cat . . . huh . . . help me, please . . . ," the man chortled and choked and quickly died. There was nothing Wes could have done for him.

Wes was about to rise when he considered the wisdom of moving forward with his flashlight. He pictured the catlike eyes the man had described and considered that whatever was down here may not have needed light, but his "torch" would make him a perfect target; he would have to go farther into the tunnels blind.

He reached into his jacket and found a pair of weapons that would not be easily knocked from his hand should a fight arise in the darkness. He chose custom-made throwing stars, razor-sharp steel weapons the size of a large hand, with a round hole in the center and five pointed blades radiating outward. Most people only used the weapons as throwing stars, but they had a more deadly use, as Wes had come to learn recently. Fitting his thumbs in the center holes of each large throwing star, Wes closed his fingers over the dulled notches between the cutting blades and swiped at the air before him. He silently gave thanks to the weaponsmaster whose work had served him so well in the past—and, he hoped, would continue to do so for a long time to come.

Continuing on along the dark tunnel, his back brushing against the damp wall, Wes held his hands before him as weapons. There was no sound, no hint of movement from the tunnel. The shuddering walls at his back indicated he was getting close to whatever was causing the strange disturbance down here. The harsh force of the silent winds from the tunnel buffeted the exposed side of his face, and he was unable to stare fully into the harsh gusts.

The wall at his back suddenly gave out. The intensity of the dark winds faded to a mild breeze that seemed to emanate from several different sources. He had reached some type of juncture. Feeling his way with the backs of his hands, Wes discovered five separate tunnels leading off from the main trunk. The vibrations in the walls were identical, the force of the power-charged winds equally distributed. Suddenly the back of his hand found something dark and cold, chiseled like marble, but alive.

"Where do I go from here?" the creature before him said.

Cold determination closed over Wes. Before Wes could thrust his hand upward, plunging the razor-sharp points of the round blades into the exposed throat of his enemy, he was lifted from his feet and thrown against the wall. There was a hollow crack as his back struck the wall, and his hand raked across his own thigh, opening a thin wound.

"I asked you a question. Answer it, and I might let you live." The soft slosh of putrid water beneath the attacker's massive feet and his rich baritone voice revealed the killer's position. "There is food to be had on this world. Thinking meat, like you. But fresher, far fresher, not so riddled with age and encroaching death. Young and vital meat. Take me to it."

He reached out with the weapons, locking his upper arms straight into place, then bent his arms at the elbow, crossed one arm over the other in the attack position as his weaponsmaster had taught him. His flashlight had slipped from his waistband, rolled, and flicked on, providing a thin shaft of light pointed in the opposite direction, which nevertheless revealed something of his attacker's rough form.

His eyes, bloodred with black, catlike slits, revealed only a dark, evil hunger. The giant's flesh was bluish-black, with bulging red and green veins. His skin, upon close inspection, revealed a surface that was covered in dark bruises, giving the illusion of a unified complexion from a distance. His chest was wide, his musculature developed to the point of exaggeration. The creature's long, silky black hair whipped about in the supernatural breeze that was now fading, a remnant of the dimensional doorway he had certainly taken to get here. He wore only a wolf's pelt and bracelets.

"I'm as blind as you are," the eight-foot-tall creature said, "but I can smell you. I can smell your fear. And your blood."

Wes forced his body to shudder and shake, drawing the huge, inhuman, man-shaped thing closer. It stopped directly before him, apparently unaware of the weapons Wes held.

"You're like an old man with palsy," the towering killer said as he laughed. "I can hear your teeth chattering—"

Wes struck, lashing out with one hand closely following the other in an upward arc. The blades bit deeply into the monster's flesh, carving an "X" in his chest as he roared in pain and surprise. Wes's hands were on either side of the murderer's throat, about to cross and tear open his bluish-black neck with the piercing double blades, when the killer punched him hard in the ribs, a blow that surely would have cracked several of them had the fight not been taken out of the creature somewhat by its injuries. Still, Wes was bounced against the wall by the force of the blow.

The assassin's massive hand caught the side of Wes's head with an openhanded slap that left his ear ringing and upset his equilibrium. Wes stumbled, then fell to the ground, the dark cloak of the world spinning above his head. He heard a faint dripping.

A heavy, bare foot connected with Wes's shoulder. It was a glancing blow, obviously aimed at his head. As he had been trained, Wes spun with the force of the kick and rolled twice in the smelly water. His right arm was numb.

"You made me bleed," the creature said in disbelief. "I am Nayati of Rien, follower of Threshandra. I claim your soul—"

Before the creature could finish, Wes rose to trembling knees and swung the gore-drenched blades in an angry swipe. He was amazed when the weapons caught the thick flesh of the creature's upper thigh and severed an artery. Blood spurted into Wes's face, and the monster hopped backward, holding one hand over his wound to stem the bleeding.

"Let me do the honors," called a young, familiar voice.

Both whirled in the direction of the newcomer—just as the newcomer's long sword sped in the direction of the creature's neck. Its head was severed with a single blow, flopping into the air and landing right in front of the flashlight's beam, the face still twitching in surprise, the catlike eyes going wide, staring, and vacant. The headless body stumbled around, tripped over its own feet, and went down, shuddering a few times before it, too, went still.

"Connor," Wes said cautiously, eyeing the blade dripping gore that Angel's teenage son still held out before him.

Unlike his lantern-jawed father, Connor had a heart-shaped face wreathed by long, straight brown hair. His soft, childlike features might have suggested innocence, but the intensity in his eyes revealed a warrior whose skills had been attained in the fires of a hell dimension.

"Were you going looking for the old man?" Connor asked.

Wes nodded.

"Don't bother. I've been there. He and Gunn are gone—they're working on cutting this off at the source."

"This," Wes repeated dully.

"Well, *yeah*," Connor said, aiming the sword at the now cooling corpse he had created. "I've seen dimensional doors open before." His brow furrowed. "Actually, only twice. And the first time I can't remember, 'cause I was just a baby at the time. You probably remember it, though. You were there, right?"

"Yes," Wes said, practicing an ancient method of

breathing to make himself combat-ready. Connor was now aiming the sword vaguely in Wes's direction. Wes wondered if this moment would ever come, if the two of them might fight because of what had happened in the past. It was Wes, after all, who had been manipulated into delivering Connor into the hands of a madman's servant, who then took him to her master and delivered the boy into a life of living hell.

"Guess we can sit down and talk about that some other time," Connor said, making a show of lowering his sword.

"Then it's true," Wes said stiffly. "There are more doors opening up, more things like this coming through."

"Oh, yeah. Keeps a person occupied. . . ." Connor shrugged. "Cordy didn't feel like coming out. She's still pretty wasted. She and Lorne are gonna try to do what they can from the hotel. I've got text messaging and everything so they can let me know where these things pop up from police reports and stuff. What would be nice, though, would be to have some idea ahead of time when and where these things are going to hit."

"Leave that to me," Wes said softly. "I know a way of finding out."

Connor turned and eased off into the darkness, quickly merging with the shadows. Wes took out his cell phone and called Lorne to check up on Fred.

"No, no, she's fine, lovechunks," Lorne assured him. "She's spending some time with another old pal of hers, someone else who knew this poor Alicia girl."

"I see," Wes said cautiously. "And you expect her to be out all evening?"

"For her sake, you bet. And frankly, I think it's *great* that she's getting her mind off all things demonic and wacky for a while."

Wes thanked him, hung up, and leaned against the wall in the near darkness. *Am I really trying to be part of the solution, or am I part of the problem?* he wondered. *Perhaps I need to just give her space, let her come to me if she needs help. I can more than keep myself busy pursuing this other business.*

Wherever Fred is, I'm sure she's just fine and, unlike the rest of us, in no danger at all. . . .

Fred met Mitchell in the parking lot. She wore a new business suit, and the company ID she had snatched from Sharon was pinned to her lapel. Fred had expertly worked it over, inserting her picture for Sharon's, and a fake employee name and a clearance level that she had been able to insert by hacking into Norris's system. "It's just us. There's just one person I wanted to bring in on this, but I couldn't reach him."

"Do you want to wait another day?"

Fred wondered why she hadn't been able to reach Wesley. She'd even gone to his apartment and taped a note to his door, then gone back later to see if it was still there. It was gone—yet he hadn't contacted her. Had some kid in the building snatched it away? Maybe she should have slipped it under the door. . . .

"No, I don't think I can wait," Fred told him.

"Good, me neither."

They approached the front entrance, Mitchell swiping his security card through the slot of a box next to the main double doors. They were inside the lobby when a husky security officer stopped them and made them sign in while he verified their company IDs.

A few moments later they were riding up in a private elevator to the lab where Alicia had worked. Their ruse had not been questioned.

"Easier than I thought," Mitchell said, breathing a sigh of relief.

"Sometimes it works out that way," Fred told him. "Not often, though."

The elevator stopped, and the doors opened. They stepped into a lobby that looked more like it would belong to a Fifth Avenue advertising agency than a scientific research lab.

"We play at being grown-ups, yet when we're grown-ups we forget how to play," Mitchell said, almost to himself.

Fred looked at him oddly.

"That's something Alicia told me once. I mean,

this whole thing . . . doesn't it feel weird to you?"
he asked. "It's like playing detective. Being spies,
whatever. That's what it feels like. I know that's not
what it is."

"No, this is deadly serious."

"But it doesn't feel real somehow. You know
what I mean?" he shook his head as he led them to
another set of glass doors. This security gate required an access code to be punched in, as well as
a card swipe. "I keep wondering if maybe the only
reason I'm doing this is as a form of therapy, working through my grief in a funny way."

"I promise you, Mitchell, I wouldn't put you in
this position if I didn't *really* have a sense that
something's not right about Alicia's death."

Mitchell nodded as the doors hissed open. A
long, dark, antiseptic corridor beckoned. "I just
feel so numb. I haven't cried. I've been wanting to,
it's there, but there's just this part of me that says
you have to hold it together. You have to. And at
some point, I know I'm just going to break. I know
it's all going to come out."

"I hate to ask, but do you think that you can
keep doing it? Just a little while longer? So we can
get through this."

"Yeah, of course, of course."

Without another word, they entered the corridor,
the doors hissing shut behind them.

Sealing them in.

"Well," Lilah said, looking away from the telemetry screen. "I've gotta admit, this is a little more efficient than running around town watching people from rooftops and wearing camouflage gear."

She was in a small room on one of the lower levels of Wolfram and Hart's offices, standing behind a chunky, unkempt techie with a fondness for plaid. Computer screens and gadgets that could do who-knew-what lined every wall from floor to ceiling. Even getting in and out of this small room was like taking one's life into one's hands. One misstep and junk would clatter from some shelf and cave in on your head.

Lilah wondered if it was set up that way on purpose. Leopold, the man who was helping her, certainly didn't get many visitors.

"Yeah? Have you been running around in black leather like some surveillance ninja?" Leopold asked, his words getting kind of slushy as if he was getting hot and bothered just picturing it. "How did that work out?"

"Terrific. The camouflage suit is fantastic. As long as you just hold still, no one even knows that you're there. You just blend right into the background. Kind of like you. Must be where you got the idea from."

Leopold shrugged. "I don't like to brag."

"Then you shouldn't." Lilah had assigned the

tracker she had disciplined earlier to watch over Wesley—but *Fred* was her personal project. Well, her personal project for fun, anyway. Her whole "bid to control the universe" side venture was pretty much all work and no play.

She gestured at the screen. "You've actually figured out how to lock this onto someone's aura," Lilah said in genuine wonder.

"An aura is as distinctive as a fingerprint. Takes a small fortune to keep a system like this running, and to keep the tech hidden from other people around here, but . . ."

"The finances aren't a problem," Lilah said reassuringly. And that was true. Lilah could always guarantee ready funds because she never spent her own money on these things. She always had a list of people that she could steal from at any given moment. Billionaire clients worldwide never noticed the loss of a quarter million here or even a million or two there. "So this picks up psychic signatures through any wall—stone, steel, whatever?"

"Oh, yeah," Leopold said. "The only thing that kind of messes with its head is bad karma."

"You've got to be joking."

"*No.*" He frowned. "That's weird."

Lilah leaned in closer. "What?"

"I was able to keep following the Burkle woman until she went into that building and rode up in the elevator. But now that she's gone a little deeper into this 'Norris' building, I'm losing her. The place is just dense with . . ."

"Bad karma?" Lilah suggested.

"What can I tell you?"

"Fine," Lilah said, standing back and crossing her arms over her chest. "Just catch her on the way out again."

"No problem."

She reached into her purse. "Now, about your fee . . ."

He smiled thinly. "I was thinking about that."

Those were not words that Lilah wanted to hear. "Listen, you do *not* want to renegotiate with me. I hate that."

"Don't get upset!" Leopold urged. "I had an idea . . . and it's to *your* advantage."

"Really?" Lilah asked, dubious.

"Yeah, I was thinking about the whole promotion and moving-up-the-ladder thing and, I dunno, I kind of like it here. No one bothers me."

"You want to play it safe. I can respect that. The corporate climb can be pretty steep. And slippery. It's not for everyone." She leaned in close. "So what do you want?"

Leopold grinned. "You know that redhead on the third floor? Katya Manheim?"

"The one who administers our personality tests?"

"Yeah, I get sent up there a lot, for some reason," Leopold told her.

"What about Ms. Manheim?"

"*She's* what I want as payment."

Lilah was intrigued. "Specifics."

"You want me to get graphic?"

"Well . . ." Lilah raised an eyebrow. "You *do* realize about her quirks, right?"

"I like quirks."

Lilah leaned back in so that she could stare right into the inventor's eyes. "She's a reanimated corpse. I mean, literally. Soulless, mindless . . . she might as well have a windup key on her back."

He smiled. "Think she'll marry me?"

Lilah chortled. "You're one sick and twisted little creature," she said admiringly as she pushed off from his chair and went to the door. "I'll see what I can do."

"Yay," he said, sounding like an eight-year-old at a birthday party. Then his businesslike demeanor returned. "Oh, do you want me to keep scrambling any calls the target makes to Wyndam-Pryce?"

"Definitely. Let her think he's ignoring her, or unavailable like everyone else."

"You got it."

Lilah looked back at the screen. Sure enough, the Norris building, as seen in this schematic-style view, was filled with a dark, swirling mass that looked like evil incarnate. All things considered, that was not surprising. In fact, in its way, it was reassuring.

The darkness on the screen meant everything was proceeding according to plan.

It was an hour before midnight when Angel left Bliss's chamber. He allowed Archiel to guide him to a vacant room that the mage assured him was soundproofed of any kind of eavesdropping magic. Most of the rooms were protected to help ensure the privacy and secrets of their occupants. Angel told Archiel all that Bliss had revealed about the victims.

The mage, now visible once more, nodded gravely. "Yes, my thoughts are clear again, and I can confirm all she told you."

"So, when it killed Dagort, it used skills it had picked up from its victims in the club," Angel observed. "Fighting style, knowledge of human anatomy—even how to handle edged weapons." That last bit had been in the dossier of the fighter who had been shot to death. "When it came after Symes, it used powers that were unique to Dagort."

"I wouldn't say unique," Archiel said, "but Dagort was an undisputed master of them, yes. And now it can do anything Symes can do, presumably. That means that with power such as it possesses, the air could be sucked from a room, leaving all within to die gasping for a single breath. Or the ions could be drawn from it, leaving one giddy and unable to think correctly. The molecules of the air could be massed tightly together, like a fist, used to press an enemy to death, to crush them against a wall like an invisible hand."

"That covers Dagort," Angel said, still thinking about all of this.

Archiel went on: "With control over water, it could boil the blood of an enemy, or turn that blood and other vital liquids to nothingness, killing them instantly. And those are just its newly acquired powers. No human, no matter how skilled with a sword or any conventional weapon, could stand against this thing. Wielders of magic, however, stand a far greater chance."

"And someone like me?"

Archiel could not meet his gaze. "We shall see what we shall see, Angel. We shall see what we shall see. . . ."

CHAPTER TEN

The computer lab looked to the untrained eye like a huge open studio with dozens of small cubicles. Everything in the area was white, including the floor, desks, cubicles, and even the chairs, so that any dust that could affect the delicate systems could be easily spotted and removed. Each cubicle had a state-of-the-art computer workstation, including flat-screen monitors with the best graphics software on the market. Some of the work stations had scanners or digital cameras connected to them so that crucial written and visual data could be quickly added to the live computer system.

"This is . . . unbelievable," Fred whispered. She had hacked deeply into the system and had access to all of Alicia's files. It had almost been too easy—which worried her.

"Science has advanced—," Mitchell began.

"No, it's not the science," Fred assured him.

"Believe me, I've seen theoretical physics applied in ways that would sear your eyes right out of your skull."

"Okay, a little too graphic . . ."

"Sorry. What I find unbelievable is that anyone would be this irresponsible."

"I don't get it. What's happening?"

"The short and simple is that people in this department started something they didn't know how to finish. And if I believe what I'm seeing on the screen, Sharon was one of them. They started something . . ."

"Started what?"

"Basically, a chain reaction." She struggled inwardly, not quite sure if he would be able to fully grasp the truth if she told it to him, or if she needed to dress it up in more reasonable terms. . . .

Reasonable meaning not involving a complex series of doorways or gates between folded and unfolded N-space, or multiple demonic dimensions that the fabric of reality itself seemed to be attempting to isolate. No way in, no way out. At least, not before these jokers got started.

In other words, what was going on here was linked up to what was happening at the abbey where Angel and Gunn were undercover.

She certainly hadn't gotten all the details of their mission when they left the hotel. But all the spatial tectonic data on the screen in front of her made the mystery easy enough to unravel. The mages evidently were gathered because the walls between the dark-matter worlds were damaged and in need of bolstering. The dark-matter worlds . . . the ones where evil was just another way of saying, "It's in our nature to destroy all of existence or at least feed on it, subjugate it, recreate it in our image."

"There's some heavy duty tech somewhere in this building," Fred told Mitchell. "An enhanced particle reactor. This thing is working on a whole other level, and it's engaged in an operation that's having unexpected side effects."

"Like what?"

Oh, I don't know, Fred thought, *tearing up rifts between our reality and the dark-matter worlds, letting things like whatever killed those people at the nightclub come here?*

"It's unstable. It can't be shut down until it's first brought under control."

"Are you talking about some kind of gene bomb? Are we being exposed to anything right now?"

"No." And that was kind of true. One murderous netherworldly beast loose in Los Angeles *was* minimal when compared to a few hundred thousand, a million . . . it was all in how you crunch the numbers.

"Fine. We burn some proof onto a CD and take it to the proper authorities. Right?"

Fred wished it were that easy. "Even if we managed to get out of here with evidence like that, convincing the proper authorities takes time. Chances are that someone will alert these guys and all this will be moved before anyone can do anything about it."

"While it's still operational?"

"Uh-huh."

"And unstable?"

"And dangerous, right."

Fred could tell that the people at Norris had been at this for a while. In fact, it could very easily have been all their tampering that created the need for the mages to gather in the first place. All their poking and prodding and tearing down things that should just be left alone had created a situation she wasn't sure she could stop without help.

Fred heard the distinctive sound of a gun being cocked, and saw Mitchell jump as a man eased out of the shadows and placed the weapon to his head.

Mitchell tensed. "I—"

"Don't move, don't talk," Fred commanded Mitchell.

He obeyed.

"Hello, Fred," the man with the gun said. A dozen people stood behind him, men and women.

The development team.

"We were wondering how long it would take you to get here," the man with the weapon told her. "It's indeed a shame about your friend Alicia, but she had been sent to bring you in on the project.

Instead, she was going to try to gain your help in stopping it. That would have been unfortunate. So . . . no more Alicia."

Fred shuddered. Not only had she been right about Alicia's murder, she had been *played* from the beginning. "What do you want?"

"It's what *you* want that matters. I see this as a contest of wills between the two of us. Are you willing to see another of your old friends *die,* or will you do what you now know must be done and stabilize the process?"

"I do that, and then you'll just kill us both," Fred said, hoping she sounded as fearless as she was trying to come across.

"Worse than that. Help us and we gain control over all the doors between the worlds. Imagine the power that will give us."

"You could do anything," Fred agreed. "Destroy worlds. Control them. Anything."

"*W-worlds?*" Mitchell said, his voice breaking. "Fred, what are you talking about?"

The man with the gun struck Mitchell on the head with the butt of his gun, knocking him out instantly. Before Fred could move, he had the barrel aimed at the back of the unconscious man's skull.

"Interruptions are rude," he observed. "My proposition is simple: Help us stabilize the process, help us save *this* world, at very least, and you never know, you just might find some way to beat us all and shut off the mechanism completely . . . or I kill your friend. Then I make you help us and it will be torturous for you, and provide unpredictable results for us."

"Well, when you put it that way," Fred said, taking off her glasses and rubbing her tired eyes, "how can a girl refuse?"

The answers came to Angel in the middle of the night. He woke Gunn, and soon they were in the hallway trying to find their way to the quarters of the next two possible victims. Angel called out to Archiel repeatedly, but no answer came. He had abandoned them again, it seemed. Three strikes, so he was out. Angel would talk to Shanower about naming a replacement in the morning—should they survive that long.

"I should have seen this before," Angel snarled, furious with himself.

Gunn was still wiping the sleep from his eyes. "Hey, you want to clue me in?"

They turned a corner and faced a corridor exactly like the one they had just been down, and there were no doors, no windows, no stairwells leading to upper or lower floors. This wasn't the layout of the place as he had memorized it earlier. Either magic was being used to confuse and slow them down, or the abbey itself operated on principles like those in Bliss's room, its exact construction changing all the time, sometimes in subtle ways, other times, not so subtle.

"It hunts at night," Angel said sharply.

Gunn wasn't getting it. "Yeah, most of them do—vamps, demons, creepy crawlies."

"No, the *dead* of night," Angel elaborated. "When there's hardly a star in the sky."

Gunn had to work hard to keep up with Angel's purposeful strides. "So there's a special time this thing comes out to play."

"Yeah," Angel acknowledged. "It's different every night. Humans can't even tell the difference. They just look up at the night sky and say, 'Oh, pretty.' They don't have a clue what they're missing."

"Yes, we people with pulses do tend to be pretty slow on the uptake."

Angel was exasperated. "You know what I'm saying."

"I'm worried that, maybe, yeah, I do."

Angel sometimes just couldn't understand his friend's posturing and preening. They were all on equal footing. All anxious to serve the same cause. Yet Gunn so often acted as if he had something to prove. Why?

Racing on, Angel said, "Bottom line, this thing wants power. It takes knowledge, skills, and abilities. We know this from the way it attacked the second wizard using abilities that it took from the first one."

"Yeah, along with some pretty mean boxing moves."

"And skills with projectiles."

"In other words, the shooter who took out the boxer," Gunn said. "How do we stop this thing?"

"Haven't really figured that out yet. But I think I know who it's going after next. It's so obvious, I should have seen it right away. I'm just so used to things being indirect." Angel stopped at a fork in the corridor. Each way that they could go looked identical, and when he looked behind him, there was nothing but a brick wall. "I'll go to the right, you head left."

"No way, we're not splitting up. If someone is turning this place into a maze to slow us down, that's got to be just what they want."

Angel went to the left, Gunn right behind him.

"Okay, okay. So which one?" Gunn asked. "Which mage is the next victim?"

"Work it out," Angel urged. "I think it's looking for power. Pure primal energies. Every one of these wizards has his or her own specialty. The first wizard that was killed had mastery over the air. The second one, water."

"The four elements," Gunn said, the answer coming into crisp focus for him. "So fire and earth are next. One tonight and one tomorrow."

"Right. We've already seen two wizards who can do pretty cool stuff, one with fire and one with earth."

"Marekai is always using fire," Gunn said.

"Uh-huh. And Archiel had that special bond with the golem, a creature made of earth and stone."

"Who watches the watchmen," Gunn whispered as the maze before them grew even more complex. "Archiel was supposed to be guarding us, but he was the one in trouble the whole time."

"He or Marekai," Angel observed, choosing between three barren corridors before them.

Gunn looked around. "You know, looking back on it, this is actually a pretty sucky time not to have our resident science whiz with us."

Angel stopped as they reached an intersection of *six* corridors. "There's got to be a mathematical element at play here."

Suddenly a flickering light shone at the end of one of the six corridors. A young man bearing a torch came into view at the end of the hall.

"Hey, you, stop right there!" Gunn commanded.

The boy, a flaxen-haired youth, did as he was instructed. Angel and Gunn caught up to him. The corridor behind him was normal, with windows and doors and entrances to stairwells.

The lad bowed and did not meet their gazes. "How may I be of service?"

"We need to find Marekai and Archiel," Angel said.

"Their chambers are some distance away, yet in

opposite directions," the boy explained. "I can take you to one and direct you to the other."

"We'll probably just get lost," Gunn admitted. "Angel, we'll have to pick."

"Marekai," Angel said without hesitation. "It'll want to control fire."

"You sure?"

"*No.* But that's the one I'd go for next. If I were, ya know, evil."

The boy nodded toward a stairwell. "This way."

Ten minutes later they burst in upon Marekai, who was instantly woken from his slumber, a pair of fireballs manifesting in his hands. There was no sign of Nemesis anywhere.

"You're . . . you're okay," Angel said in confusion and alarm. "But it's feeding time."

Understanding creased Marekai's inhumanly handsome face. "The killer. You thought it was after me."

Screams sounded from the hall.

"That can't be good," Gunn said.

Angel looked to the boy. "I thought Archiel's place was supposed to be a hike from here."

"It is," the lad said frantically.

"That was a mystical calling," Marekai said, the fireballs fading. He grabbed at his clothes, pulling on his tunic. "Every upper-level mage in a thousand yards would have heard it."

"I heard it," Gunn said.

Marekai shook his head as he jammed his feet into his boots. "Perhaps some magic has been worked upon you that none of us are aware of."

"That or I've got skills you don't know anything about," Gunn added.

Angel hissed, "Gunn, not *now*."

"Yeah, yeah," Gunn said.

Marekai touched the boy's head. "Forget." The lad slumped onto the bed. "I'll take you to Archiel's room." The sorcerer waved his hand, and all his assistants and acolytes who had been awakened by the commotion also fell back into their deep slumbers.

Angel, Gunn, and Marekai soon arrived at Archiel's quarters and watched with horror as they saw the mage attempt to battle the shadow monster. Archiel fought against Nemesis with all the power at his disposal, his goal clearly to prevent it from touching him. The mage used his power over earth to create a pair of golems to protect him from the soil that he stored in his room. The golems lumbered toward the shadowy Nemesis, but before they could even reach it, Nemesis used its control over water to send a flood of gushing liquid at the golems so they were unable to maintain their solid form and turned to mud.

Archiel quickly looked around for another weapon at his disposal. He found a pile of huge stones that he used to train his acolytes. Archiel raised the stones with his powers and hurtled them toward Nemesis. None of the stones reached their target. Nemesis had created hurricane-force winds with its power over the air to blow the stones back at Archiel. The mage desperately tried to protect himself from the brutal attack, but he was helpless against the shadowy creature's power. One of the stones rammed into his side and knocked the mage down onto the floor.

All this took place in the few seconds the newcomers needed to get their bearings. Marekai launched himself into Archiel's quarters and loosed a dozen fireballs at Nemesis. But the shadow creature easily doused them with water and rendered them harmless. At the same time, Angel and Gunn ran in after the mage and attacked Nemesis from the rear with a sword and staff that they found in Archiel's room.

Gunn tried to hit Nemesis in the back of its head with the staff, but it only passed through the monster, leaving only a temporary gap between the head and the rest of the body, which was soon filled in. Angel attempted to stab Nemesis in what should have been the creature's heart, but his efforts only created a hole in the shadow, which was quickly sealed up once the sword was removed.

Nemesis watched with amusement as Angel tried his clumsy maneuvers to injure it. Turning his head toward the vampire, the shadow creature's maw opened, revealing razor-sharp teeth. It grinned at the vampire. "We are . . . the same."

"No chance," Angel snapped as he again swung his sword "through" Nemesis with no effect.

"We both . . . live . . . off the life-essences . . . of others," said Nemesis as it re-formed itself after Angel's latest injury.

"I don't kill," Angel said. "Not anymore."

"Who said . . . anything . . . about killing?" asked Nemesis.

"You talk too much," said Angel.

Footsteps sounded from the hallway, and Bliss burst into the room. She surveyed the situation and immediately saw that this "battle" was way too one-sided. It was time to even the odds a bit.

Ahead, Nemesis gestured and started to use its power over air to change the battleground.

"Am I the only one who's starting to feel light-headed?" Gunn asked dizzily.

"Nemesis is using the power over air to remove the oxygen from the room," said Bliss. "Everyone come over here."

Bliss gathered everyone around her and projected a barrier that would protect their air supply from Nemesis's magic. Nemesis glared at the female mage and switched over to using its power over water, sending huge waves of water at Bliss's barrier. They fell away quickly and harmlessly.

"We need to imprison this thing," Marekai said as he stepped out of the ring of protection and created rings of fire around Nemesis. The shadow laughed at this display of primitive magic. It created a great wind and sent the fire back on Marekai, who withstood the blast without being harmed, screaming in frustration and rage.

"I agree with your sentiments, Marekai," said Bliss. "But I think we need to take *firmer* action first."

Bliss proceeded to conjure a spell that forced Nemesis to take on a physical form so that it could be injured and captured. The shadow creature changed. Its color went from a shadowy gray to deep black. It developed substance and depth. The "sunspots" within it faded.

"Now that's what I call magic," Gunn said as he proceeded again to go after Nemesis with his staff. Gunn swung the staff into Nemesis's midsection, and the creature doubled over with pain and let out a howl.

"Don't fade out on us, Nemesis," Angel said as he joined Gunn with his sword and slashed at the monster's arms and legs.

Nemesis desperately tried to avoid their blows, but it was clearly not used to being in solid form and moved slowly. Finally it gathered enough strength to use its water powers to make Angel's sword rust so that the blade was dulled and could no longer slice into its gleaming black flesh. But neither its water nor air powers could do anything to diminish the blows from Gunn's staff. Only the skills it had taken from the fighter in the club kept the warriors at bay.

Then Nemesis turned its attention to the real cause of his suffering, the mage Bliss. Nemesis turned his full power of water on the mage.

Bliss felt her blood boil inside her body, and she screamed in agony. The sorceress desperately fought to maintain control over the spell on Nemesis. She knew that she couldn't let it turn back into its pure shadow form.

Angel and Gunn tried desperately to distract Nemesis with blow after blow on its corporeal form, but its concentration was locked on Bliss. Marekai sent a couple of fireballs at Nemesis, but it ignored the pain of the burns on its body.

Finally Bliss could no longer remain conscious and collapsed from the pain inside her. Once Nemesis was no longer bound by her spell, it turned back into its shadowy original form and used its power over the air to fly out of Archiel's window and away from its tormentors.

Angel joined Gunn, where they checked on Archiel's and Bliss's wounds after the fight.

"I vowed that I would win back your trust," Archiel said, gasping and holding his side where he had been wounded. "I hope that my actions can be counted toward that end."

"They do count," said Angel confidently.

"That's all good, man. But we've gotta get a medic!" said Gunn.

To Gunn's surprise, Bliss stood up. "Allow me," Bliss said, pushing between them.

"Looks like we're going to need another protector," Gunn said as he watched Bliss examine Archiel's numerous wounds.

"I'll assume his station," said Bliss. "I mean, why not? I've already made you my mission."

"Can you be invisible?" asked Angel.

"It's not in my nature, no," Bliss admitted. "But you're right, there must be some reason why we are to be seen together so much." She thought about it. "I know . . ."

She kissed him, hard and full on the mouth. He gasped, pulling away.

"There. I'm known to always take a lover at these functions. This time, it will be you."

"Pretend," Angel said warily. "It's all pretend, right?"

She only smiled. "Pretend all you like, Angel. Pretend *all* you like."

CHAPTER ELEVEN

Close to dawn the next morning, Wes was standing in a dank and darkened underground chamber, a wizened man in chains at his feet. The man wasn't exactly a man, however. His naked flesh was mottled, his eyes shone bright crimson, and he had gills in the side of his neck. When rewards had not been enough to coax his services as a seer from him, he had been tortured by those who had captured him for a decade or more until he finally broke and set his "sight" on whatever problems they or other paying clients brought to him. Wes had come to the chained man for help, and the seer had already known Wes would be coming, and precisely what information he desired.

"The doors that have opened between our realm and the dark-matter universes are little more than a portent of things to come. *All* the signs point to this only being the beginning." The seer told him exactly where each of the next two dozen manifestations would take place on the earthly plane.

Wes nodded. "Thank you."

The seer tensed as Wes stood and turned his back. "Wait!" the seer called. "I have performed the services you required, accurately, fully, and without guile. What of my price?"

Wes hung his head. "It may be too high."

Seething with anger, the seer said, "You readily agreed when the need was yours."

"Is there no other way?" Wes asked, his tone surprisingly gentle as he turned to face the man. "It seems there's so much more that can be done."

A terrifying smile etched itself upon the seer's face. "You *mean* so many more uses that I can be put to." He laughed bitterly. "Honor your word. If you do not, only misery and misfortune will come to you."

This time, it was Wes's turn to be darkly amused. "Misery and misfortune? They've already arrived. And I'm fairly certain I already have the crib notes of what I have to look forward to: more of the same, until a somewhat early—"

"*No.* Where there is life, there is hope."

"It's ironic that *you* would say that, considering—"

"Free me, damn you!" the seer shouted.

Refreshing his grip on his blade, Wes readied himself. "Very well."

The first blow came crashing down on the top of

the demon seer's skull, slicing his head in two and killing him instantly. The second—and third— destroyed his eyes. Wes felt the seer's soul leave his body. The room, warm and close, filled with the undeniable fire of his life-essence, suddenly grew cold and barren. There had been a tingling in the air, the sensation of a silken butterfly's wings touching his mind, his heart, and then it was over. The seer's immortal essence was gone, released from his torments, and would one day be reborn to a better life than this.

Already, Wes could hear the guardians of this place racing his way.

If he managed to escape, he would be hunted down until the end of his days. They would kill anyone he had ever cared about. His only real option was to stay here and fight them, to either kill them all or die trying.

The seer was rumored to be the greatest of his kind in several generations. Yet he was kept here, like an animal, tortured and coerced into doing anything his captors told him to do.

Oftentimes he had been used to disseminate false information and, in the process, lead great champions to their destruction. Wes thought it flattering that they had chosen this fate for him.

Pulling off that particular ruse had been easy enough. Like others before him, Wes had been carefully drawn to this place. It wasn't hard. A word here, a whisper there. And he had known the moment he had set foot in this place that strange magics permeated the walls, the floor, the ceiling, the air itself. As a result of that magic, he would be unable to speak of this place and divulge its location and what transpired here for the rest of his days . . . not that he would have many, if the guardians on their way here now had their way.

Getting their hands dirty was distasteful to these people. Wes understood. He had been like that once himself. Now he rather enjoyed the mess.

"Come then," he whispered as the guardians massed around him, "I'd like to see if all the lessons I've been paying for have been worth it or not. . . ."

Later that morning, Angel stood before his acolytes once more, with Gunn sitting off to the side, brooding. Bliss was there, leaning haughtily against the far wall.

"It's time for a field trip, boys!" Angel said with false excitement.

Logan crossed his arms over his chest and said, "I thought we weren't allowed to go out."

"We're not," Angel said agreeably, trying to "get into" his role as both the sorcerer Kano and as a teacher and mentor to these lads.

"What's she doing here?" Marco asked, adjusting his collar uncomfortably as he pointed at Bliss.

"I'm here to see him work his magic," she said in her typically sultry voice. "Isn't that right, honey? Just like you did last night."

All three boys burst out laughing, and Angel shot Bliss a warning glance. She deflected it, her desire for amusement overriding all other concerns—except the task before them. The mage Angel was pretending to be was certainly capable of the task ahead; Angel himself was not, unless he received a little help. And that's what she was there for. Her cloak was parted in various strategic locations to show cleavage, neck, and leg. With all that to look at, no one would be noticing what she was doing with her hands, or so went the plan.

Angel gestured, his actions somewhat over the top, and the small room he shared with the largely absent Ord disappeared and was replaced by a golden-and-emerald-hued forest. The trail Angel stood before was narrow and covered in a blanket of beautifully colored leaves. The trees were spaced closely together. The students looked up. The branches high above crossed one another's paths and seemed to fold together like the arms of lovers. Intense white and yellow streaks of light pierced the spaces between broad coverings of leaves and filtered downward. Tiny chirps sounded from birds nearby. Soon crickets would wake and create their own music.

"This place is beautiful," Daniel said. "It's so quiet."

Logan chortled. "Daniel likes the quiet because it reminds him of what's in his head: empty air."

Marco laughed, and Daniel looked away, his frown giving way as he took in the incredible sight of Bliss once more.

"I feel a deep sense of peace here," Angel said, walking about, twigs snapping beneath his feet. "But I prefer the night."

He gestured again, and soon the shafts of sunlight diminished, then faded altogether. Above, a deep blue sea dotted with bright stars came into view.

"There's a brook about fifty yards in that direction," Angel said as he pointed westward. "Logan, that's the direction I want you to head in .... for the hunt."

Logan sat up straight. "What hunt?"

"I want someone to go and bring us back a prize," Angel said calmly. "Today, that someone is you."

Marco shoved his arm. "None of it's real."

"Actually, it is," Angel informed them. "Come on, Logan. Unless you're afraid . . ."

The boy's gaze narrowed as he left his seat, went a few feet into the woods, then stopped and turned. "Shouldn't I take something with me? A weapon of some kind?"

"I didn't ask you to kill anything, Logan. Just catch some small animal and bring it here."

"Yes, lord," Logan said wearily, deciding there must be a point to all this—and that point was that he was being punished for mouthing off at Daniel in class. Fine.

Logan waded into the woods. He could barely see where he was going. Soon the darkness became even deeper, and Logan had to move very slowly to avoid tripping on low-lying branches or roots. On several occasions he began to get impatient and found himself nearly slamming face first into the body of a tree.

Though it had been unearthly quiet only moments before, the woods were now alive with odd sounds. There were creatures moving up all around him. Every now and then he saw a blur of movement, a dark stain against the deep gray of the woods.

He suddenly thought of something that another of his teachers had told him in the days before he came to the monastery. It was about achieving one's goals: *Sometimes the harder you chase that which you most desire, the farther it will run from you. Try to be very still. Be at peace with yourself; be grateful for all you have, all you are. The object of your desire will become curious, and will come to you in time.*

Logan knew that it was silly to think this motto would apply to the matter at hand, but he felt he could stumble around in these woods most of the "night"—no, morning—and fail to achieve the task that had been set: capturing a beast with his bare hands. Kano either had a great deal of confidence in Logan or he was testing him. This had to be about something other than Logan's hunting skills.

Finding a comfortable spot, Logan sat down and waited. He recalled a free lesson in acting he had won at a carnival some years back and tried to apply what he had learned.

I will be a tree, he thought, attempting to ignore how foolish the sentiment may have sounded had it been spoken aloud in the company of his friends. He pictured a tree, then tried to imagine what he must look like to the small creatures of the woods. Using his artist's imagination, Logan changed the image he held of himself, melding it with that of the tree. He slowed his breathing, forced away all conscious thought.

Several minutes passed.

Suddenly, he felt a tiny leathery tongue licking his finger.

He had been so entranced by the exercise he performed that he did not jump at the unexpected sensation. Instead, he waited and felt something small and furry climb into his lap.

Now, he thought, and made a desperate grab for the animal that had fallen into his trap. His fingers closed on something soft, like a pillow. Its heart thundered as it wriggled free and leaped away before he could get a proper grip. Logan jumped to his feet and ran in the creature's direction. It was a hare.

Logan ran exactly four feet before his foot caught on a twisted root and he went down, his face mercifully falling in a nest of leaves. He felt ridiculous.

Other concerns came to him. What would happen if he broke his leg out here? Or if he was walking and one of these damned branches snapped back and tore a gash in his face?

Was any of this real?

He felt the first icy touch of true fear and did his best to banish it. Kano said nothing would happen to him. He had to have faith in the man's words.

Faith.

There it was again. This was another test of Logan's faith. God knows his own father had tested him on that score often enough, and it drove Logan half out of his mind.

Picking himself up, Logan suddenly felt that he wasn't alone. Two small orange orbs sat before him in the darkness. Logan strained for a better view and realized that it was the hare.

A part of him said, *What difference does it make?* The only way he was going to capture an animal was if he fell on one by accident and managed to knock it unconscious.

Refusing to give in to such pessimism, Logan lunged forward.

The animal evaded his clumsy attempt to catch it, and Logan fell facefirst on a downed branch, bruising his forehead. The hare skittered deeper into the woods.

"No you don't!" Logan cried as he scrambled to his feet and gave chase. He ran after the hare, somehow managing to keep it in sight while avoiding the tree trunks that kept leaping out at him.

The chase lasted for several minutes, until the hare disappeared beneath a collection of thick roots. Logan leaned against a nearby tree, out of breath. The fourteen-year-old froze as he suddenly realized that he was lost. Until he had seen the hare, he had been cataloging his movements so that he could find his way back to the clearing. His maniacal determination to catch the animal had driven all such thoughts from him.

Suddenly, Logan felt light-headed. He lowered himself to all fours before he could fall and hurt himself again. What color he could detect in the forest retreated. His vision improved radically, as if the sun had impossibly chosen this moment to appear. Logan's breathing slowed and became much deeper.

The clothing he wore felt horribly oppressive. Overwhelmed by an urge to be naked, Logan stripped off his clothing.

His skin felt almost unbearably sensitive. New sensations cascaded over him. A light breeze blew in from the north. The scent of decay wafted up from the dead leaves on the ground. The sounds of crickets and a chorus of other night creatures swelled to a crescendo before returning to a manageable level.

What was happening to him?

Thought came slowly and with difficulty. He felt hunger and could smell prey somewhere close. The hare appeared.

He could hear its heart beating. As he concentrated, the noise became louder. The creature moved, and Logan matched its every step. The stink of fear reached Logan and made him angry. His dark, animal side rose up, and he ran for the hare. Although he couldn't see it yet, he could hear it and smell its blood. His own footfalls were graceful and elegant, his scent pure, blending in with the strong but wonderful smells of the forest around him.

Instinct allowed him to select the proper spots on the ground for his feet and hands so that he would not snap any twigs or rustle any leaves as he chased his prey. The hare tried to run up the side of a tree. Logan leaped high into the air, grabbed a branch, spun, and kicked at the bark just above the creature's head. He could have struck the hare, but that would have brought the chase to a close far too easily.

Finally, after more than ten minutes of stalking the meat, Logan closed for the kill. He feinted to one side, then moved in the opposite direction and snatched the hare from the ground. His hand closed over its neck, and the madness that had gripped him faded as suddenly as it had arrived.

No. He had been charged with bringing the beast home alive, and that is what he would do. But—was that only so that Kano could have the pleasure of the kill? What had this creature done to deserve death? Magic provided for their needs.

Suddenly, he couldn't feel the animal any longer.

Logan looked down and saw that he was naked and standing in the small cell with his fellows, who were laughing their heads off.

"Oh," he whispered, turning and speedily snatching up the clothing he had removed. Daniel and Marco couldn't stop laughing, and Bliss was regarding him with a single intrigued raised eyebrow. Gunn didn't look his way, and his teacher simply stood like a stone, arms crossed over his chest.

"Good," Angel whispered, ignoring the boy's embarrassment.

"How was any of that good?" Logan snapped.

"You felt the urge to kill, you were completely in touch with your basest animal instincts, but you overcame them. In fact, when it came down to a choice between being a predator or a protector, you let the animal go to save it from me."

"None of it was real," Logan said, pulling on his leggings. "None of it."

"Don't be so sure," Angel added. "I'm not."

Class ended shortly thereafter. Angel wandered over to Gunn. "That Logan kid . . . he challenges me. He doesn't listen. But I see something in him."

"Really?" Gunn said, surprised that Angel had finally decided to share his thoughts.

"It's gonna sound crazy, like maybe I'm just seeing what I want to see, but I think he could do the world a lot of good. I think he's seen so much greed and avarice—not to mention bad manners—that he's not hot on the path his parents have him on. He's looking for something else. He wants to make a difference. I think that went pretty well," Angel said, pleased with himself.

Bliss came over, all smiles. "Perhaps better than you know."

"What do you mean?"

"The magic was mine. The idea behind the scenario was entirely yours. You just *gave* that boy something, whether you know it or not."

"Yeah, like getting razzed by his buddies the rest of the time he's here."

"No," Bliss said. "Well, *yes,* there's that. But you also gave him something to think about: his own basic nature. You were the one who felt that was important. Why is that?"

They were interrupted by Logan, who had doubled back. "Lord Kano, my father has asked me to tell you that he wishes a private audience with you before the great ceremony tomorrow night to discuss my progress."

"Um . . . sure," Angel said. He suddenly had a very bad feeling about this. There was something dark and haunted in Logan's eyes when he spoke of his father. "So—your dad. What's he like?"

"What are any of you like?" Logan asked bitterly. He stood up straight, suddenly emboldened by his earlier lesson. "You're the masters, we're the slaves."

"We teach you," Angel said, his confusion deepening.

Logan laughed. "Didn't you hear? We serve a purpose. If you would like, *Lord,* I will recite the litany on this subject for you."

"Actually," Angel said, his concern growing, "I would."

At high noon, Angel and Bliss stood before Shanower, the head mage, in his private chambers. His quarters consisted of a garden made of ice that confounded all reason by generating a comforting warmth and a rosy glow. The darkness of so much of the abbey was defeated in this place, impossible though it seemed.

The outer darkness, anyway.

"These kids are *hostages?*" Angel shouted.

Shanower gestured expansively. "They're not

children, not as you would think of them. They are the heirs of the great houses. They are our successors. And, as such, they must be prepared for the life that fate has chosen for them. By exchanging acolytes, the mages manage to keep squabbles from escalating into bloodshed."

"They also act as spies," Bliss added.

Shanower did not seem at all pleased by her statement, but he did nothing to deny it.

"Why wasn't I told about all of this?" Angel asked.

"The feeling was that if you knew everything, you might shy away," Shanower told him. "I think that would have been a terrible loss."

Angel was still struggling to take this in. "So everyone brings acolytes and then you exchange them like hostages."

"Correct."

"I didn't bring—"

Shanower cut him off. "You did. Kano did. Or so everyone thinks. Do you want to see them?"

Angel was wary about this, but he had to know the truth. "Okay."

The head mage waved his hand, and a crystalline flower blossomed before them, growing to the size of a looking glass. It filled with a sparkling clear liquid, and once its surface settled, an image took shape.

Angel gasped as he saw three teenage boys who each looked eerily like Connor studying with a kindly faced, pudgy, red-bearded mage.

"They're what we call sendings," Shanower explained. "Soulless but intelligent animated organics."

"Intelligent, you mean they're self-aware, they have—"

Shanower stopped him. "They're soulless, like golems but they have to believe that they're alive."

"And when I go . . ."

"Yes, they go. They'll be unmade. It's of no consequence."

"To you, maybe." The idea of three beings walking around who looked like Connor, each thinking he was alive, that he had a past and a future, disturbed Angel almost as much as the mages' practice of using the children to keep one another in line.

Angel was surprised when he returned to his quarters to find the elusive Ord in residence. "So that's the deal with these kids," Gunn told Ord, nodding and thoughtfully absorbing the information he had just been given.

Bliss's face lit up at the sight of the slightly mad, blue-tattooed mage. She raced at him, throwing her arms wide, and gave the man a hug that left him speechless and slightly embarrassed.

"Gunn, I just talked to Shanower," Angel informed him. "I'll fill you in later—"

"No, I got it," Gunn assured him. "It's like the Pact in the 'New Gods.' Darkseid and Highfather exchange sons to keep the peace. There's lots of historical precedent. The Romans, the Turks, you name it."

Angel was floored. He pointed at Ord. "*He* told you that?"

"Yeah, man . . . he only looks crazy," Gunn said, and then quickly reconsidered. "Okay, he acts and talks a little nuts, too, but he's got depth, if you know what I'm saying. In fact, he's got a whole theory about our three students that you really oughta listen to."

Angel looked to Bliss, who nodded her head vigorously. She was like a taken schoolgirl in the clueless Ord's scholarly yet scattered presence.

"You've been observing Logan, Marco, and Daniel?" Angel asked. "When?"

"They wander, I wander, we see one another," Ord said with his typical rapidfire delivery. "Do you want my, ah, psychological assessment of them?"

Angel wasn't exactly sure what he was getting himself into, but he couldn't deny that he was taking an interest in these teenagers. "Well . . ."

"All right, then!" Ord hollered, flitting about, jumping onto the desk and perching like a bird, then bouncing from cot to cot as he spoke. "You have these three boys in your care. Two of them are very similar in personality, one could not be any more different."

That was true enough. Daniel didn't belong with Logan and his follower Marco, but circumstances seemed to have thrown them together.

"The two that have, ah, bonded," Ord said, finding some blank parchment and quickly making origami figures from it with little light blasts from his fingers, "are *highly* insecure. They believe that everyone is judging them, or they fear as much. They do not subscribe to the theory of 'judge not lest ye be judged.' Instead, they are all about judging others *before* they can judge you."

Angel had picked up on that as well.

"They see themselves as very strong, independent, and capable," Ord went on. "That's not necessarily how they are, but it's how they view themselves. When they meet someone new, they do an assessment, they judge whether that person is like them, strong, or *not* like them, weak. The category one falls into depends on a variety of factors, most notably, ironically enough, is if that person will stand up to *them* and put *them* in their place. Or if that person, for whatever reason, will let them run around undisciplined, doing whatever, getting away with murder, perhaps literally."

"Whoa. You think the kids have something to do with what happened yesterday, or Nemesis, or—"

"I think *anything* is possible," Ord said, setting down a petting zoo of origami figures and leaping to the wall, which he paced upon as if gravity had no hold on him. "I hope it is not them. They are looking for order, discipline, structure, much like the fabric of reality itself is constantly seeking. . . . Your Fred whom you have not been able to contact is a quantum theorist, yes?"

"I guess," Gunn said, embarrassed that he couldn't answer that simple question about Fred's abilities and interests.

Ord nodded sharply. "Einstein believed that we live in a world that is made of wood. He wished to see that world transformed into marble."

"I don't understand," Angel told the mage.

"Wood is chaotic, unpredictable," Ord said, allowing Bliss to bring him down from the wall and plop him down in a chair. "Trees grow in unique, independent ways. The makeup of wood is undisciplined. Marble is strong, structured, immutable. It's densely packed, simple to replicate and predict. These boys live in a world made of wood. They, too, want marble. No one is giving it to them. So their behaviors, their beliefs, grow more destructive, more self-centered. Not at all like those of, how do you say, a *champion*. None of them."

"But they've got potential," Gunn reiterated. "And mad skills, right?"

"Oh, right!" Ord said, flushing as Bliss finally gave up on holding him in place with her powerful arms and instead sat down in his lap. "Emphasis on the mad!"

"You know what?" Bliss said. "I'm starved. I think we should all go to the Silver Dagger and get something to eat."

Gunn jumped up. "I know I'm ready to strap on the feed bag."

Angel just shook his head and followed the group out the door.

After a delicious magically conjured feast, Angel, Bliss, and Ord decided to take a walk through one of the abbey's gardens. Returning to his room alone, Gunn saw that the door was slightly ajar and he heard noises within. Opening the door slowly, he peeked inside and saw a shadow moving on the wall. He steeled himself, worrying that Nemesis was here, and wondered what he could possibly do against the beast on his own.

Instead, the figure casting a shadow was Daniel. As Gunn shoved the door all the way open, the teenager turned, a collection of scrolls in his hands.

"Hey, what do you have there?" Gunn asked.

Daniel tensed, then handed over the scrolls. Gunn was upset to see the story he had been writing among them, but his agitation and concern gave way to surprise and admiration as he surveyed the other scrolls and realized that Daniel had taken the comic book pages and quickly sketched them out.

"Pretty pathetic, I know," Daniel said in a voice that reflected his lack of confidence.

Gunn had no idea what the boy was talking about. "No, these are great! I had no idea you could draw, or draw so well."

"My dad doesn't like when I draw or paint or anything. He thinks I should spend all my time studying what he wants me to be interested in."

Gunn sighed. "That's a tough one. On the one side, at least it's good he's taking an interest. On the other, though, he doesn't sound like he really cares about what you want. Or is it more complicated than that?"

Daniel looked away. "A little more. I'm the seventh son of a seventh son. I have all this destiny garbage I have to deal with."

"Really? How does that work?"

"It's complicated," Daniel said, clearly not wanting to discuss it.

"Yeah, that's cool," Gunn said, closing the door and laying the pages out on the table so he could get a better look at them. "So . . . you like comic books?"

"Yeah. Couldn't you tell?"

"Sure, I just . . . here's how it is. You're not like other teenagers. Any other teenager would be worried about looking cool and detached and all that stuff."

Daniel hesitated. "I'm not cool?"

"You are!" Gunn said. "You're very cool. See,

when you *are* a certain thing, you don't have to *act* like you're that thing. You just . . . are. That's all there is to it."

"Oh," Daniel said softly.

"The worst is when you have to announce what you are to the world," Gunn said sagely.

"Like Logan. You should hear the way he talks when there aren't any adults around. It's like he thinks he's better than all of us, like he deserves more than everyone else."

"Exactly," Gunn told him. "The strongest people I know, the smartest people I know, the coolest people I know, don't go around saying they've got this skill, they've got that skill. . . ."

Gunn flinched inwardly as he realized *he* did that sometimes. "The thing is, that's the kind of thing where, if you have to ask for it, it doesn't mean anything when you get it."

Daniel fell silent, his gaze shifting to the images he had drawn of Angel. "He respects you. He really does."

Gunn nodded. "I know. I'm just not sure if it's for the right reasons, sometimes. That's all."

"Tell him."

Gunn cocked one eyebrow. "Hey, dude, I thought *I* was giving *you* advice."

"Oh, yeah," Daniel said. "That's right."

They both laughed.

Gunn waved at the comic book pages. "That was

just . . . I was passin' the time, that's all. You know Ang—I mean, Kano . . . you know he's not really some—"

"He's not Kano. He's a vampire."

"Pardon?" Gunn said, tensing.

"A vampire with a soul. I could smell it. That's cool."

Gunn considered arguing with the boy, but there was a larger issue at stake. "Wait, there are all these spells and things that are supposed to make it impossible for anyone to figure it out."

"If it was impossible, I wouldn't have known."

"Good point."

"Don't worry about it. I don't think anyone else is going to get it. I'm more sensitive to things than most, that's all."

"The whole seventh-son business?"

"Right. That's part of it."

Gunn didn't tell him how important it was that Daniel not say anything to anyone about what he'd learned, nor did Daniel push things by asking why Angel and Gunn were here in the first place.

"What does your father do, anyway?" Gunn asked.

Daniel hesitated. "He's . . . I suppose you'd say he is an engineer. He knows about the design of things."

"So he wants you to be all practical, not a dreamer, is that it?" Gunn asked.

"Pretty much."

Gunn looked at the pages Daniel had drawn. The teenager definitely had chops. "You want to draw more of this thing?"

"I don't know," Daniel said, barely masking his excitement. "Do you have any more that I *can* draw?"

"Oh, yeah," Gunn said. "I know just where this story is going."

PAGE EIGHT

Day. Wide establisher shot of W.W.P. Enterprises, a Los Angeles high-rise office building that puts Wolfram & Hart's offices to shame. We go inside, where we find Gunn and Angel emerging from an underground service elevator. Angel has a black GLAD bag over his head and shoulders like the hood of a cloak. He looks out at the hallway with an uncertain expression. Gunn continues to roll his eyes.

ANGEL

Is my being here really necessary?

GUNN

He likes you. He thinks you're . . . interesting.

They step out of the elevator, Angel looking around frantically, worried he might step into a shaft of direct sunlight.

ANGEL
Interesting why? How?

GUNN
You ask too many questions. But, for the record,
the whole vampire-with-a-soul thing? There aren't
many of you guys running around.

ANGEL
I have this curse. It's like a rash. Only—

GUNN
Enough. It's time to go see . . . the man.

CHAPTER TWELVE

Wes parked his SUV in front of the hotel, shielded his eyes from the glare of the setting sun, and glanced at himself in the rearview mirror before getting out. The reflection in the mirror surprised Wes. He felt horrible but looked like his normal self. For a moment, Wes pulled down the collar of his shirt and stared at the scar on his neck. It was healing pretty well with the mystical salves he had applied, but every once in a while it still ached as if forcing him to remember what he had done to Connor.

Wes carefully got out of his car, trying to avoid aggravating his injuries from the daylong battle in which he'd been engaged after he had slain the seer. The shower and change of clothes had made him feel human again, but all the bandages that he was wearing under his shirt and pants were restricting his movements. He hesitated in front of the main entrance to the hotel and forced himself to stand up straight even though the pain was excruciating in his back and bruised ribs.

Wes was grateful that he didn't need to worry about running into Angel or Gunn on this trip and silently hoped that he might meet up with Fred and be able to console her about her loss. He opened the front door and walked inside, prepared to hand over the information that he had obtained from the seer to Lorne and Cordy. Lorne stood behind the reception desk of the hotel, but Cordy was nowhere in sight. She was probably in one of the inner offices listening for police reports and checking items on the Internet.

"I was able to obtain some intelligence about the strange things that have been going on across the city," said Wes. He handed Lorne a typed copy of the information that he was able to get out of the seer before releasing the man's spirit to be reborn in freedom. "I believe this covers every dimensional rift that is due to strike the city over the next few days."

"Good, that's just what we need since it's just me and the ex-Powers-That-Be girl holding down the fort," Lorne said in despair.

"Isn't Fred here with you as well?" asked Wes, trying to hide the pain he was feeling—and his concern.

"No, she didn't come back last night. And before

you ask, *no,* we can't seem to reach her by cell phone. In fact, we can't reach Angel or Gunn, either. We're on our own on this one."

Wes let out a deep breath, forcing some of the tension from his body. "She met with a Detective Moffat yesterday, didn't she?"

"Yeah, that was his name. Why?"

"Perhaps he has some intel about where Fred might have gone."

"And you think he's just going to tell you what he knows?" Lorne laughed. "He is a police detective, you fuzzy Babboo. It's unlikely that he'll be forthcoming with this stuff."

"No, but I'm sure he can be persuaded," Wes said with a dangerous look in his eye.

Lorne shrugged. "Hey, give it a shot."

Wes picked up the phone on the reception desk and dialed the police station's number from memory. "Hello, can I please speak to Detective Moffat? This is regarding the woman who was murdered at the restaurant a couple of nights ago."

The receptionist transferred Wes's call to the detective's personal line immediately. He answered directly.

"Detective Moffat, my name is Wesley Wyndham-Price, and I am a friend of Winifred Burkle. I understand that she came to see you yesterday."

"That's right," the detective said, a strange wariness in his voice.

"She didn't come home last night," Wes explained, "and I am concerned, given how upset she has been. Can you help me? Do you know where she might have gone?"

The detective sighed. "First up, let me tell you what I told her. I know all about you guys, so let's not play games. We've got kind of our own version of *The X-Files* in this office, and all of your names are in it, along with a lot of things no one here would want to discuss, at least officially."

"Ah, so you're more . . . open-minded?"

"I've seen things and, unlike some, I can't and won't just explain them away or ignore them. You folks have done a lot of good down there. You've also been a major pain in our backside at times. But I believe we can and should work together when things get rough."

Wes was impressed.

"As far as Miss Burkle is concerned," Moffat continued, "I can't get anything done officially unless someone wants to come down and fill out a missing-persons report, and even then there's a waiting period. But I like the kid. I know she's been through a lot. Listen, I'm off the clock in an hour and I can think of one or two places to do some nosing around, the kinds of places I don't think you'd get very far without a badge. I can give you one place, though, where you can start look-ing, then you can give me a call after you're through checking it out. We can meet up and work together on this."

"I'm . . . I'm sure it's nothing to really be worried about," Wes lied, "it's just—"

"My radar's up on this too," the detective commiserated. "And, with the kind of things I've seen, it's better to be safe than sorry, if you know what I'm saying."

"I do," Wes said hoarsely, wishing that he did not. "Let me get that address from you, and I'll let you know what I find out."

Angel and Gunn sat with Bliss in their room before the wildly gesticulating Ord, who restlessly prowled around the small cell he shared with the detectives.

"You think I'm mad," Ord said, sounding breathy, gasping between every few words. "And, by any standards you might possibly apply, you're right. That doesn't make me incapable of clear thinking. Give me a problem, I can solve it for you."

"I don't think so," Angel said. He rose, and Gunn followed him to the door.

The mage raced around them, blocking their way. "I bet I know where you're going and why."

Angel looked back to Bliss, who watched the madman contentedly. He was only enduring this audience because she assured Angel that Ord had great wisdom to impart.

"You want to contact the world outside," Ord said.

"Cell phones don't work," Gunn explained. "There must be a direct line somewhere in this place."

"You want to call the scientist," Ord said. "You regret how you treated the woman. Winifred, yes? You thought bringing her here would mean putting her in danger. But there's danger everywhere. We're fighting a shadow. Shadows aren't confined to any one place. Anywhere there's light, there is shadow. And from what I've heard you say about her, there is a great light within her."

Angel asked, "How is that thing going to escape with so many people looking for it?"

Ord smiled, the light glinting wildly in his eyes. "It traveled the doors between dimensions, yes? Can you do that?"

"Not easily," Angel admitted.

"The shadow thing is as alien to you as it is to me, as we are to each other," Ord told them.

Gunn rubbed his temples. "What's scaring me is, I think he's making a lot of sense. We keep judging Nemesis by human standards, as if it thinks the way we do. But it's not one of us."

Ord danced like a court jester. "It can walk among us, it can blend in around us, and because of the things it takes from the people it feeds on—language, knowledge, power, skills, desires—it can emulate us. Pretend to be like us by using whatever it has stolen in the first place, and that is probably just to keep us guessing."

"All the more reason to bring Fred in," Angel said. "Is there a way to call out or not?"

"There *is*," Ord said. "But there is a price that would have to be paid in order to use it."

"Fine, I'll bite," Angel said. He winced inwardly. "I mean . . . fine, tell me. What does it cost to make a phone call around here?"

"You can't call out for the same reason you can't just walk out," Ord explained. "No one gets out at this point."

"Wait a minute, we're *trapped* in here?" Gunn asked. "Nobody said anything about being trapped in here."

Leaping around some more, Ord told them, "The rite that must be performed has to take place in a dimensional nexus, as the energies necessary to perform the binding mount all around us. Travel from this realm to yours becomes increasingly difficult and dangerous. At this point, only one crossing may be permitted."

"So there is a way out?" Gunn asked.

Ord shrugged. His tattoos were so thickly packed that he looked as if he'd been painted blue. "But there isn't a way back."

"And if we take advantage of that way out—," Angel began.

"Then the rest of you don't have a way of getting

out yourselves if everything falls apart," Gunn finished.

"Exactly!" Ord said, rushing over and doing his best to give them hugs. They brushed him away, and he leaped upon the table, perching once more like a great blue bird. "We would be the ones who are trapped. *That* is the cost of making a phone call from this place."

Angel shook his head. They were in this, alone, to the finish.

Wes used his lockpicks and let himself into the apartment Alicia Austin once lived in. He had knocked for several minutes and received no answer. He knew it was unlikely that he would really find a clue as to Fred's whereabouts in this place, but it was his only lead, and according to Detective Moffat, Fred was highly likely to have come here earlier.

Once inside, he heard a low wailing and a strange scratching sound—*and* he felt the telltale winds that marked the passing of a dimensional doorway. This place had not been on the list of "hot spots" the seer had given him, but Wes had a sinking sense that it should have been.

A sound came from the bedroom. Drawing his sword, Wes surveyed the darkened apartment. "Hello?" he called. "Sharon? It is Sharon, yes? You were Alicia Austin's roommate, I believe. I'm a friend of Winifred Burkle. I'm hoping you can help me find her."

The sound grew louder. A hissing and a tearing. Picturing some creature ripping the poor woman apart in her own bed while Wes was caught up in his own caution, Wes barreled into the bedroom—and slipped on something thick and wet on the floor. He landed hard, but caught sight of a woman who matched Sharon's description attacking her own bed. Only . . . the woman didn't exactly look like Sharon was supposed to. There had been no indication, for example, that Sharon had spidery limbs and other inhuman features.

Whatever had come through this rift must have *bonded* with the woman. In fact, there were severed ropes on the bed where, he presumed, she had been tied up and held in place to receive exactly this fate. Or perhaps she was simply meant to be an offering of food. Either way, she was no longer remotely human.

Issuing a curse that came out as little more than a hiss, Wes grabbed at the door handle, trying to bring himself to his feet despite the slippery floor. The monster was ripping the mattress to bits, screaming in its high-pitched wail of frustration, and a cloud of feathers rose into the air. A slight laugh that sounded like a catch in his throat escaped from Wes's mouth, and he wondered if he had gone mad, being able to laugh at a sight such as this.

His smile faded as he realized the woman-spider was transforming again, replacing some of its monstrous aspects with human attributes that would allow it to free itself and take full advantage of the close space. It had sprouted long, sinewy human legs that were covered with fine, brownish-black hairs, and its torso had reduced in size. The monster's face had become more human, but it had retained the pincers and four of its eight spider-limbs. Wes knew that in the time it would take for his hand to pull the door open, the monster would be upon him, driving its swordlike arms through his body.

I'm going to die, he thought. *I'm going to die for nothing.*

The thought gave him the determination to fight. Anchoring himself, Wes raised his sword and waited for the woman-spider to leap from the bed.

The creature moved with blinding speed. It went from standing still into attack mode in an instant, and then vanished in the time it took Wes to make a single swipe with his sword. There was a large gash in his upper arm, and he looked up to see the woman-spider sticking to the wall beside him, wiggling her tongue obscenely. Wes turned and struck with his weapon, the sword slamming into bare wall where the monster had been only moments before. He heard it skittering across the ceiling and he wondered how he could win in a battle against this creature.

Then he spotted the possible means of his salvation. On a nearby dresser sat a hurricane lamp. Suddenly, thought and action were one for the fighter as he snatched the lamp from the dresser and threw it—hard—against the headboard. The glass shattered, and flammable liquid splattered all over the bed. He drew a lighter from his pocket and lit the bed on fire. A cloud of flames rose up and scorched the ceiling. He felt his lungs strain to deal with the sudden lack of air in the room as the woman-spider began to wail. Keeping his sword before him, Wes opened the door and felt the rush of air from the hall as it briefly sucked the flames in his direction. Before he could escape, though, he felt a slight impact on the back of his neck and he was yanked upward.

The woman-spider was staying close to the ceiling, having transformed almost entirely into a seven-foot-long spider with pincers that opened and closed in rapid, hungry movements.

Threads had caught Wes by the space between his shoulders and by the fleshy part of his right calf, as he was lifted into the air. Wes's hand closed tightly over the hilt of his blade, and he swung at the threads that were yanking him steadily upward, slicing apart the strands that secured his back when he was four feet in the air. Suddenly he was supported only by his leg and he fell back, his head scraping against the floor as he found himself hanging upside down and completely at the woman-spider's mercy. Driving his sword into the partially opened wooden door, Wes pushed the door closed, trapping himself in the room once again. Then he pulled with all his weight until he felt a section of his flesh tear from his calf. Suddenly he was free, dropping to the ground with enough impact to drive the wind from him.

Before Wes could regain his footing, the woman-spider ran down the wall and attacked. Wes raised his sword just in time and jammed it between the incredibly strong set of pincers that jutted from the woman's face. The creature screamed as Wes used his leverage to push the creature toward the rapidly spreading flames that licked at its back.

Wes grabbed the door handle with the cuff of his shirt, ripped the door open, and stumbled into the hall, hoping to pull the door shut and trap the creature in the burning room. Just before it shut he heard a scream and felt the hard wood slam against him as it exploded outward, jumping off its hinges, knocking him off his feet.

When he looked up, the woman-spider was standing in the doorway, the burning room at her back. As it advanced on him, Wes scrambled to his feet and raised his sword in time to ward off the first strike. Wes felt as if his blade had connected with an iron club. The creature was moving more slowly, its lightning-fast reactions dulled to the point that Wes and the hybrid could battle as equals.

Wes's sword flashed as he forced away his fear and concentrated on hacking at the woman-spider, which advanced on him with clicking pincers and burning eyes. The monster had retained its human legs, leaping nimbly back and forth as it pressed the attack and retreated. It used its four spider arms to fight with the skill of a quartet of trained swordsmen and refused to allow Wes an opening to drive his blade at the creature's face or the sensitive, soft places between its hard, sectioned torso.

The woman-spider advanced on Wes with a feral expression, its eyes glazed with the pure, sensual delight of the battle and the joy of the anticipated kill. Wes understood why the creature was grinning: It was regaining its strength as it launched itself against the fighter, while Wes was becoming worn and tired. Suddenly the creature used all four of its arms to gather Wes's sword-arm above his head. The woman-spider took a step forward and slightly beyond Wes, then brought one of its legs between the fighter's, trapping Wes with her dark, powerful limbs. A hoarse whisper—a would-be scream of defiance—left Wes's throat as the woman-spider brought its face close to the fighter's, its pincers moving close to Wes's vulnerable eyes.

With his free hand, Wes reached back and grabbed the woman-spider's hair, pulling as hard as he could to keep the monster's awful pincers from blinding him. Wes instantly regretted that he had not tried to put out one of the creature's eyes instead. The woman-spider's face inched closer as Wes leaned back in the deadly embrace and felt the muscles in the small of his back begin to ache. The woman-spider parted its lips and spat a stream of white ichor at his throat.

Why not my face? Wes thought, then understood that the creature had wanted Wes to see the pincers coming, desiring the numbing fear that Wes would experience instants before the crablike claws parted one last time, then closed, their sharp tips piercing his moist eyeballs.

The webs constricted around Wes's throat and slowly drew his face forward as the woman-spider allowed one of its arms to fall away from the other three, which held Wes's sword at bay. The free limb poised near Wes's stomach, the tip pricking his flesh as it bit through his clothing and slowly drew blood.

Despite himself, Wes relaxed slightly, the fight slowly trickling out of him. Then he noticed the way Sharon's head slowly moved, straining to see something over its own shoulder.

"The itsy-bitsy spider . . . ," a familiar voice sang.

Then there was a brutal and terrifying explosion of carnage. Something akin to a force of nature, though its power was certainly not of the natural world, attacked the woman-spider, tearing her limbs from her, then mashing in her skull with a single powerful kick.

Wes held still as Connor stepped forward and freed him. They left the burning room behind, Wes already reaching for his cell phone to call 911. Once he was through, and the pair had done all they could to keep the blaze under control until help arrived, Wes turned to the young, gore-covered fighter.

"You keep coming to my rescue," Wes observed. "Why?"

Connor shrugged. "Beats sitting around doing nothing. And Cordy called, said you could use my help, gave me this address."

"And that's your only reason?"

"Guess I'm curious about you. You don't seem stupid. You don't *seem* like some gutless pawn," Connor said candidly.

"Thank you. I think."

"But you were the one who took me when I was a baby. I wouldn't have ended up where I did if it weren't for you."

Wes nodded. "So you want . . . revenge."

"Naw," Connor said with a smile. "Maybe I'm just saying thanks."

"Or maybe you haven't decided what to do with me yet, and you'll be damned if anyone else is going to get the pleasure of killing me should you decide that's what you want, ultimately."

"Could be that, too. But that's what keeps life

interesting, isn't it, Wes? You just *never* know . . ."

Sirens blared in the distance.

"Let's get out of here," Wes urged. "I think we should have a word with a certain detective who sent both of us here . . . and almost to our deaths."

Together, they made their escape.

Gunn walked with Daniel down the long hallway where his father's cell lay. It had taken some doing, but Gunn had convinced Daniel to talk to his father about his desire to spend his life creating magic with a quill and a brush rather than spells and swords of power.

"Just be confident, that's all," Gunn advised as they closed on the cell. But as they got closer, they heard raised voices, and both froze when it became clear that Daniel himself was the subject of their robust discussion.

"Purefoy, you don't drive a very hard bargain, now do you?" a throaty voice declared. "He is your only son, after all."

"Fah!" another voice spat contemptuously. "He is useless to me. The fact that you actually want him, that you've come to me for him, though . . . tells me I *should* ask for more, if only to take advantage of your foolishness!"

A chorus of laughter accompanied this remark.

Gunn leaned in close to Daniel and whispered, "What's happening in there?"

Daniel's face was ashen. "He's bartering for power . . . spells of some kind . . . objects, territories, possibly. . . ." The lad shuddered. "He's *selling* me."

Gunn couldn't believe it. "That's crazy. He's your dad. He doesn't *own* you."

"This happens," Daniel said, dazed. "When a child fails completely, it happens."

The "buyer" emerged from Purefoy's cell, a young, balding man with hawklike features and dark, swirling robes. He noticed Gunn and Daniel in the hallway, surveyed Daniel appraisingly, then grinned and walked past the pair without a word.

"My God," Gunn whispered. "I thought if we talked to your dad, we could make him come around . . . but that's not going to work. What he just did, I mean—there's no going back from this."

Next to Gunn, Daniel was shuddering.

Gunn put his hand on Daniel's shoulder to steady him. "What happens if you don't agree? If you just won't go with that guy?"

Daniel looked up at him with sad eyes. "Can he be any worse than my father?"

The look Gunn gave him in return was chilling. "Believe me, there's *always* worse."

"Freedom, breaking with the path set down by our forebearers . . . ," Daniel said reverently, treating each word like it was as delicate as it was strange to him. "I don't know. I've never heard of it being done."

"There's a first time for everything," Gunn said,

urging Daniel toward his father's cell. "Come on."

They came to the cell and entered it. Purefoy and his friends were of the diehard warrior caste that Gunn had seen wandering around outside, the pale-fleshed, dark-eyed, dreadlock-wearing crew. Purefoy himself was weighted down with so much armor and adornment that he probably *had* to use magic just to move around. The whole group was laughing, and their merriment did not stop when Gunn and Daniel entered the room.

"Father, I need to speak with you," Daniel told the man.

Purefoy laughed. "What's the servant for, boy? Were you afraid you'd lose your way?" He turned to his friends, a half-dozen in all. "He's always afraid of something!"

The laughter reached a crescendo.

"I won't do it!" Daniel suddenly shouted, his hands moving quickly, a fiery matrix of energies blasting from his fingers and enveloping the room, creating a laserlike spiderweb that settled around each warrior, the bonds forming squares of empty space around their heads. If he were to bring them together, he might decapitate them all.

"Whoa," Gunn said, impressed.

Purefoy was not. He waved his hand, and the crimson lattice of arcane energies vanished. "You were in the hallway, I presume. And you heard me strike a deal for your destiny?"

"Please," Daniel said, edging away from Gunn. "Father, I need you to give me a chance. . . ."

The laughter had ceased, and the other warriors were looking disapprovingly at Purefoy.

"You would defy me in this?" Purefoy roared at his son.

"I'm begging you, Father," Daniel pleaded. "I want to do what I care about. What makes me happy. Why is that wrong?"

"Arrogant little pup," Purefoy snarled, a sphere of bloodred energy forming around his gauntleted right hand. "I made you. I can unmake you. The bond between us goes deeper than blood. It reaches to the very fiber of your being."

Purefoy pointed at his son—and the ball of rippling red fire shot forward and engulfed him!

Daniel quaked and screamed as the energies worked through him and he slowly, painfully, came undone. The spells of unmaking that he had described were being worked on *him*.

"Stop it," Gunn shouted. "You're killing him!"

Purefoy smiled. "Such is my right."

"Not while I'm around," Gunn declared, surging at the mage. Then something gripped his back, holding him in place. Gunn looked over his shoulder and saw the sorceress Bliss in the doorway, her hands spread wide in conjuring.

"Wait," Bliss urged, casting a spell that dragged him away from his charge. Meanwhile, Daniel's body was still shaking, and his flesh was coming apart, his entire body transforming into a whirlwind of tiny puzzle pieces struggling to remain as one.

"Let me go," Gunn yelled. "I can't let him—"

Bliss touched his arm, and Gunn felt ancient power flare from her hand. It was as if she was lending her strength, her resolve, to him.

Or was she just controlling him?

"Trust me," she coaxed, removing her hand, allowing him the freedom to choose.

Gunn studied Purefoy's face. The warrior mage's features were twisted up in a mask of hatred and malice. Yet . . . his eyes betrayed none of those harsh feelings.

What game was Purefoy playing?

"Come now," Purefoy whispered. "You don't mean to say this little hobby of yours is worth your life?"

"Go to hell!" Daniel screamed defiantly.

The boy's shimmering body was on the verge of disintegration—when his father grunted and released him, allowing Daniel to fall to the floor, his body quickly reintegrating.

"Well," Purefoy said dispassionately as he stood over his son. "You have some spirit after all. Not that it will do you much good. Your will can be broken." He shrugged. "I'll leave that task for your new master." He motioned to his companions, and they all left the cell with him.

Bliss and Gunn went to Daniel, Bliss cradling

him in her lap and she worked healing magics upon him.

Yet there was something in Daniel's eyes that Gunn did not expect.

"Okay, help me out here," Gunn requested as he stared at Daniel. "You look happy . . . why, exactly?"

"He showed his hand," Daniel said with a triumphant grin, one he mustered despite his great pain and weakness.

Gunn felt a little of the young artist's enthusiasm and excitement touch him. "You're saying you can keep him from ever doing that to you again? You can get free of him?"

Daniel nodded.

"Do it," Gunn urged. "Don't waste any time, man. Do it now."

"Timing," Daniel said softly. "I must wait until the time is right."

Daniel turned. It appeared there was something else on the lad's mind, something he wasn't sure if he wished to share or not.

"What?" Gunn asked.

Daniel leaned back, luxuriating in the softness of Bliss's lap. "Nothing," he said, sounding happy and a little sleepy. He smiled up at her. "This is nice."

Without another word, he settled back to sleep. Bliss brushed his hair, kissing his forehead, and looked at Gunn.

"You may not think so now," Bliss told him,

"but you have won a great victory this day."

Gunn thought of the horror he had just witnessed—and wondered how Bliss's words could possibly be true.

Detective Moffat went to the door of his small rented house, a baseball bat in one hand. He didn't live in the best of neighborhoods, and the kind of knocking that was battering his front door now usually spelled trouble. He opened the door—and Connor hit the man hard enough to knock him across the room, but *not* to knock him out. His baseball bat flew from his hand.

Wes and Connor stepped inside. Connor closed the door as Wes advanced on the man.

"I want to know what you've done with Fred," Wes said.

Moffat's nostrils flared. He looked up at the pair in shock. "I haven't done *anything* with her."

"Wrong answer," Connor said, grabbing the man and lifting him into the air.

"If you two would cut it the hell out and just listen for a second, I could tell you exactly where she is," Moffat shouted.

"Can't I just keep hitting him while he's talking?" Connor asked.

"Let's see what he has to say first."

Connor dumped the detective into a motheaten old couch. "Talk."

"Why did you send us to Alicia's apartment? Did you know what we were going to find there?" Wes demanded to know.

Moffat looked confused. "I told you before: When I had Miss Burkle in my office, she gave me reason to think that *she* was going there at some point. You're the one who volunteered to go there tonight to check it out. I didn't 'send you' any-where."

"This is the problem with giving them a chance to talk," Connor said. "They talk and talk and don't say anything."

"He's right," Wes added, still staring at the de-tective. "We were both nearly killed in that place. We're not here to argue variances in phrasing—"

"I tracked her down," Moffat said abruptly. "And she's fine."

Wes was startled. "You mean Fred?"

"Yes." The detective frowned. "Listen, I don't know what happened at the Austin woman's apart-ment. If I need to send a unit there, then let's stop messing around and let me get on the horn!"

Wes studied the man's face carefully. The detec-tive looked sincere, but that didn't mean anything. "The police were already on the way when we left."

Moffat shook his head and muttered. "I thought we could all work together. I told Fred that. Maybe I was crazy."

"When did you see her?" Wes asked. "Where is she now?"

Connor grabbed his arm. "This guy set us up! You can't believe anything he says."

"Maybe he set us up, and maybe he didn't," Wes told the lad. "In any case, I want to hear what he has to say."

Moffat relayed the details of his encounter with Fred at Norris Industries the previous afternoon, and told them how he had gone back to Norris just an hour ago and had actually seen Fred there.

"You spoke with her?" Wes asked.

"She's *fine*," Moffat said, caressing the bruise on the side of his face. "She's pitching some project they've got going over there. Don't expect me to explain the details of it. You're better off asking her."

Wes frowned. He looked to Connor. "Do you believe him?"

"No." Connor shrugged. "But I never believe anyone. What do you want to do with this guy?"

Moments later, Connor was helping Wes manhandle the detective into a nearby closet, where they used his own handcuffs on him and bound his ankles with electrical tape they found lying around.

"What are you people thinking?" Moffat hollered. "You're assaulting an officer of the law!"

"Yeah, yeah, *quiet*," Connor commanded, slam-

ming the door on him and smashing the lock so
that it would take a handyman to get the detective
out again.

"If he's telling the truth, this is going to be quite
embarrassing and difficult to explain," Wes counseled.

Connor shrugged. "Tell it to someone who
cares."

"Good point."

Wes and Connor left the detective's house, got
into Wes's car, and headed for Norris Industries,
where the detective claimed he had last seen
Fred.

Detective Moffat waited until he heard the front
door slam shut, and then he leaned back against
the wall of the closet, closed his eyes, and whispered a few arcane but powerful words. The detective heard a skittering sound coming from outside
of the closet. The closet door started to shake on its
hinges and was then ripped free. The detective
glanced at the legion of foot-long onyx scorpions
that had responded to his summons.

He said another arcane word, and a few of the
scorpions came toward him, tearing away the tape
that held his ankles and breaking his handcuffs.
The detective rose from the floor and walked out
of the closet and over to the phone in the living
room. The creatures cleared a path for him, the

man barely acknowledging their existence now that he was free.

He had some calls to make.

A half hour later, Wes sat on the edge of an over-sized black leather chair while he waited for the security guard at the reception desk to reach "Miss Burkle" upstairs. He had been relieved to hear that Fred was indeed here at Norris and that the security guard recognized her name without having to search a database.

Wes turned as he heard the chime of the elevator and the *whoosh* of its doors opening. He was *amazed* at what he saw come out of the elevator. There was Fred, wearing her hair up in a bun to keep it out of her face, and a white lab coat over her dark blue dress. She had a broad smile on her face and waved happily at Wes as she walked over to meet him.

"Wes, I'm so glad you're here," Fred said breathlessly. "You're one of the few people I know who could appreciate what I've been working on upstairs."

Wes couldn't believe it. Fred was standing right in front of him, lit up by an inner excitement and radiance he feared he might never see in her again.

The sight was actually unnerving. He thought of how distraught she had been at his apartment and all she had been through. Her "perky" new appearance made him think she was either in shock or in pathological denial of all she had experienced.

He forced a smile in place and hid his reaction to her current state.

"You're all right, then?" asked Wes. "No one had heard from you and we were worried."

"I'm sorry," Fred said, apologizing. "The work that I'm doing here is just so amazing that I sorta got caught up in it, but I *promise* I'll call over to the hotel tonight."

"Great," said Wes softly. "So—what have you been working on over here?"

"Oh, it's amazing!" said Fred. "We're working on solving the gravitational anomalies of supersymmetry . . ."

Fred proceeded to talk in detailed technobabble that went over Wesley's head a few times.

Suddenly, with no warning at all, she looked away and said, "I guess this seems pretty weird, huh? My being here and kind of losing myself in all this stuff?"

That statement took him by surprise. He reacted honestly. "Actually, yes."

"I guess I'm hiding out." A smile flickered on her beautiful face, then faltered completely. "I should be helping out with all this craziness that's going on, I know that. To be honest, I don't know if I can handle it right now. But, look . . . you know where I am. If I can help, let me know, come get me. Is that okay?"

"Well, of course," Wes told her, not sure of what else to say. Goodness knows, there had been enough times in his life when the darkness around him had been so terrible that all he wanted to do was run and hide. It was a human reaction. In a way, it reassured him far more than her initial calm.

Twenty minutes later, Fred looked at her watch and rose abruptly.

"I've got to go now," Fred said hurriedly. "But I'll let you know if our theories are correct. Keep me in the loop with stuff, all right?"

Fred waved good-bye to Wes as she got back in the elevator to go to the lab, and Wes went back to the car where Connor was sitting on the hood.

"Well," said Connor curiously. "How did it go? Was she there? Is she okay?"

"Yes," Wes said, smiling. "I saw her, and she's fine."

"That's great. One problem solved."

"Unfortunately, we created a problem in order to solve one," Wes said uneasily.

"What problem's that?" asked Connor.

"We harassed a police officer for no reason," Wes said guiltily.

Connor just stared at him. "Yeah, so what's your point?"

"We have to make sure that he's not going to take action against us or Angel Investigations for what we did."

Wes's cell phone rang. He answered it and was surprised to hear Detective Moffat's voice on the other end. "Detective, I want to apologize—," Wes began.

"Save it," Moffat said gruffly. "A couple of my neighbors heard the racket. They just came over and let me out. Believe me, it wasn't easy to explain away."

"I see. And . . . are you considering pressing charges?"

"No. I'd never hear the end of it down at the station. What I *am* considering is how I don't want to see or hear from you people anymore. Pass the message on to all your friends, all right?"

"I'll tell the others," Wes said, and before he could add anything else, the line went dead.

Connor glanced at Wes. "So what do we do now?"

"The location of the next disturbance is near here," said Wes. "I'm going to drop you off there and then I have some business that I need to take care of on my own."

"That's okay," Connor said, nodding quickly. "I'm used to being abandoned."

Wes dropped Connor off at the location of the next disturbance and headed on to Lilah's condo. He felt miserable. He had been on a wild goose chase, worried that Fred was in some kind of danger, and it had turned out that she had just gotten a cool job. She needed a place where she could lose herself in the work, in the purity and rationality of science, and escape the chaotic terrors of the world. Still, just to cover all the bases, he would check out Norris thoroughly. He thought Lilah might have information, and decided to drop by her place before continuing to the seer's next destination.

Wes parked his car in the parking garage of Lilah's building and rode the elevator up to her floor. He walked quickly to Lilah's door and knocked. It took a few minutes before the lock turned from the inside and the door opened.

Lilah peeked her head outside and gazed at Wes. Her brunette hair was tousled, and her face gleamed with sweat. From what little he could see of the rest of her body, she had on one of her skimpiest negligees. Sounds came from inside her place. She was entertaining.

"Uh . . . I need to ask you something," said Wes.

"Sorry, lover—I'm kinda busy."

"But it's about—"

"Work can wait. You know how it goes. Raincheck, though. Kiss-kiss," Lilah said as she quickly closed and then locked her door.

Wes stood there for several long moments, remembering the way he had blown Lilah off at the warehouse a couple of days ago. He had wanted her to move on from their relationship. Now it seemed that she had, though the timing was hardly convenient.

Turning from her door, he considered the list he had acquired from the seer. There were monsters coming, and while he had coordinated an effort to control the situation, there was nothing like getting one's hands dirty.

Or, in this case—*bloody*.

CHAPTER THIRTEEN

Angel prowled the halls of the abbey, considering how to stop the shadowy assassin when his own shadow suddenly elongated, and raced a dozen feet away.

No, it hadn't been *his* shadow at all.

It was Nemesis.

Angel grabbed a torch from the wall mount and instinctively held it out before him. The living shadow darted and merged with others. Wherever he shone the torchlight, the shadow retreated and ended up elsewhere.

Angel tried to think of a way to fight the living shadow. It rose up before him, its body growing to twice his height, its egg-shaped head elongating, its jagged teeth stretching to the size of short-swords.

"You always kill the ones you love, vampire," Nemesis said. With a laugh, the shadow streaked down the corridor. Angel ran after it, horribly certain that he knew exactly where it was heading.

In a solitary chamber, a sharp blade descended in a silver streak that shredded the darkness. The blade was gripped by a young man with so much rage in his heart that he was overflowing.

A powerful hand caught the knife-wielder's arm and the tip of the blade was halted less than half an inch over the throbbing jugular of the sleeping man for whom it had been intended.

"Yah!" the boy cried in surprise and alarm.

"Don't think so," Angel said softly as he grabbed the youth. "Come on—let's have a little talk."

Angel dragged Logan out of his father's cell and anxiously surveyed the hallway. He had followed Nemesis to this room, where it had paused appreciatively in the partially open doorway, and then merged with a mass of shadows a dozen yards ahead.

Wondering what the creature had seen that had intrigued it so, Angel had doubled back—and had been just in time to prevent Logan from making the mistake of his young life. Angel took the blade from the boy and slipped it into the lining of his duster.

"That's a pretty nasty weight you would have been carrying around if no one had been there to stop you," Angel told the lad.

Logan's laugh was filled with contempt. "I would not have been punished. *You* would."

Angel was taken aback. "Okay, this works *how*, exactly?"

"As if you don't know, *Master* Kano," Logan said savagely. "Although, sometimes I think you don't. Your roommate's mad, and you're simply stupid. You must be an intuit, a mystical idiot savant. No wonder you're so reclusive. You don't want anyone to find out your secret, to understand what an imbecile—"

Angel grabbed the boy by the neck and hauled him up until they were at eye level.

"I'm talking now," Angel informed him. He trembled with rage and had to struggle to keep his vampire face from showing. This boy was so much like Connor, it nearly killed him. "Let me see if I've got this straight. You kill your old man, but I get blamed because I let you out of my sight, because I trusted you."

Logan grinned. "We are the eyes and ears of your enemies. That's what they always say about us acolytes."

"Not in this case."

"No," Logan admitted. "I could care less if you live or die, but that doesn't make me your enemy." He nodded toward the doorway, where his father slept. "My enemy's right in there."

"Why?"

Logan shook his head. "He won't give me what I want, what I'm entitled to."

"And what's that?" Angel asked.

The boy's eyes suddenly sparkled with dark, terrible magic. He smiled again. "Power."

Angel let Logan down, then hauled him down the corridor. He collected up Marco, then Daniel, and banged on the door where Archiel was being safeguarded.

"Take these three and keep an eye on them," Angel commanded the closest guard. "They can sleep on the floor, if need be, and they don't leave here until I say. Got it?"

The guardians smiled, and roughly dragged the youths inside.

Angel stood outside, his back to the wall, wondering which was worse: Nemesis, a creature that was little more than a wild beast acting on its predatory nature, or a boy who had a soul, had a choice, and was willing to put a knife in his father's neck for the sake of power.

Both seemed monstrous . . . and he would somehow have to deal with each of them.

Morning sunlight shone brightly in the halls as Gunn followed the winding corridor back to his cell. After a few moments' thought, he withdrew his scrolls and quickly went to work. There was only one person Gunn could think of who could make him as crazy as that Marekai dude, only one who was so . . . arrogant.

"Come on, Wes," Gunn said, scribbling away. "Time to play."

PAGE NINE

Gunn and Angel stand in a spacious and expensively appointed office, with marble floors and tall, elegant Roman-style pillars leading up to a two-story-high ceiling and a panoramic view of Los Angeles beyond. Wesley Wyndam-Pryce, in an expensively tailored suit, stands with his back turned to the two heroes. He looks out at the stormclouds and lightning strikes as he speaks.

ANGEL
Whuh-oh. Window.

WESLEY
Have no fear, little vampire. As you can see, it's an overcast day.

GUNN
Don't trust anything he says or does.

Laughing, Wesley turns to face them. He is wreathed by the furious storm outside.

WESLEY
Come now. You don't actually expect me to say dastardly and devilish things, now do you?

Gunn draws his sword.

GUNN
I expect you to tell me where my woman is.

Wesley smiles.

WESLEY
Lost track of her, have you?

Angel leans in close to Gunn, tugging a little on his sleeve.

ANGEL
Okay, you *did* leave yourself open for that one, you've gotta admit.

PAGE TEN
Gunn moves closer to Wes. They circle around his desk as they speak. Angel cowers in the background.

GUNN
You know what I'm talking about. I know what goes on here.

Wesley shrugs.

WESLEY
I run a respectable business. Pharmaceuticals, periodicals, produce. Anything that begins with the letter "P," come to think of it.

GUNN
Quit stallin'. I want answers. *Now.*

WESLEY
So you're here playing detective? Showing off your "big brain"?

GUNN
I don't have to show off for you . . . but, yeah. I had Lorne run a mystical trace on the sending I got. The one that said Fred was in danger. It led back to this place.

WESLEY
In danger . . .

Wes looks away, distracted. His arrogant facade slipping just a little. Is it an act? Maybe. Or could it be that he still has *some* human feeling left in him?

WESLEY
Your woman is missing. Now . . . which of your

"bitches" are we talking about? That *is* the technical term, yes?

GUNN
I'll gut you.

WESLEY
You will try. No, seriously. Is it the Asian American with black hair, red streaks, and amply enhanced bustline? The leggy Scandinavian? The hot saucy Latina from the French Quarter? The one who is so good with the sais and other—ah—pointy things?

GUNN
They come with the outfit and the job description. They don't mean anything to me, except as soldiers, and Fred knows that. Same with my boys.

WESLEY
Your boys are aware of this, or you also have your boys hanging lasciviously all over you when—

GUNN
That's it, dawg. Enough of this dancing around.

Wes's eyes brim with white-hot mystical energy.

WESLEY
As you wish.

PAGE ELEVEN

Full-page spread of Wes readying himself for battle. Lightning leaps from his body as he levitates, the palms of his hands open, even more mystical energies gathering within them.

GUNN

We were friends.

WESLEY

That's what makes us killing each other that much more poignant, don't you think?

Off to one side, Angel cowers like a frightened little lamb.

ANGEL

Why isn't the fake shrubbery big enough for me to hide behind? I just don't like this magic stuff. I bruise easily!

Scribbling away at his table, Gunn smiled at that one. He couldn't *wait* to see how Daniel would render these pages, and he also couldn't help but wonder how Angel would react if *he* ever saw them.

And *that* gave him an idea.

Angel and Bliss were alone in her room. It was nearly noon on the final day, and they had no leads to run down. Tonight, the ceremony would commence, and Angel still had no idea what Nemesis was planning, or where it was hiding.

"It could be anywhere," Angel said, careful not to look into the mirror on the other side of the room. "Anywhere there's darkness."

"You don't think we'd be aware of its presence?" Bliss asked.

Angel shook his head. "You know, I've been here three days and I don't feel like I've accomplished a damn thing."

Bliss leaned against an illusionary waterfall, smiling as she bathed in its sparkling stream. "You established the link between the first two victims that led us to Archiel in time. Marekai is now always kept in places where this shadow thing, Nemesis, cannot strike without revealing itself to many, something it apparently is not willing to do. Whatever its plan was, it's having to change it."

"I don't know about that," said Angel. "When we were fighting Nemesis, I noticed that it has one limitation. It can only use one power at a time. If it's in defensive mode, it can't launch an attack. When it's launching an attack, it's vulnerable. We've been able to hurt it but not kill it. I think it's playing us. I think it's playing everybody here."

Bliss sat on a marble bench that had suddenly appeared. "Why do you think that?"

"It let Rabbit go. It wanted to be seen. It wanted to send a message."

"I'm listening."

Angel paced agitatedly. "Okay, if it wanted to take down all of you the way it took down all of those people at the nightclub, it would have done that. If it wanted that and it was capable of it, this whole thing would have been over by now. By letting the boy live, it sent a signal that it wasn't capable of killing everyone—not that it didn't have the desire. That might not be true. Maybe it's being selective for a reason, and that reason has something to do with the ceremony tonight."

"But why attack any of us at all if it wants the ceremony to go on?"

"Maybe because it's planning on being a part of it, somehow. But it needs certain powers to pull off whatever its real game is."

"You think this is a game?"

Angel nodded. "For Nemesis? Yes. I think it's just as Machiavellian as any of you. It picked that up from one of the people at the nightclub if it didn't have it already."

"And from the mages it slew," Bliss reflected worriedly.

"Yeah, that probably didn't help."

Bliss looked up. "All you have are theories."

"I know."

"Theories that might or might not be correct."

"I *know*."

Rising to face him, Bliss put her hand on Angel's shoulder, keeping him still. "What course of action are you suggesting?"

"Find it. Kill it. Send it home in a box." Angel grimaced. "The question is *how*."

They were interrupted by a knock at the door. Bliss squinted, and seemed to see *through* the heavy door. "It is a servant of Logan's father," Bliss said. "He has come to tell you that the audience you both desire may now be granted."

Angel just looked at her. "You people can be kinda scary with your powers, do you know that?"

"Know it?" She grinned. "I thought that was the whole point."

Unlike many of the other chambers within the mystical abbey, the one assigned to Logan's father, the warrior mage known as Zeal, was as austere as Angel's cell. Zeal was a powerful-looking man with long, blond hair who looked and dressed much like an ancient Viking warrior. He glowered at Angel, displeased with the news Angel had delivered.

"Commenting on such affairs is highly irregular," Zeal said.

Angel was thunderstruck. "Yeah? Well, screw that. Your son is looking to *slit* your *throat*."

Zeal sighed heavily. "Of course."

"You knew that already," Angel declared, studying the man's pained, haunted expression. Zeal's anger was barely kept in check.

"I plotted against my father," Zeal said resignedly. "He against his father before him. All I want is for my son to prove worthy of the gifts I have to give him."

"Worthy by *your* standards?"

Zeal smiled—and the sight was chilling. "Oh, I see. You've made decisions about me and the relationship I have with my son based on little or no information."

Angel approached the stone table behind which Zeal was sitting and took a seat across from the man. "So tell me what's going on."

"Logan is my son," Zeal explained. "I love him and I will accept him no matter what he may think of me or what he might do. No, the standard I refer to is one set by more ancient and powerful sorcerers than myself. When I say worthy, I mean worthy by the standard that with great power comes even greater temptation; worthy meaning he won't be corrupted or destroy others. It *kills* me that I cannot give him what he wants."

"Your power."

"My power, my position, my 'kingdom' as he reckons it." Zeal's mouth twisted up in disgust. "How I loathe all of it and would have this burden lifted from me if only it could happen safely. But I must wait, and so must Logan, even though he has no desire to do so."

Angel ran his hand through his hair. "Last night—"

"Last night, that blade would have turned to dust the instant it touched my skin."

"You knew we were there," Angel said.

"I haven't slept in a century," Zeal practically chortled. "It is part of *my* curse. I must be ever vigilant. I must answer when I am called."

"So you're some big-time warrior?" Angel asked.

"I am a man bound by chains you cannot see."

"Where were you when Nemesis was attacking?"

"Here," Zeal said again. "Waiting to be called."

Angel didn't understand.

"Only Master Shanower or a consensus of the council may summon me. Otherwise, I am bound to this cell." Zeal shook his head. "When I was young, I bore my duty proudly. I lived for the days when I served my true purpose. Logan, I believe, may one day feel that way too. I pray every night that he will grow into the man he now believes himself to be. Yet . . . this is a matter of great sadness to me."

"I have a son too," Angel heard himself saying.

Zeal looked up. "There is much we wish to give them, yes? And yet, what can we do when they are not yet capable of receiving what they desire? And when they can't see what is clear to us. We become the villains."

Angel knew that, in Connor's eyes, that was

absolutely true. Perhaps that was why he felt so drawn to Logan . . . he saw his own son in the boy.

"But it worked out okay in the end, right?" Angel asked. "I mean, you went through this with your father, and you didn't just kill him and—"

Zeal cut him off. "This is not something I wish to discuss any longer."

Angel realized that he had pushed it too far. "To be honest," Angel said, "I thought all you wizards were the same."

"In ways, we are." Zeal leaned closer. "Don't be deceived by anything that anyone here tells you or shows you . . . not even me," he added laughing.

Fred walked uncertainly down a long corridor with no doors and only a single window in the distance. Barefoot and wearing a thin white shift, she had no idea where she was, or how she had gotten there.

She suddenly became aware that she was not alone in the corridor. Something rose from the darkness and flew at her. Her view of the light at the end of the corridor was obscured by whatever had just taken flight, though she could not make out anything more than a vague, large shape in silhouette and could not tell how far away it had been when it began its flight. She could hear the beating of leathery wings and a steady, high-pitched squeal that grew louder with each passing second.

Fred heard the squeal before her grow more intense, and she redirected her gaze to the corridor. The flying creature was almost upon her. By the dull, caressing glow reflected from the walls beside her, she caught a glimpse of the monster in the light. But before her mind could assimilate what she had seen, the creature was upon her and she was overcome by its hot, sweet breath, which smelled of honey.

She raised her hands to ward off the thing before her, but it did not attack. Instead, it hovered in place, studying her. She was surprised by the strange beauty of the monstrosity. It had four clear, colorless wings with the intricate designs of a butterfly. The creature's body was black and gold, shaped in segments, with dozens of tiny arms branching off, each with distinctly human hands. She looked up at the creature's face and saw a child with red eyes containing black, catlike slits. Its pouting Cupid lips suddenly drew back to reveal sharp, glimmering, carnivorous teeth.

Fred screamed—and the creature was upon her!

"Okay, why does she keep doing that?" Lilah asked as she gestured at the woman lying on the cot before her, who was convulsing, straining at her bonds, and biting down hard on the bit in her mouth, the fiberglass helmet covering most of her head and making dull slapping sounds against her pillow. Cables as thick as a man's wrist led off from the helmet to a machine that was half the size of the room. Technicians monitored the woman's blood pressure and other vitals at all times.

"The twitching around?" the man in charge of the operation asked. "Well, right now, she is tackling a complex, nearly impossible mathematical conundrum that has defeated every great mind of the last century. However, she is wrestling with it on a metaphysical as well as theoretical level. From the looks of her reactions, she has found a way to visualize the dilemma, a frightfully nasty one, and she's doing her best not to be skinned alive by it."

On the cot, Winifred Burkle settled down. Lilah saw a string of equations suddenly appear on the flat-screen monitor of the computer a few feet away, a machine that was connected to all the weird tech the guys here at Norris had dreamed up.

The equation went on for 1,103 screens full of text.

"Good," the man said. "Now we'll let her rest, then set her to work on the next big problem we're facing. We should have the gateway system that we've talked about ready in plenty of time."

Lilah nodded. Thousands of doorways to forbidden worlds, all hers to regulate, and to charge fees for using.

Glorious.

"As we discussed, I wasn't thrilled with running the process again so soon," the man said. "The effects were unpredictable. We might have torn open a dimensional door in this room and all became demon food."

"Blah, blah," Lilah said. "All I care about is the stick of asparagus here. Can she see or hear us?"

"Of course not."

"Good. I hadn't really intended on things going this route with her, although now I see that you did, great master planner that you are."

He smiled. "I have my moments."

"Just in case, though, I don't want her to have any knowledge of my involvement in this, any memory of my visit here."

"Again, not a problem."

Lilah tilted her head to look at Fred more closely. "What exactly *are* you doing to her? Ultimately, I mean."

"I'm freeing her mind," the man said, "in a way no one's mind has ever been freed before."

Lilah nodded. As she said, she hadn't *meant* for harm to come to the stringbean. She'd always worried that Wes would somehow find a way to blame her if something happened to Fred, even something with which she wasn't even remotely connected.

On the other hand, a world without Fred . . . there were worse things.

"Carry on," Lilah said brightly. "And give me a call when it's all over."

Turning, she left the lab, feeling the kind of happiness inside that she hadn't felt in a very long time.

CHAPTER FOURTEEN

Angel returned to his quarters and was *stunned* to find the array of scrolls that Charles had left behind. He quickly read the story they told, then detected the scent of his companion as the man stood in the hallway, then entered the room and quietly shut the door behind himself.

"Now see, that's more like it, don't ya think?" Gunn asked. "A hero readers can relate to, and his bumbling sidekick for comic relief."

Angel faced him. "You didn't draw these pages."

"Naw, that was Daniel."

"Wait a minute," Angel said, incredulous. "This kid knew *everything*? And you didn't think that was worth mentioning."

"I trusted him," Gunn said levelly.

"Yeah, like I trusted you to not go off and do something stupid."

Gunn circled the vampire. "Something stupid . . . I do that a lot, is that right?"

"Don't put words in my mouth."

"Feels like the only way they're gonna get there."

Angel went back to the pages. "Fine. This *is* stupid."

"I thought this kid needed somebody he could talk to," Gunn said earnestly. "Someone who would really listen, whom he could trust."

"I mean that you did this at all . . . and that you left it where people could find it."

Gunn threw his hands up. "Fine, well that's *me*, isn't it? Just the muscle. Don't have a brain in my head."

"Come on," Angel said in warning. "Are we going to do this now? I promise you, it won't be fun."

"Naw, man. We're not going to do anything. We're just going to let it go, just like we always do."

"All right, that's it," Angel said, shoving over the hard wood table as if it were little more than a stage prop, causing the scrolls to fly up into the air, the bottle of ink to smash against the far wall. Earlier, Gunn had tried for ten minutes to move the heavy table even a few inches to give himself more work room, and had failed. "Tell me, Gunn. What is your problem?"

"What's yours?"

Angel snatched one of the scrolls from the air as it lazily drifted back to the floor. "I don't know." Angel held up one of the more pitiful versions of himself from the comic book. "Is *this* how you see me? How you'd *like* to see me? Just—all cut down to size or whatever? *Why?*"

"It was just a goof, we were just—"

Angel slammed his fist into the wall so hard that he left a crater. Dust and rock drifted down next to Gunn's head.

"We don't have time for this now," Gunn said quietly.

Angel advanced on him. "I think we're going to have to make time. I need to know that I can trust you. Need to know that your head is in the game and not up your ass."

"Oh, that's it," Gunn said, his heart racing, the fight he was burning for now before him. "That's exactly what I was saying."

They circled each other. "Come on," Angel offered. "First shot's free. After that, you're paying for it. With interest."

Gunn smiled. "Well, if you put it like that."

Ducking down in a blur, Gunn snatched up a chunk of stone that had been dislodged from the wall and threw it at the nearest darkened window. It shattered, allowing shafts of brilliant sunlight to stab into the room, every one of them directed at Angel. The vampire leaped out of the way, rolled once, and came up in a crouch in the shadows. Then, slowly, Angel emerged from the darkness, his hand touching the light.

It didn't burn.

"See, that's just it," Gunn said. "In your head, you know the sunlight isn't going to burn you, not with all those hexes they put on you. But what's the first thing you do?"

"Run," Angel said.

"Right. 'Cause, in your heart, you know this isn't right, you know it can't last."

"Your point being?"

"Point is, we made a deal," Gunn told him. "I wasn't joining your crew. I wasn't just another name on the books. We were supposed to do this together, as partners. That's not how it's been. Not lately. There's one thing being said, another thing being done. It's like knowing one thing in your head, but feelin' something else in your heart."

Angel scratched his head and looked away. "Two people can't drive one car at one time."

"Excuse me?"

"Something Howard Hawks told me once. A movie guy. He meant that someone has to lead."

"And that means someone has to follow. How come it's always you taking charge?"

"Hey," Angel said, "*Wes* had the agency for a good, long time—"

"This isn't about you and him, it's about you and

me. It's about you trusting me to do more than back you up in the tight scrapes. Sometimes I need *you* backing *me* up."

"I tried that with Marekai two days ago and *you* told me to back off. What is it you *want*, Charles?"

Gunn hesitated, the fight draining out of him. "I want to know I'm making a difference."

Angel thought of Zeal, trapped in his cell, waiting to be called upon so that he could unleash his power. Then Angel recalled the words Bliss had spoken so many times around him: *my penitent.*

Time moved so very differently for Angel. The idea of waiting in the darkness until he was needed, of knowing that he was making no movement that might somehow bring harm to others, was a comforting one to him. But to someone like Zeal . . . or Gunn . . . it was a nightmare.

He had inflicted a nightmare upon his friend and hadn't even been remotely aware that anything was wrong.

Angel looked down at the drawings. "The kid's good."

"He is. But his father wants him to fulfill some big destiny. He doesn't care what he wants."

Angel thought of Logan and the fierceness in the boy's murderous eyes. "No compromise, no middle ground?"

"Not the way the old man sees it."

Angel looked genuinely impressed. "You actually

got one of these kids to talk to you? And listen?"

"Yeah."

"Then let me tell you something," Angel said sincerely, "you *are* making a difference."

They talked for close to an hour, comparing notes on the case and finally coming up with a plan to see if one of their many theories might just be the right one. Then Angel gestured at the renderings lying about. "Gunn, you understand . . . all this has to be burned. If I found it, someone else could too. We've already got enough problems with our cover."

"I hear that."

Angel glanced at the cowering version of himself. "I'm not *that* dorky."

"Naw, man. You think I'd partner up with some complete loser. I was just ticked off, that's all."

After Angel left, Daniel entered, anxious to draw more pages. Gunn gave him the news, which the lad took with the same air of resignation that he greeted so many things.

"I've got an idea, though," Gunn told him. "That magic you guys were talking about the first day we were here . . . pulling things apart, unbinding them . . ."

"Unmaking them," Daniel ventured.

"Yeah. Could you undo it again, later? I mean, remake something you've pulled apart?"

"Sure."

"All right," Gunn said, looking at the comic book pages, "here's what we need to do. . . ."

That afternoon, Angel and Gunn walked along the very same courtyard in which Bliss had fought her "battle" with the strange creature days earlier. The acolytes were with them: Daniel, Logan, and Marco. All three were as moody as could be. Bliss followed behind at a comfortable distance, ready to work her magic when the need arose.

Daniel stopped as he spotted his father and two of his warriors clustered in a nearby shadowy alcove. Their eyes met—and Daniel saw Nemesis rise from the darkness. Sharp, black claws sprang from the vaguely manlike nightmarish form.

"Father!" Daniel screamed.

But it was too late. There was no prolonged battle this time, no further taunts or warning of an attack. The shadow creature struck at Purefoy, its hand darting through his chest. The man's eyes widened, his body buckled, and he fell.

Then the shadow merged back into the darkness and was gone.

Angel looked to the sky. Nemesis only struck at the time of deepest night. But now it was the opposite of that time, the brightest day.

Which meant it *was* darkest night somewhere else in this dimension.

Dozens raced to Purefoy, who lay still and dead,

his warriors gathered around him in shock. Bliss and several other healers did their best to revive him, but it was too late. She looked to Angel in confusion, and he nodded. They would discuss this soon privately. Nemesis, it seemed, had either outwitted them from the start by leading them to believe he was after certain mages when this one was his true target, or the creature had changed its tactics because the other possible victims were too well guarded. In any case, Angel felt as if he had failed.

"Purefoy was the keeper of the pattern," a high-level mage said. "How can the ceremony proceed if he is—"

Daniel touched his father's cold face, his hands trembling. "What he knew, I know," the teenager revealed. "I am the seventh son of a seventh son. I have his power, if not his experience. All I've lacked, until now, is the proper motivation to use it."

Gunn shook his head. "But you wanted to be an artist."

"I will be," Daniel assured him gravely. "In a way."

There was no pleasure in Daniel's eyes as he beheld the prospect, no hint of anything but a cold, savage sense of satisfaction as he contemplated revenge.

"My father gave me the means to seek my freedom," Daniel said, "and he did so in the only way he knew how, the only way in which he would not lose his station and still be able to protect me if I went down a path of my own choosing, defying tradition. What seemed like an act of hate . . . wasn't. I won't rest until I stop this thing. And the only way I can do that is to fulfill my destiny."

Close by, Logan stared at the scene in horror. Just last night he had thought to take his father's life to gain the man's power. Now Daniel, whom he had never even liked or respected, had gained exactly what Logan *thought* he wanted. The age-old phrase "Be careful what you wish for" ran through Logan's mind, making him consider everything his teacher had been telling him about his ambitions.

Breaking from the side of his friend Marco, Logan raced to Daniel and put his hand on the boy's shoulder. He bowed his head in a gesture of servitude and obedience. "You can't do this alone."

One of the dreadlocked warriors who had been with Purefoy said, "He won't be alone. As I served his father, so shall I serve—"

"Yeah, and look where it got him," Logan said.

"I don't understand," Daniel said. "Why would you want to help me? What's in it for you?"

The other lad took a long time answering. Finally Logan answered, "I . . . nothing."

"The funny thing is," Daniel said, his voice hard, "I *believe* you."

Logan was about to say something when Daniel raised his hand to cut him off.

"Just don't get in the way," Daniel told him.

Together, they left the killing ground, Angel studying them carefully while he looked around for signs of the shadowy killer.

Early that evening, Angel was alone with Shanower in the head wizard's chamber. Preparations were now fully underway for the ceremony at midnight.

"The beast is still loose," Shanower said gravely. "Three of our number have now perished, giving it power almost beyond belief."

"But the ceremony goes on," Angel observed.

"It must. What choice do we have?"

Angel paced about the chamber. "The worst thing is, I think there is either someone or something who's working directly with this thing or, at the very least, wants to see it succeed with its plan."

"Ridiculous," Shanower said angrily. "Why would any of us do such a thing?"

"You said it yourself: power."

Shanower glowered at the vampire. "Whom do you suspect?"

"I don't know," Angel said, shaking his head. "There are just too many possibilities right now. I have to narrow down the choices."

"In my experience, there is usually a simple and elegant solution to such seemingly complex riddles."

"Yeah, well I'm open to—"

Sss-shunk!

Angel gasped and looked down. He hadn't seen the wooden stake that had been in Shanower's hand until it was lodged deep in his heart. The identity of Nemesis's ally was now painfully clear.

"You?" Angel said with a final gasp, reaching for his murderer.

"Me," the head mage replied matter-of-factly.

Angel threw his head back and screamed as his body burst into an explosive shower of ashes.

Shanower brushed a few stray ashes from his robe and willed the stake, the murder weapon—if murder was the correct term when it came to an undead thing like an ensouled vampire—out of existence.

"You've more than served you're purpose, Angel," Shanower said softly. "The council was divided before you came along. Having you amongst us gave them something to think about beyond Nemesis, and held our ranks together so that the ceremony tonight *will* proceed . . . albeit with a few surprises. Enjoy the peace I have given you, creature."

Shanower laughed. "Enjoy it well."

Wes launched himself, sword swinging, at the latest in a long line of creatures he had battled today.

This one resembled a shark that had adapted to land. It was gray, ten feet tall, with two muscular legs and two primary fins that were elongated and curved to look like arms. Of course, these arms also had razor-sharp blades along their edges.

The shark creature easily batted away Wes's attempt to pierce its tough hide.

Wes was tired and in no mood to fight this abomination so hard. No, this was simply *not* going as planned. He had been fighting this creature for over an *hour,* and it showed no signs of weakness.

Breathing hard, Wes glared at the monstrosity. The creature just stood there in the middle of the parking lot of an abandoned strip mall, then, with contempt, sat itself down on the roof of a derelict car. Wes heard the metal straining under the great weight of the beast. This creature was not going anywhere, and it had already declared its antisocial intentions by eating two homeless people just as he arrived.

Traffic had been hell, otherwise, he would have been there sooner.

There was only one thing left to do: use the "holy hand grenade." Or, in this case, a mystical hand grenade. He was hoping not to resort to this kind of weapon, but his sword had proved useless and he couldn't think of any other options. At least there weren't any other people around the abandoned mall to get injured in the explosion. Wes just had to hope that the creature didn't move before he could get into position.

He took out a cobalt sphere from his pocket, whispered the grenade's "pin-number," a minor conjuring, and chucked it at the land shark. The moment the grenade left his hands, the Englishman turned and ran for the safety of the strip mall. The grenade landed in the driver's seat of the smashed-up car. Wes had just enough time to slip behind a huge concrete pillar and then the grenade went off.

Car and shark debris flew in every direction. From behind the pillar, Wes saw pieces of the car's dashboard and the shark's fins fly past him and smash into the front window of an empty card shop. Several bits of debris hit the other side of the pillar.

When everything seemed to have settled, Wes came out and surveyed his work. The entire parking lot was covered in debris, and he was glad that he wouldn't have to clean up the mess. At that moment, his cell phone rang. Answering it, he was surprised to hear Cordy's voice on the other end.

"Wes? Is that you?"

"Hello, Cordelia," said Wes. "How can I help you?"

"Remember Detective Moffat?" asked Cordy.

"Actually, I'm trying to forget him," said Wes, exhausted.

"Well, here's the funny part, and we're not talking

funny 'ha-ha.' I tried to reach Detective Moffat today and he wasn't around. Know why?" Cordy asked, bemused.

"No idea."

"He was on the firing range, practicing."

Wes still didn't see her point. "That's normal enough."

"I thought so, too, until the cop I was speaking with made a joke out of it and told me what Moffat's nickname is. Ready for this?"

"Um . . . fire away?"

"Deadshot," Cordy said earnestly. "I pulled his firing range results, and he's got one of the best records in the department. He also used to be in the military: special ops, closed file, but plenty of citations for marksmanship going back to when he first joined up."

"Alicia was killed by a single shot through the heart," Wes said worriedly, seeing it all coming together now. "A perfect killshot."

"Yeah, and when Otakun and his supposed shooter got clipped at the same time, Moffat was off-duty. I'm sure he's got some bought-and-paid-for alibi, but—"

"Thank you, Cordelia," Wes said, his mind racing. "I think I understand the situation."

He thought back to how Fred had not quite seemed herself at first, but then she had recovered and explained away her odd behavior. In truth, the reason for her behavior could easily have been that she was under a spell of some kind, or it might not have been Fred he had spoken with at all. There were shapeshifters all over Los Angeles, or someone skilled enough in the mystic arts could have created a doppelgänger of Fred for their brief encounter.

"Get Connor for me, will you?" Wes asked Cordy. "I think we have a situation he'll quite enjoy taking on."

Angel gasped—and was reborn.

He sat upon the small cot in his quarters, surrounded by Gunn, Bliss, and Ord. Bliss touched his face, working her arcane energies into his body, his mind, his soul . . . healing him as best she could.

"So that's what it's like to have a 'sending,'" Angel whispered, his body still convulsing from the shock of having his consciousness split between two physical forms—one of which had just been destroyed. "Never again."

"We heard your conversation with Shanower," Bliss said gravely. "It seems you were right to suspect him."

"No way is he alone in this," Gunn added. "My money's on Archiel, and maybe those women guarding the place."

"Why Archiel?" Bliss asked.

Gunn listed his reasons: "Power over the earth. The ways those rock corridors kept twisting and turning, keeping us lost until he was ready for us to find him, then that scream to make *sure* we'd be drawn in the right direction, which only the right people heard, it turned out . . . and that fight with Nemesis wasn't like any other time that thing went after people. It doesn't waste time. It usually pulls quick, surgical strikes. But, with Archiel, it put on a show. And Archiel's the only one who survived against it."

"They must have made some kind of deal with Nemesis," Angel decided.

Gunn shook his head. "Shanower, though . . . he was the one who wanted us here in the first place."

"And look how much concern that caused with the council members. Everyone was watching us—" Angel started.

Gunn finished the notion. "Instead of him."

"It put more attention on Nemesis, too, and suggested something was being done about it, so the other wizards didn't run off."

"What do you think he's after?" Bliss asked.

"He laid it out for us right in the beginning," Angel said. "I'm betting that, in the right circles, which is where he wants to be, it's considered an embarrassment that the Powers That Be still have to directly interfere to keep us on track, that we still have to be guided like children. If this threat turned out to be real, and humans were the only ones who had believed in it from the beginning, the only ones who tried to make a difference, the whole balance of power would change. Humanity would move up—way up—on the magical food chain. Everybody else would have to take us seriously from then on."

"Yeah, and the only way that can happen is if the ceremony fails," Gunn added. "And that'll turn our world and a couple of million others into a hell dimension. At least for a while."

"We're talking about billions of people and . . . other things . . . dying in just the first few days," Bliss observed.

"Right," Angel said. "But not the wizards."

Gunn nodded. "So that's the game. How do we stop it?"

Ord finally spoke up. "There's a flaw. A structural weakness in this place. I know exactly where it resides."

"So this flaw would allow passage, communication between this place and our world?" Angel asked.

"Yes," Ord told him.

"The pathway is being used now?" Bliss asked.

"Oh yes, but it's well hidden, well guarded."

Angel stared at the mage. "You seem . . . I dunno. Different."

Ord shuddered. "Ah. Yes. That is the rewarding

thing about being thought mad. You can go anywhere, do anything, ask any questions, and no one
thinks of you as a threat. Shanower, you see, used
you as misdirection. So did I."

"So," Angel said, picking up his sword, "you two
project a couple of 'sendings' to take your place at
the ceremony . . . and then let's find the hidden
room and see if we can't end this thing before it's
too late."

Wes and Connor dove for cover from the bullets
that were flying toward them in a couple of the
white freestanding cubicles in the computer lab.
They had already fought past the security guards
and the development team who were unconscious
on the floor. Now they had a bigger problem to
deal with. Detective Moffat was on the other side
of the huge white lab, standing before a doorway
from which a blinding white light was escaping.

"He must be protecting that entrance," Wes said
to Connor, who was in the next cubicle over. "I'm
willing to wager that's where Fred is being kept.
The problem is, he's a deadshot. How are we going
to get past him?"

"You leave that to me," said Connor. The lad
turned and leaped onto the top of the computer
desk that was behind him in the cubicle. He then
used his enhanced speed and agility to jump from
computer desk to computer desk in a blur. Moffat

fired at the boy but could barely even see him, never mind hit the target.

Wes watched in surprise as Connor at one point stopped his movements. The young man stared directly into the cop's eyes, winked at him, and then was a blur of constant motion once more. Angrily, Moffat shouted something in a language Wes had never heard before. Suddenly, a collection of nasty skittering sounds came from all around. Wes stole a quick look around the cubicle and saw a swarm of onyx scorpions the size of Dobermans coming from Moffat's direction, as if the cop had summoned the creatures. Wes also saw that Detective Moffat's jacket had fallen open and a mystical medallion was hooked to Moffat's belt, an item that was bound to be connected in some way to the scorpions. They needed to smash that thing! Wes searched his clothes and found a single knife in his pocket. He took aim and determined that it was too far for him to accurately hit the target. But he knew someone who could.

"Connor, take this," Wes shouted as he threw Connor the knife. "Aim for the medallion on his belt. Not his heart. We don't know what other spells of protection that he might have."

Connor nodded to Wes. He hefted the knife and threw it with expert aim. The blade spun end over end in the air, and the handle smashed the medallion on Moffat's belt.

There was a sound like a thousand screams as the medallion was destroyed.

Just as the onyx scorpions were about to launch at Wes and Connor, they stopped, turned, and raced back toward Moffat. They swarmed him, covering him with their stingers. Wes heard his dying screams from inside the mass of black scorpions as they quickly ate him alive and then faded from existence.

Wes and Connor rose, looked at each other, and walked over to the entrance.

"That was fun," Connor said, letting out a deep breath. "Let's see what's next."

They passed through the doorway into the brilliant white light.

The abbey was awash with light. Hundreds of sorcerers gathered at the perimeter of the vast jade meeting hall. They waited patiently, many taking in its wonders for the first time. A handful of mages had seen this place in dreams. Some had called it the hall of the slain. It was said to have 540 doors, each so wide that 800 mages could walk side by side. Images of battles fought long ago were carved into the ivory walls. The roof was made of golden shields.

Even the acolytes and the sorcerers' assistants were present, though Daniel and Logan did not stand with them.

They were with the great mages.

"Are you ready for this?" Logan asked Daniel.

"Sure," Daniel said somewhat unconvincingly, which didn't seem to inspire much confidence in Logan.

Shanower stood in the center of the room with the other mages around him in a semicircle. Zeal, Logan's father, stood to Shanower's right.

The head mage raised his arms. "It is time."

Daniel was brought forward. He knew what he had to do. This vast chamber had to be transformed into the proper arena for the energies that would be tapped into and released this night. Tapping into the collective power the assembled mages had placed at his disposal, he tried to imagine the place they would need. He had already seen its wonders in his dreams.

There would be no walls, no boundaries, Daniel decided.

(The walls of the chamber began to melt away.)

The River Lethe itself, which held the healing waters of all infinity, would run through this place.

(Shimmering streams came into view around him in labyrinthine configurations.)

There would be places of amusement and challenge. He imagined massive coliseums and theaters made of glass.

(The constructs rose about him.)

Closing his eyes, Daniel felt as if he were walking upon the air, his body changing, its strange fires pulsing with a power and a majesty that was not to be denied. The room started to change. The walls vanished into a mist. The ceiling began to glow a golden color, and patterns of light and colors appeared in the air. The patterns slowly started transforming into the shapes of buildings with many doors. The air was filled with the crackling of static electricity.

Suddenly, everything changed. He felt control slide away in a heartbeat, an emerald lattice rippling out from him, releasing an ugly, brutish sight: A series of ziggurats climbing on the shoulders of one another in a vain attempt to reach the heavens. The stars themselves appeared, only to scream and catch fire—

"No!" Daniel screamed, releasing his hold on the magic and dropping to his knees as Logan rushed forward to steady him.

The proper arena had not been created, and that had been the simplest of tonight's tasks.

"We will wait a few minutes for the boy to recover and then we will try again," said Shanower with determination.

A murmur went through the crowd of sorcerers.

The shadow of Nemesis rose from among the crowd of observing sorcerers. It came forward and stood before Shanower and the other mages.

"The boy will fail again," stated Nemesis. "You know I speak the truth."

"It's because of you that we are even having to use a boy," Marekai yelled, stepping forward to confront Nemesis.

Shanower put an arm in front of the mage to hold him back.

The other mages and their followers looked at one another in confusion. "What is this thing? What business does it have here?"

Shanower ignored them.

"I offer you a deal," Nemesis said confidently.

"Go on," said Shanower.

"I have the powers and memories of Purefoy, who knew how to perform the ceremony," reminded Nemesis. "I can help you complete the ceremony, but there is a price."

"What price is that?"

"My people are starving," said Nemesis. "I will help you restore the walls between worlds *if* you allow my people to pass freely among all the worlds so that they can feed and survive. All the other dark dimensions, what you call the 'dark-matter' universes, will be cut off once more."

"No deal," shouted Marekai.

Nemesis turned to the man. "I suppose you would rather that, instead of having a few of my kind roaming around, you will have thousands upon thousands of every kind of demon and monster passing through to this and every other dimension whenever they please."

Marekai said nothing in response to this statement.

"The choice is yours," said Nemesis evenly. "Either I help and my people cull your herds, or you have death and destruction on a scale that will mean an end to all any of you have ever dreamed of for yourselves."

Shanower nodded to Nemesis. "I agree to your terms."

CHAPTER FIFTEEN

Ord had led Angel, Gunn, and Bliss through a series of twisting corridors, each section of which required a complex series of runes drawn upon its surface and spells pronounced in its presence before it allowed the next bit of branching corridor to appear. Finally, they had come to the room Ord had discovered—only to find the way blocked by Archiel himself.

"Still alive, vampire?" Archiel said, vexed. "I did mention to you once before, I believe, that we mages are not *all* alike." He smiled, and the walls began to shudder. "Some of us, you see, are far *worse* than others."

Ord took the lead. "Archiel, you metal-headed nit. I just want you to know that I have *never* liked you."

Archiel opened his mouth to speak, but he was too late. The crimson sphere Ord had suddenly brought into being behind his back was flung at the darksome mage. It sailed in Archiel's direction and exploded on contact, enveloping the sorcerer.

Angel saw a vague shadow that had been Archiel, then the light faded quietly and Archiel stood, unharmed, but clearly annoyed.

"That was impolite," Archiel said with a grin. His eyes burst into flame, and he raised his hands to gesture, but before he could release a single incantation, Ord struck again. Ord blew slightly, and a creature made of vapor with talons branching out from its arms and legs streaked across the distance separating it from Archiel. The monstrosity doubled in size as it reached him, then seemingly vanished. It took Archiel a moment to understand that he had had actually *breathed in* the vapors. He fell to his knees, hands reaching up, eyes rolling into his sockets, as very loud crunching sounds came from somewhere within him. Dropping to the ground, he shuddered with indescribable agony.

The burning mage writhed and spun himself over on the ground, his hands clasping together as if in prayer.

"Bother!" Ord said. He put his hand out, clasped it into a fist, and the burning Archiel collapsed into a pile of ashes.

"How do we know that's not just a double?" Gunn asked.

"This one had a soul," Ord told him. "I can smell such things."

Bliss surged forward, tore at the door before them, and hauled it open, engulfing them all in a blinding explosion of pure white light, heat, and roaring wind!

"Okay, this is different," Connor said as a gust of wind blew his hair out of his face, then subsided. He and Wes stood upon the roof of a great abbey that was situated somewhere in the middle of nowhere.

Truly *nowhere*.

Wes looked out of the abbey's reaches and glimpsed Los Angeles as a city of madness. In another moment, he was granted a vision of a gigantic torch being tossed down through a rend in the sky, engulfing the city with its flames. And far above, the horizon was reshaped into the form of a cobalt dragon, who spread his wings and marked this place as his dominion.

"None of it's real," Connor said shakily.

"Oh, I think all of it is real enough," Wes amended. "The question is simply if it has anything to do with *our* reality. We can only pray that it does not."

A group of warrior women stood near a great tower upon which an ancient sigil had been drawn in emerald-and-gold flames.

"The abbey and the lab are connected," Wes said, almost to himself. "Whatever Fred has been forced to work on must have something to do with the ceremony taking place here tonight. They're probably looking to take the energies released and use them for their own ends."

"That, or they're all scum and they're working together," Connor suggested. "I mean, those Amazon women don't seem happy to see us."

The warrior women, two dozen in all, turned to look at the newcomers—and the closest of them *changed*.

One moment the woman looked like a Valkyrie from ancient myth—then her true face and form were revealed. Connor stared at the demon witch in wonder. She was beautiful beyond belief. Her flesh was dark blue, almost black. A wealth of eyes stole up and down her arms, legs, and flank. They blinked rapidly, vanishing from existence as they did so, only to reappear in other places upon her magnificent form. Her hair was alive, reaching down to the ground and groping in every direction.

Gossamer veils, shimmering plates of armor hid much of her body, and a collection of weapons forged from black steel and adorned with rubies hovered within her reach at any time. She smiled. Her teeth were sharp.

"Ever kiss a woman?" she asked. Laughing, talons exposed, she launched herself at him, not bothering to wait for an answer. "Now you never will!"

Connor met her attack, Wes moving forward to fight at his side.

In a strange way, Connor was comforted by conflict and carnage.

It was what he did best.

Archiel was dead, and Angel was bathed in his blood. The sigils of binding, the mystical runes that had been painted onto his flesh, kept Angel's bloodthirst at bay, despite the fresh splattering of the life-giving fluid.

Bliss turned back to the doorway and continued to struggle toward the blinding white light ahead. Ord and Gunn were behind her.

Angel rested his palm on the jamb of the white doorway, shielding his eyes from the glare with his free hand. The waves of force no longer felt like a lover's caress; now they were the raking talons of a demon.

Angel stepped into the room, his eyes adjusting to the harsh light. Shanower's hidden lair, where he had breached the gap between the trans-dimensional space in which the rest of the abbey existed and Earth itself did not appear to exist solely on the material plane.

Twelve identical "sendings" of Winifred Burkle were at the core of the swirling mass of confusion, a dozen perfect replicas of the young woman sitting

cross-legged in a circle, hands linked. Only—
Angel had a sense that one of them was real, but
the terrible magics Shanower had unleashed were
dulling his senses, making it hard to tell which she
might be.

A column of swirling bluish-white light rose up
at the apex of the room, leading up to a cyclone
that grew in diameter until it filled the sky far
above: the walls, floors, and ceiling were gone. All
around, the many Freds were constantly shifting
images that seemed to be ripped from the memories of a multitude of people. Men and women
made love, others murdered one another, children
were born, people wept in disappointment over
love or money—portraits of envy and greed were
matched by scenes of unbelievable kindness and
charity. The images were contained on large cubes
that had been pressed together to form a surface
for Fred and her many sendings to sit upon.
Beneath the first layer were a half dozen more, all
receding in size, until they vanished.

Beneath them lay an endless white abyss. Angel
looked down and saw that he was standing on one
of the cubes.

When he instinctively stepped from it, another
formed beneath him.

"Angel!"

The vampire looked up and saw Shanower
standing behind one of the Freds, presumably the

real one, a tangle of brown hair flowing from his left hand. He was holding her up by the hair, a knife to her throat. Fred's head lolled from side to side, but her eyes were closed.

Tentatively, Angel walked to the circle where Shanower and Fred waited, the cubes winking in and out of existence to create a bridge for him to cross.

Shanower sighed. "You know, when I kill things, I actually expect them to stay dead. I suppose, in my arrogance, I should have sniffed that duplicate you sent to see if it had a soul or not."

"It happens," Angel said.

"Look at you," the wizard said. "You're covered in blood. Hardly a state that befits a champion and savior."

"Let her go," Angel commanded.

The sorcerer laughed. "I intend to. I have been working very hard, in fact, to free her mind from the unfortunate constraints of the flesh. You see, I'm known as many things in many places. Here, I am the head mage, called Shanower. At Norris Industries, I have another name and title altogether. Dividing my time between these two lives has been something of a drain, but worth it, I expect. Right now, my 'second self' is at the ceremony itself."

"You don't want to shore up the walls between the worlds at all, do you?" Angel growled.

"I do, actually, but with a catch. While restoring

the walls, I intend to create a series of doors that only I can control. Those doors will make me the most powerful being in all of existence. The problem has been subverting the will of so many mages, bending their work to my specific ideas. This is where science plays a role. I can't control so many minds at once. But, with the right technology, I can divert and reshape the outcome of their efforts."

"That's why Fred's here," Angel said.

"She's quite brilliant, you know, but she wastes her thoughts on matters of no real consequence. If she were nothing *but* thought, a living, thinking, *machine*, her potential would become limitless."

The others burst into the room. Gunn hollered Fred's name and had to be held back by Ord and Bliss.

"That's not the real Fred," Angel told him.

"Are you sure?" Shanower asked. "If you are, I'll go ahead and slit her throat. To achieve my ends, her corporeal form must perish ultimately, so it's a win-win for me. If you're *not* so certain, I would advise standing down and letting the natural and unnatural order of things unfold as destiny itself has foretold."

Angel seethed inwardly; this guy was certifiable, but Angel couldn't take the chance. He stepped back.

"You know what the funny part is?" another of the Freds asked, looking up from her "trance" state and smiling. "*He* actually thinks that's the real me, but it's not. He grabbed the wrong one."

Shanower stared at her blankly. "*What?*"

Fred stood up, yanking her hands out of the grip of the doppelgängers flanking her, and the moment that contact between the twelve Freds was lost, the magical circuit severed, everything in the room began to change.

For a time, the ceremony had proceeded as planned, despite the addition to their ranks of the creature that had killed Daniel's father. Remaining quiet, not challenging Shanower's decision, had been one of the hardest things Daniel had ever done. But his instincts, which Gunn had urged him to trust, were screaming at him to hold back, to wait for his moment.

Now it had arrived. He could see the pattern of creation that was being formed as the mages chanted and loosed their incredible power. A "City of Doorways" was coming into being even as the walls between worlds were shorn up. Thousands of doorways were being chiseled into those walls, and no one but Daniel was able to see it.

"You should have killed me, too," Daniel whispered as he looked upon Nemesis, which wielded his father's great power. Then it all started to fall apart. Even before Daniel could act, the doorways were faltering, closing up one by one. Sealing themselves up, never to be opened again.

Daniel sensed another will at work here, another mind controlling what was happening.

The mind of a woman.

Winifred.

Good. That left him free to deal with the *thing* that had taken his father's life.

Daniel turned to Logan. "Do you have any of the power they granted your father?"

"Some."

"And do you really want to help?"

Logan nodded.

"Create a sword of pure light," Daniel said, gazing at Nemesis. "We have a shadow in our way. . . ."

In the white room, the momentarily startled Shanower gestured and a wall of pure force slammed into Fred, tossing her back. More of the strange cubes winked into existence, keeping her from plunging into the depths below. Then they lifted her up, and tendrils of force suddenly wove themselves into the air between Shanower and Fred.

"I said I could force you to help me if I needed to," Shanower said. And with that, he sent a mass of mystical lightning into her body, instantly shattering her defenses, leaving her mind and soul bare for his use.

Bliss, Gunn, Angel, and Ord all surged at the

mage, but he kept them at bay with a single command.

"Harm me and she dies," Shanower said. He relaxed, sensing that the damage she had done was not complete.

The City of Doors would be smaller now, but still large enough to suit his purpose.

On the rooftop, Wes and Connor were locked in mortal combat with the demon women. Even though they had killed three of the guardians, there were so many more that Wes and Connor were losing ground, and being forced closer and closer to the edge of the rooftop—and farther from the tower with its now blazing sigil. A stream of pure white energy shot from that sign, penetrating the mad heavens above.

"You know the funny part?" Connor asked as three more of the women came at him, mystical energies coalescing around their hands. "As much as I like killing things? I like ticking them off even more!"

With that, he leaped over them and took a run directly at the tower. Turning, the sorceress demon women, who had been the powerful guardians in Shanower's employ, spun and loosed their sorceress energies at the teenager.

"Connor!" Wes yelled in warning, but it wasn't necessary. At exactly the right moment, Connor fell flat, the energies flying over his head—and striking the sigil on the tower, blowing it to bits!

The rooftop shuddered as the tower fell, revealing a mass of strange ruined machinery inside.

Eyes wide, the remaining demon women stared at the tangle of wires and circuitry in shock—then looked to one another in panic, linked hands, and vanished as one.

"Score one for the good guys," Connor said, not really sure of the havoc he had brought about but hoping he had caused all kinds of hell.

He had.

In the white room, Shanower's hold on Fred was severed, and the panoramic phantasmagoria that had surrounded the place vanished, sending all the combatants to the jade ceremonial hall. Gunn went to Fred, who was still unconscious, while Bliss and Ord took positions on either side of Angel. Shanower was on his knees.

"My engine," Shanower murmured, "my Quantum Engine of Creation—destroyed!"

No, there were *two* Shanowers now, one involved in the ceremony, and one in the white room.

Which was the real guy?

Angel was startled by the sudden, shifting reality, but he was not so disoriented as to be blind to the even greater fight ahead. Near the circle of mages, he saw Logan and Daniel approach Nemesis, a glowing sword in Logan's hand.

"Do it!" Daniel commanded. He had felt the doors opening once more, then felt them shut completely.

With a smile, Logan drove his sword into Nemesis's body. He dragged it from the circle, and Daniel surged forward, instantly taking its place. Daniel had explained to Logan that the power needed to manipulate the pattern was great, and so Nemesis would be weakened while wielding it.

"Let's do this," Daniel said, praying that he would get it right on his second and final chance to honor his father's memory.

The sudden changing stresses in the magical circle had a secondary effect: the Shanower who was participating in the ancient rite fell away from his fellows, clutching his head. As he did so, his sending, the being Angel had confronted a moment earlier, splintered and faded from existence.

Now there was only the one true mage—and he was plenty ticked off.

In fury, Shanower pointed at Nemesis in its weakened and disoriented state. "Our chance has come!" he shouted, attempting to recover the situation as best he could. There would be other opportunities for absolute power, he was certain. What mattered now was destroying his enemies, and that meant everyone who knew the truth. "Zeal! You are needed."

Zeal, Logan's father, stepped from the circle. "At last," he said with a shudder, his body suddenly transforming into a shining mass of blue-white light, a reaping scythe of energy manifesting in his hands.

Nemesis pulled itself away from Logan's sword and gestured, calling up hundreds, then *thousands*, of mystical sendings of its own shadowy form and launching them at the warrior of light.

Marekai entered the fray with Zeal, the light of his flames helping to cut through the ranks of shadow demons that spread as far as the eye could see. Logan fought them, too, along with Bliss and Ord.

Angel knelt by Gunn and Fred.

"Take care of her," Angel said.

"It's what I do," Gunn said with surprising tenderness. "What I always try to do."

Then Angel raced toward Shanower, sword in hand—but Nemesis got to the mage first.

Shanower released one fiery blast of energy after another at Nemesis, but the living shadow was unaffected by Shanower's power. Nemesis hissed a phrase in an ancient tongue, then thrust both of its claws into the body of Shanower. Angel could do nothing but watch as Nemesis, wearing the form of Shanower, arched back and screamed in agony!

Then a torrent of blinding energies erupted from Shanower and flowed into Nemesis.

Shanower placed his hands on the face of the living shadow and released a magic that was toxic to the creature. It withdrew, and the wounded Shanower fell to the floor. The moment Shanower's outstretched hand touched the ground, a jagged fissure opened with a wrenching moan and a river of light appeared, making Nemesis shrink back.

Before the fissure could open any wider, Nemesis reared back as a ragged hole appeared in the living shadow's head, quickly filling with jagged, razor-sharp teeth. Its jaws extended, growing wide enough to swallow up any mortal.

With a laugh, it consumed Shanower.

For long seconds a war was fought within the body of shadows. Light and shadow raged until finally the last flickers of illumination were stilled and Shanower was gone.

"That's better," Nemesis said in a low, deep voice that shook the foundations of the great hall.

Within the circle, a being made of light was cutting through the last of a series of shadow demons with a fiery scythe—Marekai, Ord, and Bliss fighting at his side. He turned to face Logan.

"Forgive me, Father," Logan whispered. "I'm so very sorry . . ."

Zeal willed the scythe into nonexistence and stilled the burning fires raging in his heart. His son was not beyond redemption. Opening his arms, he embraced Logan and began to weep.

Beside him, Ord wasted no time. He hurled an array of spells at Nemesis, leaping at the creature with his sword drawn. All his life he had dreamed of one day confronting the avatar of ultimate darkness and evil. His chance had finally come.

Nemesis recoiled from his attack, crying out in fear and surprise. Ord swept forward with his blade and sent a stream of crackling light and fire into the heart of the living shadow.

Falling to its knees, Nemesis reached up feebly to protect itself as Ord raised his sword overhead and prepared to bring it down upon the abomination. With a sharp, high cackle, Nemesis extended his claws and pierced the man's armors, five ebony blades running through the warrior at once. Ord teetered for a moment, then dropped his blade and fell back. Ord shuddered and held his arms before his wounded chest.

Angel stared at the fallen sorcerer in shock. If he could be felled so easily by Nemesis, what chance did they have?

Leaving Fred's side, Gunn went to Ord and knelt beside him. Ord whispered, "Know all that we have learned."

Gunn gasped as Ord's gauntleted hand touched the side of his face. Sights and sounds exploded in his head. Suddenly, he possessed the answers to the great secrets of a thousand ages, and a multitude of ancient incantations and a vast array of arcane wisdom burst into his mind. Then the flood of knowledge stopped. Gunn looked down to see Ord staring at him, eyes wide with wonder.

"It's within you," Ord said to the fighter. "I can feel it. The Gift that had been granted to me, the power to complete the ceremony, the Strength of Binding, is now within you. How could this be?"

"I don't know, man," Gunn said, startled at what he felt inside himself.

"No matter," Ord uttered as he fell back.

"No!" Gunn shouted as he tried to get his arms under Ord. If he could just drag the man to the River of Healing, the flowing waters the boy had brought into existence in this chamber, maybe the warrior could be saved. Ord's armors made him too heavy, and Gunn was too weak. He cried out for Angel or Bliss to help him, but before either could make a move in Gunn's direction, Nemesis extended its body and blocked the path to the healing waters.

"Let it go," whispered Ord.

"No, you can't die," Gunn hissed. "I won't let you!"

"Sometimes it's better when it's over with quickly. Go to Angel. He needs you now."

Reluctantly, Gunn got to his feet and joined Angel as Nemesis rose up in a triumphant stance.

Bliss called out to the others, "The ceremony is failing. The walls between worlds are falling!"

Strangely it was Charles Gunn who knew exactly what to do about that. "Get my back," he said to Angel.

"You got it . . . partner," the vampire said.

Gunn smiled, and raced for the circle.

Angel and Bliss were left alone to stop Nemesis.

"I won't let them succeed," Nemesis declared. "I had wished to keep the many worlds of your kind free from other predators, to make them our hunting ground alone, but I will not let my people die. Stand aside, or I will be upon the woman before you can even try to stop me. Perhaps, with her mind, I can still accomplish my goal."

"The more someone has to tell you they are something," Bliss whispered, "the less truth there usually is in the statement."

Angel nodded. Gunn had said the same thing on many an occasion. If Nemesis could strike them down and take Fred so easily—why didn't the beast just do so and be done with it?

"We're the same," Nemesis said again. "Stand aside, and we will give you worlds to prey upon."

Fred was stirring. "Angel . . . ," she said breathlessly, "the two of you are nothing alike. Of course, you do take from us—we *all* take from one another. But we *give,* too. Yeah, our lives would be different if you weren't in them. But that doesn't mean they'd be better. I'd still be in hell if not for you."

Angel took Bliss's hand. "I'm in a giving mood."

"I think I know exactly what you mean," she said.

With that, Bliss raised her free hand and struck at Nemesis with a blast of pure energy. Angel fell to his knees as he felt all that Bliss was drawing from him.

Angel was an avatar of good, a shining light in a world of darkness—who was, himself, cursed never to see the sun. His own inherent paradoxes were just as powerful as those that kept the abbey from falling into ruin. His potential, both as a champion of good and as a being of unending evil, made him unique among the known worlds . . . unique and filled with raw energy that was more than Nemesis could take.

Angel gave of himself freely—all the love, all the hate, all the triumphs and sorrows that were his existence—and Nemesis, a being who could *only* take, was overwhelmed by the sheer power blasting away at it.

With a final, horrifying scream, Nemesis exploded into a cloud of darkness that dissipated in the light, and did not form again.

Angel went to Fred, who was adjusting her glasses. She shook her head. "I've got one word for you—trippy!"

The ceremony lasted until dawn. When it was done, Gunn staggered off to the sidelines, Fred at his side. They still had much to work out, and who knew if they ever would? But, for today, they were together.

She frowned at her cell phone, which she wanted to use to get the police over to the Norris building, but she couldn't get a line out.

Then, suddenly, she had a dialtone. Her voice mail lit up, and she checked her messages, relieved to hear Mitchell's voice on the other end. The cops had been by hours ago, and he was just fine.

Angel was surprised to find Connor and Wes stumbling into the vast chamber. They had been searching through the place all night.

"Dad, hey," Connor said. "We could use a ride out of here."

Angel saw the way Logan and Zeal were acting, the conflict between them finally resolved. Could he hope for such a resolution with his own son?

He could *always* hope.

Wes went to Gunn and Fred and sat with them in relieved silence. Wes had no idea that, in an office in Los Angeles, Lilah Morgan was sitting by, anxiously waiting for a call that would never come.

And twenty feet away, Bliss stood over the body of Ord. Angel broke from his son and went to her. He brushed a glistening tear from her eye.

"Now that's not like me at all, is it?" she whispered, sobs threatening to break from her like waves. "Dammit. Ord might have been a fool, but at least he was a fool I could tolerate. Possibly the only one."

"Then he was a very lucky man," Angel replied.

Marekai approached. He was different now, humbled in some way. "In his madness, Ord was the most clear thinking and wise of all of us."

"Huh! You'd think that would make him fit to lead, wouldn't you?" a familiar voice called.

Angel turned and was stunned by the sight before him. Ord stood there, alive and whole.

"It was the sending," Angel said. "You were never at the battle—"

"No, *I* am the sending," Ord said. "Only a true mage could have mustered the power required there at the end. No wonder I seemed quite mad. A lot of information was being shelved in my head. Any more, and I think my skull would have exploded."

"*You're* the sending," Angel repeated, surprised.

"Yes, but . . . I am more than just an echo, a reflection. My soul, my essence, fled at the moment of my death, and was simply too contrary or confused to go to its reward. It ended up here, in this makeshift flesh." He shrugged. "I suppose I will have to start all over as far as massing true power is concerned. But—"

Bliss could take it no longer. She threw her arms around the blue-tattooed mage. "The *things* I plan on doing to you," she said huskily.

"Provided, uh, we can find the time. There is much to be done. For example—"

She silenced him by pressing her lips greedily to his. He tensed, then his arms encircled her tiny waist. Her cloak fell back, leaving her face and hair fully exposed for the first time that Angel could remember. There were aspects of her "self" she was willing to lay bare at a moment's notice, yet this most basic gesture, simply allowing someone to look upon her face when it was not draped in shadow, to touch her hair, to see her with no apparent mystery, this was a moment of emotional intimacy far more powerful than any of the wild acts she had proposed.

Angel stood alone, looking at all the people whose lives he had touched. He knew that while his mission was unquestionably righteous, he was not a righteous man and did not always use righteous methods. But he had to let go of these concerns. The humans who kept him grounded, moored to the hopes, fears, and needs of the very people he was sworn to protect, were not some necessary evil—nor were they human sacrifices.

They were friends, family . . . and, no matter what happened, they would always be with him, in his heart.

He smiled, and walked to a far window, where the sun was now blazing.

He stood in its light as long as he could.

Scott Ciencin is a *New York Times* best-selling author of more than fifty books from Random House, Simon & Schuster, and many more. He has written Buffy the Vampire Slayer: *Sweet Sixteen*, cowritten Angel: *Vengeance* with Dan Jolley, and cowritten the Angel short story "It Could Happen to You" with his wife, Denise. He has worked on the Jurassic Park, Star Wars, Transformers, and Dinotopia franchises, written for Marvel and DC Comics, and is the author of the popular Vampire Odyssey and Dinoverse series (which has recently been optioned as a feature film). He is also the writer of the acclaimed CrossGen Entertainment comic book series DemonWars. Among his upcoming projects is a prestige miniseries from IDW Publishing based on the international best-selling horror video game Silent Hill. He lives in Ft. Myers, Florida, with his beloved wife, Denise.

Denise Ciencin has a masters degree in community counseling and has worked with at-risk teenagers, displaced homemakers, the developmentally disabled, and many other populations in crisis. She was listed in *Who's Who in America's* 2001 edition. She has also written in the field of neurology and neurosurgery and worked with her husband on the majority of his fiction output, providing research, co-plotting, and much more. She is the creative consultant of the acclaimed CrossGen Entertainment comic book series *DemonWars*.

As many as one in three
Americans with HIV...
DO NOT KNOW IT.

More than half of those
who will get HIV this year...
ARE UNDER 25.

HIV is preventable.
You can help fight AIDS.
Get informed. Get the facts.

www.knowhivaids.org
1-866-344-KNOW